1

Moon Puddles

A Life of Wonder

Written by Robert R. Gamble
Illustrated by Gabriel R. Gamble

To Amma

I would also like to thank Marianne, who I'd be lost without, and am blessed to have married, my two sons, Gabriel (13), for designing and creating the cover art and all the illustrations, and Elliott (8) for suggesting the sub-title and for being patient with me. Special thanks also to Mahesvara, Simon, and Analan, who helped edit the book and made many helpful suggestions. I'd also like to acknowledge my brother Jim and my sister Terri who were too young (Jim) or not born yet (Terri) to be included in this book, but who share the loving legacy of our parents, brother, and other dear relatives. No one accomplishes anything worthwhile without many other people giving freely of themselves; I am grateful to all the friends and teachers who have helped me throughout my life.

"Love all that has been created by God,
both the whole and every grain of sand.
Love every leaf and every ray of light.
Love the beasts and the birds,
love the plants,
love every separate fragment.
If you love each separate fragment,
you will understand the mystery
of the whole resting in God."

Fydor Dostoevsky

"Why not look at the beauty your
memory holds,
so nourishing that light can be.
The past's lips are not
deceased.
Let them comfort you
if they can."

Kabir

Table of Contents

"I did not
have to ask my heart what it wanted,
because of all the desires I have ever known
just one did I cling to for it was the essence of
all desire:

to hold beauty in
my soul's
arms."

St. John of the Cross

Chapter 1

Uncle Billy

Me and Danny are in the back seat. I'm looking at a *Wonder Woman* comic. Danny thinks Superman is the best DC superhero, but Wonder Woman is number one for me. My favorite superhero of all time is Thor, but he's in Marvel comics, not DC.

Me and Danny read both Marvel and DC, but I like Marvel comics better; somehow, they seem more real. Marvel characters aren't so perfect; they have problems and flaws just like ordinary people. Look at Spiderman: the other kids call him a bookworm, he can't get a date, his family hardly has any money, his Uncle Ben gets killed, and Spiderman blames himself. It goes on and on, like real life.

Open fields of grass and telephone poles keep sliding past the car windows. We must be near the end of Texas since there's so much grass. Copperas Cove, where we live, is closer to the middle of Texas, where the only grass is what people plant in their lawns. Fields of sandy soil, rocks, and scrubby little bushes or cactuses surround our neighborhood, the stores—everywhere in fact (except around people's houses, which people water with sprinklers so their grass will grow.) If they don't water it, the dry clay of their yards cracks and puckers up like a miniature earthquake hit.

Texas is great, though; it has lizards everywhere. I keep finding different kinds all the time, horned toads, skinks, whiptails, but mostly lizards with different colors, sizes, scales, and levels of speed whose names I don't know. Almost all of them are pretty quick and hard to grab—that's why I love catching lizards, it's challenging, exciting, and when I finally trap one in my hand and feel the life pulsing in its little body, a thrill shoots up my heart. I never hurt them, of course, and I always let them go after a while.

Skinks are striped skinny slippery, and lightning-fast, some of the most challenging lizards to catch, while horned toads aren't hard to catch at all. They are kind of fat, flat-bellied and slow, but they are so cool looking with all their spikes and horns that it's like catching gold.

Once I caught a huge horned toad twice. He was a beauty, proud-looking with gorgeous horns that had a little red at the tips, so I called him my Devil Horned Toad, but I noticed one of his back feet was a little smushed and broken. After a while, I let him go in a big field. A few weeks later, I caught him again. I knew it was him because of his bad foot. It was like finding an old friend who moved away; I love that lizard more than any of the ones I've caught so far.

The most exciting lizards to catch, though, are the kinds I've never seen before; it's like finding living treasure. Just the other day, I was in a field following rabbit tracks through the rocky sand and brush. After five or ten minutes, the tracks led me to a rabbit who was sitting up sniffing the air, his ears perked upright and still. Suddenly a giant lizard zipped by.

God, he was fast, a flash of bluish-green and orange. He must have been over a foot long with his tail. When he ran, his body's front part seemed higher than his back legs and tail, like some sort of dinosaur.

I chased him under a giant flat boulder, where I lost him. I didn't even try to budge that rock as it was so huge, and digging him out wouldn't work either because the ground was hard stony soil. He was so big and such a beauty, though, that I waited there for half an hour. He poked his handsome head out once to see if I was still there, then ducked back inside; he was clever all right. Finally, I got too hungry and went home for dinner. I'll go back to that boulder when we get home from our trip; it's not over yet between him and me.

We're on our way to Kansas: flat ugly dusty chigger-bite Kansas. We were just there a year ago visiting Grandma Ludwiczak after her lung cancer operation, and I hated those chiggers biting my ankles. I couldn't see the devils, but when I came inside, hot from playing, the itches would start under my socks, and before I knew it, Mom was smearing on calamine lotion again. Now we're going to Kansas because they're going to bury Uncle Billy. A lousy sniper shot him in Vietnam.

Danny lets out a big yawn; he's reading, with his hands tight on *Superman* as the wind from Dad's window whips through the pages. Superman is great, but Wonder Woman is almost as strong, plus she doesn't have the weakness of kryptonite to worry about. She also has her lasso of truth, making villains unable to lie, and they have to do what Wonder Woman tells them. Besides, she's a princess, almost a goddess and noble like Thor.

Thor is a Norse god, but he isn't GOD. Neither is Odin, Thor's father, who they call the All-Father and who has incredible power. Comic books are a lot like school in how they treat God. God's never mentioned or talked about in school, except in the Pledge of Allegiance. In a comic book, characters might bow their heads at a funeral or look up at the sky after something that calls for prayer, and that's about it. God is off-limits at school or in comics; I think I know why, but it still bugs me.

I guess everyone believes in God, but you never hear people talking about him. They must in church, I guess (we don't go ourselves, so I don't know what that's like), but not when people bump into each other in the neighborhood or when relatives visit. It just seems like you're not supposed to talk about God.

I'm not sure what's more important than God, if anything, but I guess people don't talk about him because they're afraid someone else will have a different idea of God, and I can understand that. Maybe people are right, and it's better to keep God private, but I hope we're not missing something important.

People miss chances often—I know I sure do, I often think of something I should have said or done after it's already too late, and I could kick myself—but not Wonder Woman; she never misses with her lasso of truth. I wonder what would happen if she was alive and she lassoed President Johnson about what's really going on in Vietnam. Now that would be something Dad would love to hear. Dad doesn't seem to trust President Johnson like he did President Kennedy. I listen to him grumble at the TV sometimes after hearing the President talking about Vietnam on the news.

I also like Wonder Woman because she spends time in every comic on Paradise Island, which is full of beautiful Amazons, and Wonder Woman herself is pretty. Women tug at my heart differently than men. There's something about women that makes me want to be around them and put my head on their lap. Not all of them, of course, but nice ones and pretty ones that smile like they care about people. Wonder Woman does for sure.

I hear the metal click of Dad's lighter; he's lighting up a cigarette. He smokes Pall Malls, which have an ugly smell and no filters. Mom used to smoke Newports, menthol with a filter; she only smoked a few a day, but she quit a while ago because of the new warnings that cigarettes may be harmful to your health—I think she just smoked because Dad did anyway.

The comic page is lit up by a dusty stream of light from over the front seat, swirling down past Mom's right earlobe. Mom is wearing her white sunglasses with green lenses; she's had them ever since I can remember. They make her look like a movie star.

The wind is bouncing her blonde hair—dishwater blonde, Mom calls it. She puts pink curlers in every night, and she doesn't like the wind messing with her hair, which curls up just above her shoulders, but it's too hot to keep the windows closed. Mom has a sleeveless white blouse on, which lets me look at the pretty freckles on her shoulders—that's the only place Mom has any. She's chewing gum, probably Teaberry, Juicy Fruit, or Wrigley's Spearmint, which she likes the best.

Dad has his elbow out the window as he drives; his muscular arm is poking out of a blue and white striped shirt. He looks like he is thinking seriously about something, maybe about Uncle Billy's funeral in two days or a memory of their time together as kids.

I only have two clear memories about Uncle Billy myself. One is him playing cards with us in Germany, and the other is the day of the french fries. We lived in PA back then (that's Pennsylvania), and so did Grandma Ludwiczak in her big yellow house. Uncle Billy and Aunt Elaine lived at home with Grandma—they're Dad's brother and sister, not Mom's. It's funny, but I can't remember if Grandpap Steve was there that day, maybe he was working, or maybe Grandma hadn't married him yet—Grandma was married twice—to Grandpap Steve and Pap-Pap. I was only three or so when we visited that day, so my memory's spotty.

They had a big yellow and white collie, called Tequila, who followed me around with his tongue hanging out. Dad said Tequila was old, almost the same age as Uncle Billy. His breath was warm and terrible, and his tongue was up by my chin.

I had a Band-Aid on my chin from getting stitches—my tricycle flipped in the wet alley by our row-house apartment. It had just stopped raining, and I was eager to get outside finally, so I was pedaling hard, and the concrete was slick with water running off. Something happened—maybe I hit a big crack or a pothole—I don't know—and I flew over the handlebars chin first onto the wet concrete.

I hit that cement so hard I saw colored lights in blackness for a few seconds; the inside of my mouth tasted like I'd been sucking on rocks, and my chin was throbbing so much I knew it was terrible. I pulled myself up and pushed my tricycle home dripping blood and tears all over the puddled alley.

Dad drove me to the hospital while Mom sat in the back seat and held a bloody blue washcloth on my chin; it smelled a bit sour like a wet washcloth that's been lying on the tub ledge for a while. Danny sat in the front, looking back over the seat at me, poking his tongue into his cheek. He looked scared from all the blood, I guess, and that didn't help me feel any better.

I'd just been to the hospital a month or so before to get my tonsils taken out. I didn't like it there. The doctor told me I could have all the ice cream I wanted after the operation, but afterwards, my throat was so darn sore I could hardly get a spoonful down. Doctors are not to be trusted.

Whenever we went to see Dr. Nader, I always seemed to end up getting a shot for something. I'd sit by his desk with my nostrils full of alcohol stink as he'd rub a cotton ball on my arm. He always seemed satisfied somehow as he brought the needle close. Every time he'd say, "It will just pinch for a minute." He was a liar; my arm always ached for the rest of the day. I think he must like jabbing needles into people. He's treated all our family forever. He still makes house calls to see Pap-Pap and Grandma Babe if it's urgent, but he tells them to keep it to themselves, or other people will expect it, too. Mom said Dr. Nader is the one who delivered me in the hospital and spanked my butt for the first time. Like I said, you can't trust them; they say what they do is to help you, but what they do always hurts.

The only good thing about getting my tonsils out was that Mom and Dad went to the gift shop and bought me a red metal tractor. I had fun playing with it on the bed till I got to go home. I had that tractor for a long time because it was so sturdy and solid; it felt good to hold and push around. I might even still have it somewhere.

For my chin, we went right into the emergency room. Mom was still holding the rag to my chin till we got in the doctor's room. They put me under a sheet with only my chin showing, and the doctor sewed three stitches in—I guess he didn't want me to see what he was doing.

It didn't help because him stitching added a sharp pinching to the pain I already had. It was hard not to cry. When he finished, he showed me the crooked black thread in my chin skin with a mirror; then he put a Band-Aid on it. I still have the scar, right where the bottom of my jawbone meets the soft skin of my throat. Sometimes late at night, when I can't sleep for a long time, I can feel my chin throb a teeny tiny bit like it still remembers that hurt after all these years.

Well, Tequila kept trying to lick my bandage in Grandma's living room, and I kept trying to move away. Tequila was sweet and must have sensed that my chin was sore, but his breath was horrible.

Later, we were all watching *Howdy Doody*. Howdy Doody is a marionette who looks a little bit like Danny, but Danny doesn't have as many freckles. Howdy Doody was dancing with a giant box of Kellogg's Rice Crispies when Uncle Billy came in with a big bowl-full of french fries and squirted ketchup. He made it for a snack—all by himself, and he shared it on the floor with me and Danny and Tequila. Uncle Billy and

Danny stuck french fries in their mouths like cigarettes and let Tequila lick them away with his big stinky tongue. I handed Tequila one or two of mine, and my fingertips got wet.

Tequila followed me upstairs when I went up to Aunt Elaine's room. She had her doll collection, about ten dolls of all sizes, lined up on a shelf about two feet from the ceiling. She brought some down for me to look at. Aunt Elaine had her black hair braided into pigtails, and she was wearing a red plaid dress that showed her skinny knees when she sat on the bed with me. Aunt Elaine has a soft, gentle way about her.

Aunt Elaine was in high school, and I don't think she played with her dolls much anymore, but she let me have fun with them for a bit. One was a giant Raggedy Ann, almost as big as me with a small rip in the shoulder. Aunt Elaine just said to be careful. I also liked a bald baby doll with painted eyes that looked old, but I wasn't allowed to play with that one as it was an antique from Grandma Gamble.

Uncle Billy came up the steps with Danny and went into his room. He let me come in, too. The wooden floor had a blue and yellow throw rug that Tequila stretched out on, his long curled tongue panting and stinking up the room. Uncle Billy's bed had a green bedspread with some baseball cards scattered on it, and hanging on the wall was a triangular flag with an eye-patched-pirate above two crossed baseball bats. Besides dog breath, the room had a burnt smell, almost like someone singed their arm hairs over a gas burner.

That happened to me when we lived in a guest house in Germany. I was watching Mom heat some milk for hot chocolate when my blonde arm hair curled up and got stinky.

I guess I was standing too close to the stove, and I was surprised at the strong smell it made. Mom made me back away after she checked my arm. I stood off to the side, sniffing my arm, till Mom said, "What are you doing?"

"My arm hairs smell funny, here take a sniff," I said, holding out my arm to her.

"Get away and let me finish." She shook her head and rolled up her eyeballs like I was strange or something.

"Danny, come over here and smell my arm. My arm hair curled up." Danny was sitting on our sofa bed reading *Winnie the Pooh*.

"No thanks," he said, not even bothering to look up.

My arm hairs burning happened when I was around six, years after the french fries day—but I don't forget smells. Sometimes a smell can take me back in time just from getting a whiff of something for a second or two.

Anyway, Danny picked up a tool from Uncle Billy's dresser; it looked like an electric pen with round cork to hold near the tip. "What's this thing?" Danny asked.

"That's for making pictures," said Uncle Billy. He showed us a piece of wood with the brown outline of a submarine on it. "I just finished this before you got here. You press the tip into the wood, and it makes burn marks; you can make anything you can think of. I've only had it a couple of weeks since my birthday, so I haven't had time to make much yet."

"Wow! That looks like a real neat submarine. Can I try it?" said Danny.

"Sure, but you gotta be careful."

Uncle Billy plugged in the pen to let it warm up. It started to stink like hot radiators; then, he pressed the tip into a block of wood. The wood turned dark brown, and the smell got real strong and made my nose crinkle up.

"Danny, don't touch the white part or you'll burn your fingers real bad, just hold the cork; that's the brown part." Then he let Danny press the pen into the wood. Danny had a big grin on his face as he made a few marks on the wood, but I didn't want to try it.

Uncle Billy also had a model airplane on his desk which he probably got for his birthday, too. He said it was a B-52 Bomber. There was a paintbrush set next to it, but I guess he hadn't gotten around to painting yet as it was still model gray.

Uncle Billy sat on his bed next to Danny and me, and then Tequila hopped up, flopped down next to Uncle Billy, and smushed all the baseball cards. Uncle Billy didn't seem to care; he just ruffled up Tequila's fur and stuck his nose next to Tequila's. How could he stand the smell?

We must have gone home soon after that. That's the only memory of Uncle Billy I have in PA. Grandma probably moved back to Kansas shortly after our visit—she was always moving somewhere, well, so were we, with Dad getting transferred from one base to another.

Uncle Billy did visit us one time, though, in Germany. He was stationed in Würzburg, an hour or two from Bad Kissingen, where we lived. He stayed with us for a few days and slept on our couch. I was about eight at the time, and Uncle Billy and I were both into cards. We played war, 500, crazy eights; Uncle Billy also taught us how to play poker, blackjack, and gin. Danny, Mom, and Dad played some too, but mostly it was just me and Uncle Billy.

He taught me how to shuffle cards; Danny couldn't quite get shuffling and stopped trying after a while, but I wanted to be good at it. Uncle Billy said I had good hands and to keep practicing. Before he left, Uncle Billy said I could shuffle as good as he could; I felt proud when he told me that. Later that day, he drove away. I didn't know it at the time, but that was the last time I ever got to be with him. Shortly after that, he got stationed in Berlin; a year or so later, Dad told us Uncle Billy got transferred to Vietnam. I wish I had known Uncle Billy better. Now it's too late. Time doesn't wait for people; if you aren't ready, you can get left behind lickety-split.

The flapping noise of Danny's comic is quieting down, sounding like the baseball cards clothespinned to my bicycle spokes. They make noise like a motor does when I pedal real fast. I miss my bike so far away. I won't be back to my bike and my lizard catching for a few days. Dad tried to get more time off for the funeral, but the Army only gave him four days.

The pages settle because Dad is pulling into a gas station; it's Dino gas! There are green brontosauruses on the gas-pump bubbles. The bubbles are white, about the size of tether-balls, perched on top of the pumps. The brontosauruses look happy, their necks and tails curving like green smiles.

"Listen up, boys. If you have to go, do it now. I don't want to stop for a couple hours after this." Dad turns around and gives us the eyeball. Danny tucks his shirt in and opens the door; a flap of green plaid pokes out from under his belt as he scoots out. Dad's still looking at me, but I'm empty, as far as I can tell. "You sure, Robert?"

After a quick nod from me, Dad gets out.

The gas station guy is all dressed in green. He tips his green cap at Mom as she walks around the front of the car to stand next to Dad.

"Fill 'er up and check the oil," Dad orders.

"Yes, sir. Restrooms are round to the right."

Danny runs ahead, spraying gravel with his sneakers, his toes pointing out funny like they always do. Mom and Dad crunch after.

The gas station guy clunks the nozzle into the tank. He has a white tag over his shirt pocket that says Sinclair in red longhand. Sinclair is the real name, but we call it Dino gas, after Dino, in *The Flintstones*.

When we lived in Virginia, *The Flintstones* were on every Friday night. Fred, Barney, Wilma, Betty, and Dino all lived in Bedrock, where most everything—houses, cars, machines, dishes, TV's—were made out of stone from the quarry where Fred worked. Fred Flintstone always reminded me of Dad— Fred and Jackie Gleason, both big with dark hair—Dad isn't as fat or as funny, though. They all have tempers too, but Fred and Jackie Gleason's tempers make me laugh—Dad's doesn't.

We'd eat Jiffy-Pop popcorn and drink Dr. Pepper or Pepsi—Dad hates Coca-Cola—as we watched Fred and Barney get into some kind of a jam. Wilma and Betty were usually the smart ones who got the men out of trouble. Even Dino had more sense than Fred sometimes.

Saturday night was the *Bugs Bunny Hour*, and Mom often made a Chef Boyardee pizza from a box about the same size

21

as Kraft macaroni and cheese. It was our special treat for the week; we loved it; the dough smelled so heavenly when Mom rolled it out, even better than when she baked it. The pizza was especially great with Dr. Pepper to chug down after a hot cheesy bite. Danny chugged too much once and laughed at the same time; most of it came out of his nose. We all laughed as it bubbled and fizzed down his chin and dripped onto his shirt.

The first time I remember stopping for Dino gas was in Virginia on our way home from a drive-in movie. I was about four. Me and Danny were in the back seat, sharing a soft blue blanket that we had cuddled up in during the movie. It was a strange coincidence, now that I think about it, because the movie called *Dinosaurus* was about a brontosaurus, a Tyrannosaurus Rex and a funny caveman. All three had been frozen deep in the ocean but were hauled to the surface by giant tractors. Lightning struck them at night after the rain thawed them out, and they all came alive.

Not long after we saw *Dinosaurus,* we found this great dinosaur set in a nearby toy store. I don't know if it was just a coincidence or if they made the dinosaur set because this movie came out. The set had two tan rock formations with small caves, a few tan plastic cavemen, and half a dozen hard rubbery plastic dinosaurs. The two biggest prizes were a gray brontosaurus longer than Dad's hand and a fantastic looking gray Tyrannosaurus Rex with his little arms, tiny ears, big toes, lashing lizard's tail, and wrinkle lines on his belly and around his neck. He was so realistic looking. We loved him.

We played with that set a lot in Virginia and then in Germany. I also added some plastic animals I liked: a gorilla, a lion, a tiger, and a brown grizzly which I was particularly fond of because he felt good in my hand and looked so strong. I also had some green plastic army men who always ran for their lives from the dinosaurs and the animals.

The king of them all was the Tyrannosaurus Rex; nothing could beat him, even a sturdy green triceratops that usually gave a good fight. Then one Christmas in Germany, we got a robot, saber-toothed tiger. He was about a foot long with his massive shoulders. Soft brown fur-looking cloth covered his metal robot body—when the cloth got ripped around his neck later, we could see the silver-looking body inside. He could open and close his mouth with his big fangs slashing and shuffle forward on his paws. A cord connected him to the battery-powered controls. The Rex lost his throne.

We had so much fun having battles between all the dinosaurs and animals. Eventually, we lost the caves and the cavemen, and the saber-toothed tiger broke, but we still have the T-Rex and the brontosaurus. They are old friends of mine, and I still play with them from time to time. Danny doesn't seem to be interested in playing with them these days. He says he is getting too old for that kind of stuff anymore. I hope I'm not such a party pooper in two years when I'm twelve like him.

Well, in the movie, when the caveman wandered into someone's yard and looked through the window of a house, lightning flared and showed a woman wearing curlers and a mud pack smack up against the window looking right at the caveman. They were eyeball to eyeball; both of them screamed at each other and ran the other way. Dad laughed so hard, two tears trickled down his cheeks, and he almost choked on his popcorn.

The sad part was when the tyrannosaurus caught the brontosaurus by the neck with his giant teeth and muscular jaws and killed the brontosaurus. He didn't have a chance against the Rex—just like Uncle Billy didn't have a chance against some crummy sniper hiding up a jungle tree. I wonder if Uncle Billy's buddies shot the sniper or if they couldn't find him and he got away—or maybe Uncle Billy was all alone when he died.

What an awful way to lose your life; he was probably walking on some overgrown path in the jungle when suddenly he was shot from out of nowhere. There's no way anybody can survive an attack like that, no matter how good of a soldier a person might be, and I'm sure Uncle Billy was a darn good soldier. Maybe he saw the sniper just before he got shot and realized it was too late for him to do anything. That would be frightening to know you were going to die in a few seconds, surrounded by some horrible jungle far away from everyone you loved or cared about. Maybe his last thought was about his girlfriend or Grandma Ludwiczak and Pap-Pap, or if he would go to heaven soon and get to see God.

I think it would be better not to see death coming so it wouldn't be so scary. I hope it was quick and painless, that he wasn't laying there trying to stop the blood or part of his insides from coming out with his hand—that would be a thousand times more painful than when I hurt my chin. Maybe biting ants started to crawl over his body as giant elephant leaves hid him from the other members of his platoon, and death took its time—no one deserves to die like that, especially Uncle Billy. I'm going to miss playing cards with him—what a crummy stinking war.

On the news, we see what's going on over in Vietnam—it's a giant nightmare coming into our living room every night. Helicopters fly over heavy jungles, then land in clearings so soldiers can jump out with their weapons ready. Gunfire shatters the jungle quiet, followed by shouts and screams. Villages burn as men and women flee with their children and what they can carry.

The war is all over their country; there's no place they can go to get away from it completely. Moving from one place to another is probably just temporary relief until something awful happens to make them run again somewhere else. I'd hate to be a kid in Vietnam hearing bombs, helicopters, and machine-gun fire all the time. How can they even relax enough to sleep, let alone go to school or play and have fun?

I wonder how many kids are getting killed over there every day—women and old people, too. It's terrible what's happening, and our soldiers are being wounded or killed daily—they call it the 'casualty totals' every night on the news, but it's really death they're counting. I hate watching the news now, but sometimes I can't get away from it as Dad always watches TV so loud since his one ear can't hear so good.

I don't understand what they are fighting about over there. Dad said that they are trying to stop the communists from taking over all of Vietnam and that the North Vietnamese are getting weapons from the Chinese, who are also communists. I don't get what that has to do with us. Why are we sending soldiers like Uncle Billy over there to get killed? It makes me mad. It's their country, not ours. Dad explained about the communists to me kind of half-heartedly, like he wasn't sure about it all either.

When they show close-ups of the soldiers, they always look so grubby and sweaty in their helmets and gear. They smoke and wait around under the dense trees of the jungle—I am sure Uncle Billy played a lot of cards when he could relax—then gunfire erupts, and they all crouch and prepare to face death. It must be horrible being over there, having to kill other people, afraid of getting killed yourself. Just watching from our living room before Uncle Billy got killed made me sad about Vietnam, but war is even more terrible when you know and care about the people getting killed. The closer the people are to you, the more terrible war becomes.

Dad is tapping on the steering wheel and humming softly, sounds like the theme song from *Green Acres*; he loves that show, especially how all the country folk are always smarter than Mr. Douglas, the lawyer from the big city. Arnold, the Ziffle's pet pig, makes Dad laugh most of all. As I look at him tapping away, I realize that what's really frightening is it could have been Dad getting shot by that sniper. If Dad had gotten orders to go there instead of Uncle Billy, I'd be going to Dad's funeral. I feel sorry for Uncle Billy, and I miss him already, but I can't imagine how I'd feel if it was Dad who got ambushed and killed. I wonder if the Army will ever send Dad to Vietnam; maybe it's time I started praying that he never has to go.

Well, when we stopped for gas that night after the drive-in, not only were there brontosauruses on the gas pump bubbles, there was also a giant, inflatable brontosaurus. It was twenty feet high, bouncing upwards from the gas station roof against the ropes holding it down. The night breeze almost

26

made the dinosaur seem alive as it got whipped and tossed about by the wind.

The sky above the brontosaurus was deep and dark. Beyond the haze of light from the gas station, there were thousands of bright stars, scattered like diamond dust against the black beauty of the night. The brontosaurus's huge belly was shaking like green Jell-O. I remember wishing I could climb on its back, cut the ropes and ride up to the stars. Angels were sure to be up there. We could fly right into heaven, maybe, and see what God was up to, what he looked like, how it felt to be close to him. Then it occurred to me that once I was in heaven, they might not let me leave—a shiver shook me as I thought about being alone up there, and I was glad to be snuggling under a blanket with Danny next to me.

Uncle Billy must be up there now; I hope he's not alone and that he can be with God whenever he wants. Maybe he's waiting to get his angel wings like Clarence in *It's a Wonderful Life*. I'm sure Uncle Billy will make a good angel; maybe he'll keep an eye on us from time to time and not forget about us; I sure won't forget him.

Chapter II

Danny

Danny hops in the car and gives me a start. "You're gonna be sorry you didn't pee." He bounces up and down on the seat a few times. What a goober. Mom gets in and takes off her shoes; she's wearing white socks up to her ankles. She turns around, holding up a pack of Juicy Fruit.

"Do you want one, Bobby?" She knows that Danny doesn't like chewing gum.

"Sure, Mom. Thanks." I roll my gum up sideways so that it looks like a cigarette. I pretend to take a puff and blow it in Danny's face.

"You think you're Steve McQueen or something," Danny says, smirking.

"No, just my usual cool self."

Once we get going again, me and Danny switch comics. Superman's red cape gets me thinking about my bike. It's red with white stripes on the fenders. I loosened the handlebars and turned them up and backwards; it looks cooler that way. Sometimes I ride the streets for an hour or so, usually the same neighborhood roads over and over. It takes a while before a street becomes comfortable, and I know every dip, bump, gravel patch, and curve. I like finding streets without many cars messing things up; then I can go no-handed, curving along from gutter to gutter without worrying about parked cars or traffic sneaking up behind me.

I usually ride by myself. Danny used to have a bike; he got a red English bike in Germany with the metal tag of a castle under the handlebars. It was cool, but he never rode much, and the bike rusted up—he's not much into sports and stuff like I am.

The first time I realized that me and Danny were different that way was when Dad bought us baseball gloves one spring in Germany. They had the word Raleigh branded into the leather, and they cost over five bucks apiece. Dad took Danny and me to the field behind our apartment building; the grass was bright green from all the rain and soft under our sneakers. The glove leather smelled good, so I kept it close to my face letting the smell seep deep into my nose and lungs.

Danny should've too because one that Dad tossed smacked Danny's nose. He shrugged it off like Dad said to, but his eyes were watering, he was red-faced, and I could tell he was fuming inside—Dad didn't seem to see that. He was trying to show Danny how to throw right, but every time Danny turned his arm out funny—just like a girl, Dad said.

Part of me was happy because I could catch and throw good, and Dad wasn't yelling at me, but I felt terrible for Danny; his face twisted from fighting off tears; his hay-fever was giving his nose the drips, and Dad's voice kept getting more and more P-O'd.

"Daniel quit daydreaming and pay attention. What the hell were you looking at? Don't just stand there; go get the damn ball." That was the first and last time Danny ever wore that glove. Later on, Dad used Danny's glove to catch with me.

After a couple weeks, I joined pee-wee league baseball. I didn't play much outside with Danny then—I'm not sure what he did with himself when I played baseball, rode my bike (I had a green German bike back then with a pump attached to the bar), or shot marbles—besides read comics and listen to Beatle records.

We had a blue and white record player that we played albums of our Babar the Elephant stories on, and we could pop the middle up so we could also play small forty-fives. Those were mostly Beatle records Mom bought for us at the PX (PX stands for Post Exchange, an Army department store that sells almost everything but groceries and big appliances) that had big red and yellow swirls on the label. I must have heard *She Loves You* and *I Want to Hold Your Hand* a thousand times, along with a *One-Eyed One-Horned Flying Purple People Eater* that Danny liked to dance to. I enjoyed them, but Danny could listen to them over and over and over.

It's funny, but sometimes when I think back, Danny was nowhere around and then at other times we were real close—like when we journeyed to our castle in Bad Kissingen.

Some Saturdays, Mom would pack us each a lunch for our hike: sandwiches with a couple of Oreos or Vanilla Wafers and some chips or pretzels. We'd leave Post (the army base where we lived) by cutting across a field full of Queen Anne's lace, where on other days we'd catch milk snakes, snails, and fat gray lizards. We caught a chubby gray one once that was growing back his tail. The new part always looks different from the old tail part on lizards; their tails are never as smooth and beautiful again after they grow back. "As good as new" doesn't apply to lizard tails.

Beyond the field were about a thousand stone steps going down a steep hill. Halfway down on the left, an old abandoned three-story house sat back from a black prison-bar fence that had sharp points on top. German Peter told us it was haunted, so we always looked for witches and ghosts in the windows.

German Peter led the German gang that came on base. He rang all the doorbells of an apartment building, and I heard about kids getting beat up—once we found a wire hanging straight between two trees, throat high, next to the skeleton of some dead animal, probably a opossum from the looks of the skinny snouted skull. Kids said one of German Peter's gang, the meanest one, Herman the German, put it there to strangle unsuspecting kids. For some reason, they didn't much like American kids.

German Peter liked me, though. He had blond hair, black clothes, and a smile that made people want to be his friend. One day he asked if he could look at Charley, my monkey puppet. I took Charley everywhere with me for a while. German Peter told me not to worry, then he grabbed Charley and rode up and down the street on his bike while he dangled Charley at a brown dog that was chasing him. He tossed Charley to me when he was done and gave me a big smile.

I trusted German Peter, but I thought he was kidding about the witches and haunting ghosts until I swear I saw one sitting there one day. The window she looked through was kind of purple with a gob of rainbow colors sparkling across her cheek. She had white hair, a hooked nose, and a secret smile that shot me down those stairs like Speedy Gonzales.

I never saw her again, and Danny didn't believe me, but I know she was there. If she wasn't a witch, maybe she was a friend of Garbage-Picker Annie, an old stout German lady who came on base to pick through the garbage bins. Maybe they both hid in that house and lived there for free because they had nowhere else to go. Witch or not, though, I saw an old woman in that window, and that's a fact.

At the bottom of the stone steps, we were in Bad Kissingen. We would walk over cobble-stoned streets past shops and outdoor cafes. A fountain was in the middle of the square; it had a minstrel playing a lyre on top of a stone column. Water came out of curved bronze pipes on the bottom that emptied into a green pool.

One day we sat on the fountain lip and looked down at the sunlight sparkling on the coins at the bottom of the pool. They were mostly German coins, but I saw some nickels and dimes in there, too. They were tempting, but we never snatched any of them; I wondered if people stole coins sometimes at night.

Past the square, we'd go down a crooked street where the puppet shop was. Marionettes of jesters, kings, and queens were hanging in the windows along with puppets made of soft material that felt like fur. My monkey puppet Charley had that kind of fur, which was dark brown, and so did Danny's owl puppet, which was tan with spotted owl markings. Those puppets were so soft, and they always had a fresh furry smell that made me bury my nose into Charley from time to time.

Mom and Dad had bought our puppets at the puppet shop for Christmas. I also got a devil puppet and a jester puppet with a big nose. Danny got a cool brown wolf puppet. Our hands would fit into his big mouth, and we could bite each other; the white rubber teeth would sink into our skin a little. Danny called him Lobo. Once he had Lobo bite Dad a little too hard when we were all playing with our puppets, and Dad got mad. We had to be careful how hard Lobo bit after that. Danny also got a king puppet with a crown and a white beard.

Charley was my favorite puppet, and I slept with him most nights; his soft cream-colored muzzle and brown furry head rested next to me on my pillow. One day though, disaster struck while I was playing in the giant sandbox by our apartment building. That was when we lived in the same apartment building as my friend Walter. After a few months, we moved to a different building by a big field, where we played catch with our baseball gloves for the first time.

I was digging away in the sand, making tunnels and volcanoes for my little trucks. Charley was by my side, and we had the whole sandbox to ourselves when I heard Mom calling me to eat lunch. For some reason, I decided to dig a hidden chamber under the volcano to bury Charley in, like in the pyramids, until I came back from lunch. I'll never understand why I did that. I guess I figured since nobody was there, Charley would be cozy and safe at the bottom.

When I came back, I dug where I thought I left Charley, but I couldn't find him. I tried more to the right, then more to the left, above and below; I started to panic, digging everywhere. It was a huge sandbox, so it took me a long time to dig it all up. About halfway through, I began to realize that

Charley was gone, and sobs started slipping out of me. I felt so alone; fear was squeezing out everything good and happy as the sun kept getting lower. By the time I finished and gave up, it was getting dark. Someone must have found Charley and taken him while I was eating my alphabet soup. That was one of the worst days of my life. I cried for the longest time and refused to eat supper. I finally fell asleep in my sweaty sand-crusted clothes.

I don't know if adults understand, but toys can open up a kid's heart as much as a real person can. Once a heart is open, love just starts pouring out naturally, like cool water out of a hand pump—it doesn't matter whose hand pumps the handle—person, pet, or puppet, it gushes out wet and refreshing all the same. Charley never talked to me, but he filled up a space in me that needed filling—sometimes, I still miss him.

At the end of the crooked street, past the puppet shop a bit, we'd come to the edge of the village where there were great flower gardens along the river. We'd walk past purple, red, and yellow tulips and a giant fountain spraying water twenty feet high in a rainbow shape till we came to a small dam that was off to the side of the river. The dam was knee-high, and we liked to watch the thick green water—the color of Mom's sunglasses, spill over it. Sometimes we'd pretend we were giants throwing boulders and trees into Niagara Falls.

When we crossed the double-arched stone bridge, we always saw a couple of swans floating in the middle of the river. They must've wanted everyone to see how beautiful they were; their white bellies puffed up on the green water, but like queens, they allowed no one close enough to stroke their soft white necks.

We'd turn right after the bridge and go up the road a bit until we found a dirt path off to the left. We'd follow it zigzagging up the mountain through tall, straight pine trees on either side that stretched up to the sky. Scattered pine cones dotted beds of brown pine needles on the sides of the path. The woods also had plenty of fat, smooth trees that lost their leaves in the winter.

Giant slanted slabs of rocks were sometimes on one side of the path, with trees going higher up the hill above them. On the other side was a steep drop full of towering trees, matted layers of leaves and pine needles, rotting branches, and an occasional boulder poking up. Sunlight would squeeze its way through the trees in shafts of dusty white brightness. The air smelled like pine trees, moss, and moist earth.

We got hot and hungry hiking. About halfway up, there was a Chinese pagoda, that's what Danny called it, where we'd stop and eat our tuna or egg salad sandwiches. Danny carried one of Dad's old canteens around his belt, and we'd sip tinny tasting Kool-Aid—a chain kept the black cap from falling to the dirt.

We would eat and talk about comic books, movies, or stuff that we were experiencing at the time. Sometimes we'd talk about places where we used to live, what we did there or people we knew. One day when we were munching away, Danny started talking about our old black alley cat Buttons.

"Do you remember the day we took off for Virginia, and we tried to take Buttons in the car?"

"Yeah, that was a horrible day," I said.

"It started good though, Mom dropped us off at the movies while the movers packed and loaded our stuff, and we got to see *The Three Stooges Meet Hercules*. Remember when Hercules was cracking walnuts by flexing his muscles?" Steve Reeves played Hercules, and he was the strongest and handsomest looking Hercules we ever saw, much more muscular than the Hercules in *Jason and the Argonauts*, who made the bronze giant come to life by being greedy.

"That was cool, all right, and Curly Joe was funny when he tried to copy Hercules and crack a nut the same way. Curly Joe is nowhere near as funny as the old Curly, but he is funny sometimes," I said.

"You're right; the old Curly is the funniest stooge of all time. But it sure turned cruddy when Buttons went crazy in the car, scratching at the windows to get out. Then we had to take him to Ricky's instead of to Virginia with us. I miss Buttons sometimes; just petting him and listening to his loud purr was comforting. He used to sleep with me when he wasn't out at night fighting in the alley, and his purr helped me get to sleep."

We have a picture in one of our photo albums of Danny holding Buttons back then, squeezing him so tight it's a wonder Buttons put up with it. Danny had his giant smile beaming all cheesy at the camera—he always smiles that way when he gets his picture taken. There's a similar picture from the same time except I'm the victim, not Buttons, and Danny is holding me with his arm around my baby neck. He's about three in the picture, and he looks all proud and happy to be holding me, though I look startled from his chokehold.

We took Buttons to Ricky's because he's our cousin, a year older than me, a year younger than Danny. He has wide round eyes and dark hair like Dad. He lives with Aunt Joyce, Uncle Friday, and his sister Kathy—who everyone calls Cuppy for some reason. Ricky used to tease her by saying, "See you pee-pee why." It was pretty stupid, but it always made Cuppy mad. Sometimes we copied what Ricky said; then, I would feel bad about it when Cuppy left the room calling us creeps.

Uncle Friday was a foreman at the glass factory; it was a couple blocks from their house behind a high white fence. Three giant white silos holding sand and glass making stuff towered about a hundred feet tall behind the fence. There was also a conveyor belt up there hanging high in space.

Uncle Friday walked to work every day, and Aunt Joyce had a shopping cart that she pushed a few blocks to Petrowski's or the A&P for groceries, so they were able to go without a car for years. They must have saved a lot of money that way, maybe that's why they were the first ones in our family to buy a color TV. They had to get a car recently, though, when the glass factory went out of business and Uncle Friday lost his job. He needed a car to drive to his new job as a foreman at a paper factory in Blawnox, not far from Pittsburgh.

Ricky had one talent that I really admired; he could put his fingers in his mouth and make those kind of loud shrill whistles that reach a block away. I can whistle but not with my fingers; I always wished I could do that. Ricky said there was nothing to it, and he tried to teach me, but nothing came out but hissing air between my teeth and fingers.

Unfortunately, Ricky was kind of a trouble maker and had a knack for getting into hot water with Uncle Friday, who was taller than Dad, Italian, and starting to lose his hair already. He was a great uncle, funny and nice to us, but he and Ricky were always clashing at each other about something.

It made me uncomfortable to listen to Uncle Friday's deep stern voice when he hollered, "Richard!" Ricky never seemed too afraid though, he talked back in a way I would never do with Dad—Dad would have his belt off in a heartbeat. Maybe Ricky just acted like he wasn't scared to show off to us, and he knew Uncle Friday wouldn't hit him with us there.

They had a bathroom in their basement that I made a point of using because I liked the smell of the green painted walls down there—the floor was green, too. Aunt Joyce always had orange Dial soap in the bathroom sink that smelled good, too. I could sniff my hands for quite a while afterwards and still be able to enjoy it.

One day after using the bathroom, Ricky and me were pretending to be pirates using sticks for swords on their back porch. Danny was bouncing on a sturdy black rocking horse by the railing that was separating the neighbors half of the porch from their half—they lived in a duplex; a few times, Ricky had me and Danny listen with him to the wall in his bedroom. If we put our ears next to it and listened without hardly breathing, sometimes we could hear Mr. Davis yelling at his kids or his wife or Mrs. Davis giving him heck back.

The porch had a wooden railing with square poles spaced a couple inches apart, and for some reason, I stuck my arm between two of the poles facing their tiny backyard. I was surprised when I couldn't pull my arm out. Ricky started laughing, but it was hurting my arm, and I started to get scared—thinking maybe my arm would swell up so much cutting off the blood, it would begin turning purple or black, and once they sawed away the poles, my hand would hang limp and useless forever. I didn't want to cry in front of Ricky, but I could feel tears starting to well up. Danny came over and yanked on it, but he couldn't get it loose either.

Luckily, Aunt Joyce came out from the kitchen and saw my predicament. Aunt Joyce is skinny with a long nose, dark frizzy hair, and her voice sounds a lot like Mom's—maybe because they are sisters near the same age. She tried to get my arm out and saw that it was really good and stuck, but she told me not to worry, and she'd be right back. She returned with a butter dish in her hand and smeared butter all over my arm; it came out as easy as could be. I gave her a big hug. Women have always looked out for me, more so than men. I guess they're just more aware of what kids are up to and what they feel than men are.

When we visited another time, it rained really hard for twenty minutes, a typical spring shower in PA. Ricky had a couple rafts he had made out of popsicle sticks and triangular paper for sails. Ricky, me, and Danny ran outside when the rain eased up to race them down their street gutter. The water was gushing four feet wide as we set the rafts side by side and let them go. Then we ran alongside as they zipped and bobbed and twirled down to the gutter mouth at the corner. We snatched them just before the rafts got sucked in.

The gutter mouths in Arnold have a unique smell from the Allegheny River being just a block or two away; they smell like

41

river water and sewer stink mixed up; it's an odor that always makes me feel at home and peaceful when I get a strong whiff. That might sound strange, but I enjoy strong smells; they make me feel more alive somehow like they shake me and make me aware of what the world is putting out there for us.

We raced the rafts a handful of times before the gush turned into a trickle. One of the rafts fell into the gutter mouth—I think Ricky let it fall on purpose to see it get sucked down the black hole. As it plunged, he screamed into the metal slot like a person falling, and we could hear his echo.

When Buttons started to go nuts, Ricky's house was only half a dozen blocks away, so Dad rushed over there, hardly stopping at stop signs. Mom and Dad asked Aunt Joyce if she and Uncle Friday could take care of Buttons until we moved back. She said sure, but we found out later that Buttons ran away back to our old house in Parnassus

Somehow he found his way home from Arnold; it was at least a mile or so away. We knew because Mrs. McCutcheon, our old landlady, wrote Mom a letter saying they saw him back in the alley prowling around. They started leaving cat food out for him, but he never went in their house.

"He was a great cat," I said to Danny as a couple wearing green camping packs walked past the pagoda and waved at us. "Do you remember that Thanksgiving when he got on the table and was eating our turkey?"

"Oh yeah, I thought Dad was going to throw him out the window instead of down the steps," Danny laughed. "Buttons looked back up at Dad, like, who do you think you are tossing *me* out? Do you think he is still alive roaming around the alley?" Danny asked.

"I don't know, that was years ago, and he always came in with cuts and scratches from other cats. He was tough, but he had a rough life."

"Something tells me he isn't around anymore," Danny said. He looked sad about it, so I gathered up our trash and tossed it in the green metal garbage can next to the picnic table.

"Hey, let's go up to the nest," I said.

"Ok, you're right; it's time to get going." The climb was easier after we had full stomachs and had rested for a while.

We took turns leading the way, though sometimes the path got wider, and we could walk next to each other.

We had found the stone pit of an old machine-gun nest further up. We always stopped there and crouched in the pit for a while—neither one of us were willing to be Germans, so we'd shoot at Nazis creeping up behind the trees.

It was hard to believe there had been such a big war in Germany twenty years before; there was hardly any evidence now; the machine gun nest was all we ever saw. All the buildings seemed in good shape; the people were friendly. We'd heard about the Berlin Wall, but we never saw that. Of course, Army bases all over Germany kept an eye on things, I guess, but otherwise, it was like the war never happened on the outside.

One of my friends at school said that Nazis used to make lampshades out of human skin, and he claimed to have seen one in some old German lady's house. I'm not sure I believe he saw one, Bobby Britain was known to exaggerate, but I think Nazis did make lampshades out of skin. I heard it before somewhere. How could they do that to other human beings? I hope they killed the poor people before they took their skin off, but who knows; those Nazis were evil without a doubt.

The outside of the country looked great, but the inside must be a different story; who knows what horrible memories people in Germany might have from the war, from what they did to other people, or what soldiers did to them. Now there's another war happening in Vietnam; doesn't it ever stop?

Beyond the trees, at the top of the mountain, was a cobble-stoned road that led us to the castle. Danny said the cobblestones were a time boundary, and once we stepped onto the street, we were in King Arthur's time. I picked Sir Lancelot because he was the best swordsman, and Danny was usually King Arthur because he got to be king, and he could take command of our battles against the Black Knight or what other bad guys we fought.

I was always a little disappointed at the castle, though; it was just a giant wall of ivy-covered stones that rose from the street. There wasn't even a drawbridge or a massive gate, just an ancient-looking wooden door. The tower looked more like the steeple of a church than those cool crown-looking towers, but it was a real castle, and the wall was a hundred feet high— armies would've had a hard time busting in.

On the other side of Bad Kissingen, across the river, are a series of stone watchtowers next to each other on a high hill. Once, our third-grade class went for a field trip up there. Mrs. Budzelack must have been seventy with her wild white hair, and she was so thin all the veins in her arms and hands stood out, but she hiked up that hill even better than we did. She smiled at us with her hands on her hips as we panted with our hands on our knees. She kept telling us that we were almost there; just a bit further, we could make it.

I loved her, mostly because I could tell that she loved me—she loved all of us, I guess, but she made me feel special, that what I said and wrote was worth paying attention to. She was also so gentle and patient, especially when I struggled with writing longhand, and she encouraged me to start a hobby.

"Everybody should have a hobby, something that they love to do in their spare time. I know you love to read, and that's great, but you should also have a hobby, something to build or collect. Stamps are lots of fun; I bet you would like to collect stamps. They are from countries all over the world, and some of them are quite beautiful. Why don't you think about it?"

So I started collecting stamps for a while, and I did enjoy it. Some of the stamps even came in triangular shapes. Danny liked collecting them, too. It was exciting to see how many different countries we could get and how cool some of them were. We eagerly checked the mailbox every week for the little wax paper packets of stamps we got. Mom and Dad got us a white stamp album that we could keep them all in.

Mrs. Budzelack had a beautiful reading voice, and she often read us stories like *Pippi Longstocking* and *Charlotte's Web*. She read those so great I had to check them out of the library for myself. I cried when I had to leave third grade. Mrs. Budzelack said I would like fourth grade too, and I could visit her from time to time. I did once—right before we left Germany after two months of fourth grade, and I remember that she gave me a big hug; she felt like a skeleton, and I kissed her on her soft wrinkled cheek.

On our field trip, we walked up a huge grassy hill with white and yellow wildflowers poking their heads out of the grass, and we kept looking up as the towers grew bigger and bigger. They aren't nearly as tall as our hiking castle, but they have those cool-looking crown tops that archers could hide behind.

We found the steps blocked with chains and signs saying "Betreten verboten" (Mrs. Budzelack told us that meant keep out in German), so we couldn't climb to the tops of the towers, but they were great anyway. We ate our lunches sitting on soft grass as we leaned against the bottoms of cold stone walls, and I imagined what it must have been like to look out from the tops, searching for an enemy that might be sneaking up through the countryside with their swords out and their bows nocked with arrows.

The Romans were supposed to have built those towers well over a thousand years ago, and the thick stone blocks were huge and ancient-looking. It must have been a lot of work moving those stones up the hill or wherever they got them from. I wonder if the buildings people make these days could last so long. Some maybe, but most probably not.

Next to the towers was the Miniature Black Forest. It was all pine trees and dark and shadowy inside. After lunch, we hiked in a ways; it was so quiet, pine cones and pine needles were everywhere, making our footsteps as silent as an Indian's—unless you crunched a pine cone with your shoe. It seemed like the kind of dark forest that Hansel and Gretel lost their way in. We collected bags of pine cones to save for making Christmas wreaths in class, and Mrs. Budzelack encouraged us to enjoy the beauty of the forest as we worked.

"What a fine old forest this is. Breathe in the air that the pine trees are making for us," and she made us all stop for a second and take a deep sweet breath. Mrs. Budzelack came by me while I was picking up cones. She bent down to pick up a perfect-looking pine cone. "Look at this beauty, Bobby." She handed me the cone, gave me her lovely wrinkly smile, and moved down the path near other kids.

Well, our hiking castle was way taller than the Roman watchtowers, but there was no way for us to get inside, so me and Danny would walk back and forth along the wall and get dizzy looking up at the ivy-covered stone. After a few sword fights with sticks and last-minute escapes from boiling oil, we'd hike back down. The journeys we had up to that castle were some of the best times we ever had doing stuff together. Sometimes we talk about going back there someday, inside though we know we never will—those times are over forever, but they are still a part of who we are somehow.

I look over at Danny, who is deep into my *Wonder Woman* comic; he's not aware of me looking at him or the world outside the car we pass by. His face has changed from Germany; his nose is longer, his lips wider. His arms and legs are getting skinnier and longer, too, more awkward somehow. I guess Danny is growing up; he'll be thirteen in December— a teenager, which he often brags he almost is.

I feel kind of sad thinking about him getting older; how did it happen? Time just works away quietly under your nose until one day you're surprised to notice that someone or something has changed considerably. Danny is twisting a lock of his brown hair, sitting Indian style with his shoes off and his legs crossed on the car seat. Once again, we are on another journey together; I'm not looking forward to this one because of the funeral, but I'm glad Danny is with me as usual.

Chapter III

The Mystery

I hear the metal click of Dad's Zippo up front. "Hey, boys," he says, "look out the window. Take your noses out of your comics and look at those cows. Did you ever see horns like that? Daniel. Close the book. Look up. That's called a Texas Longhorn. Isn't that something?" Dad is holding his Pall Mall with his lips, squinting through the smoke, and pointing out the window as the fence posts and the Longhorns flick past.

Dad loves living in Texas. He's been talking about staying in Copperas Cove after he gets out of the Army—which may be soon. We live in a white ranch house with pink trim at 220 Easy Street. Dad loves the name of our street and likes to say, "We're all set now; we're living on Easy Street." It has a front yard with tall scratchy bushes next to a picture window and a roomy backyard with a big field behind our fence. The neighbors are nice and pretty much mind their own business. Dad has been talking about maybe buying the house somehow if he doesn't reenlist in October.

It's actually the first real house we've ever lived in. Usually, we have an apartment or the upstairs or the basement or a duplex, never a whole house before; it's a good feeling.

Dad said it's the best place we've ever lived in, and we all like it too—except for the cockroaches, but they seem to be all over Texas, along with black crickets.

Once we went looking for a nice place to have a picnic. We finally found a great-looking park, but when we stopped the car and walked closer, we saw all the picnic tables totally covered with squirming black crickets—it reminded me of a movie we watched with Charleton Heston called *The Naked Jungle*. Charleton Heston is my favorite actor who I first saw in *Ben Hur*. This movie wasn't nearly as good as *Ben-Hur*—no movie is, but it was interesting and gripping.

Charleton Heston was a plantation owner in South America somewhere, and army ants were on the march, swarming over and devouring everything in their path. They were heading right toward his plantation. Trees, animals, bridges, people, it was all stripped to the bone—that's why the jungle was naked. Nothing could stop the ants; there was a loud buzzing sound from the ants chewing and gnawing away without stop. As a last resort, he tried killing them with fire around the stone walls of his estate. They piled up wood and furniture around the walls, but when the fire went out, the ants kept coming, crawling up the walls while his Amazon Indian servants tried to beat them away with brooms and blankets.

Finally, Charleton Heston covered himself with turpentine or something to keep the ants off him and raced out the gate through what little was left of the jungle and his crops. After he made it to the dam, he blew it up with dynamite; the flood washed the ants away and killed them. He got swept along with the powerful floodwaters back to the wall of his plantation, but Charleton Heston was alive, of course; he was the hero. In real life, I think the ants would have devoured him before he made it to the dam, turpentine or not, but it made for a good story.

After we saw the crickets crawling on the picnic tables, the grills, and the ground around the tables, Dad said, "The hell with it, I'm tired of looking for a decent spot; let's just go home and eat."

So we drove home, and Mom put our picnic basket on the kitchen table. We took our potato salad and cold cut sandwiches into the living room—*Atom Ant* was on TV for our picnic—it really was, no joking.

Sometimes I think God must have a great sense of humor—how could he bear some of the awful things that happen in the universe he created if he didn't joke around once in a while and look at the funny side of life. I bet Jesus must have laughed a lot, too; he couldn't have been as serious all the time as the Bible makes him seem. I mean, come on, he was God's son, after all, so he must have been happy and full of joy most of the time just from knowing that.

Luckily the cockroaches aren't swarming in our house like the army ants or the crickets, so we all like living there, especially Dad. I peeked into the kitchen from down the hall as Dad talked to Mom just the other day, "Joan, my job is to teach these kids how to stay alive, but they rush them through too damn fast; they aren't ready. Some can hardly shave, and it's the first time they have been away from home. Most of them are just young kids fresh out of high school, and Vietnam is too much for them. Even for Billy, it was too much, and he was an E-5, not some raw recruit. I'm not even sure what the hell we are doing over there anymore. Maybe it's time to get out and move on to something different. Texas might be a good place to settle down; it feels good here, and there's no damn snow."

Mom's face was a little red like it gets when she is scared about something, and Dad just looked tired as he sipped some iced tea at our kitchen table. I was surprised when I heard Dad say that; I thought he loved the Army since he's been in it forever. I never considered him ever getting out and being a civilian—what kind of work would he do? I figured he must be upset about Uncle Billy, and now that we are on the road, I can tell he isn't quite himself; he usually talks more when he drives.

Dad stretches and slaps the steering wheel. "Yes, sir, those are Texas cows all right; all this room lets their horns spread out and relax!" Dad must not have noticed the WELCOME TO OKLAHOMA sign a while back, but I'm not bringing it up. I think Danny did notice because he's trying to hold back a giggle. I look away from Danny quick as his giggles are contagious, especially if he tries to hold it in, and laughter starts slipping out past his hand. If we both get started, we might have to explain what we are snickering about.

Sometimes we get in trouble at night because we can't stop giggling. Danny always sleeps in the top bunk, and I'm on the bottom. I tried the top bunk for a short time when I was four in Virginia, but even with the wooden bar that is supposed to stop you, I fell out somehow. I don't know how I fell without breaking anything; it had to be a miracle. There must've been a beautiful angel slowing me down with her soft

wings or something. Maybe she's my guardian angel appointed by God to watch over me—she has to be lovely with black or golden hair and a face shining with God's light. She saved me, I'm guessing, but ever since the bottom is for me, and Danny likes the top.

Sometimes when we move, we get a room big enough to separate the beds, so we are both on the floor, and that's a nice change, but almost always, we're in the same room. So if one of us gets the giggles, the other starts laughing, and if it's late, we both get in trouble.

Just the other day, after watching an old Cary Grant movie called *Mr. Blanding's Dream House* on the late show, Danny got goofy. Cary Grant was an advertising executive who was building the house he and his wife had always dreamed of. Of course, there were all kinds of funny things that went wrong all the time. Cary Grant also had to come up with a slogan for a type of ham called Wham, or he would lose a big account and maybe his job.

When they built the house and were about to celebrate with a house-warming dinner, the colored maid came out with a big plate of ham. Someone praised how it looked, and she said, "If you ain't eatin' Wham, you ain't eatin' ham." Cary Grant kissed her and ran to his office to use what she said for his advertising campaign.

For some reason, Danny was tickled by that, and after we went to bed, he kept saying, "If you ain't eatin' Wham, you ain't eatin' ham." Then he would say, "Wham, a homer! Wham, another homer!" Which was something that Bugs Bunny said in a cartoon once. Danny loves Bugs Bunny almost as much as he does Yogi Bear.

Sometimes Danny's humor is a bit strange, but it makes sense somehow once you think about what he says. After he said "another homer!" he would burst out giggling, and of course, I would start laughing as well. Trying not to laugh only makes it harder to hold in. After we finally managed to control ourselves, my sides had quit aching, and I thought it was over, Danny would say it again, and the giggles would erupt once more.

Suddenly, Dad swung open the door, and we could see he was hot, "If you don't get quiet, you're going to find out what WHAM means." He gave us both the evil eye and slammed the door. We quit laughing right then and settled down to sleep.

"Would you like to eat now?" Mom asks everybody.

"Sounds good to me, Hon. What do you have?" Dad asks.

"Ham, or braunschweiger sandwiches."

"Make mine ham," Dad says.

"Me too," says Danny.

There goes God again with his sense of humor; I was just thinking about ham, and here Mom is offering it to all of us. It kind of gives me the willies when something like this happens; it's a little too coincidental; it must be some sort of cosmic joke by God again, I'm guessing.

Ham is Dad's favorite meat; he can eat it every day. For me, ham has an unpleasant smell when it cooks, making my stomach a little bit queasy; sometimes, I make an excuse to go to my room or outside when Mom cooks it. The smell didn't bother me when I was younger. Maybe it has something to do with reading *Charlotte's Web,* one of my favorite books. Wilbur was such a nice pig, and he fought for his life all through the book. Ever since Mrs. Budzalack first read it to me, I've kind of lost my taste—and smell for ham.

"Braunschweiger for me, Mom." We also call it goose liver; I don't know why though, it doesn't come from a goose—what does it come from, now that I think about it? A cow—or maybe, a pig? No, it couldn't be from a pig, could it?

The sandwich Mom hands me is wrapped in wax paper. "Thanks, Mom." When I open the paper, the braunschweiger's pasty meat smell and the tang of the mayonnaise make my stomach gurgle. Mom knows I like it with Miracle Whip. "Can I have some Fritos, too?" Mom shakes up a bottle of Yoo-Hoo and opens it with the bottle opener before she passes it to me with a small bag of Fritos—you have to shake up the chocolate real good before you open the bottle.

Danny already has a mouthful of his ham sandwich. The smell doesn't bother me much when it is cold, only when it's hot and steaming. Danny smiles at me and then opens his mouth, so I have to look at chewed-up ham. He knows ham is not my favorite.

I turn away, take a bite of my goose liver sandwich, and then about halfway through chewing, I stuff in some Fritos. I remember when Fritos first came out, we were living in Virginia at the time, and they had these funny commercials with the Frito Bandito; he had a mustache and a sombrero on TV.

The first time we heard the commercial was on the radio, though; the Bandito's funny voice came on during our drive home from a fair. We had fun walking around, even though they didn't have any cool rides. There was a big tent with a giant statue of Smokey the Bear standing outside; it was almost as tall as our house. A large sign was next to him, "Only You Can Prevent Forest Fires!" The inside of the tent had all kinds of tables about how to use fire safely. They gave us pamphlets, Smokey the Bear pencils, and a cool magnet to take home and put on our refrigerator.

The best part of the fair, though, was when Dad bought us our Three Stooges puppets at one of the booths. He had tried to win them for us by throwing baseballs at these stacks of wooden milk bottles. After a couple pitches, he realized there was no way he would win, so he went over and whispered to the guy behind the counter. Dad handed him a five-dollar bill, and the guy gave Dad Moe and Curly. Danny wanted Curly, and I wanted Moe.

Moe looked just like he did at the movies with his black banged hair that he uses shoe polish on. Moe and Curly both had a little four o'clock shadow on their faces—Curly had it on the top of his head, too. I loved Moe; his rubber head smelled great. We had a lot of fun playing with them. Eventually, Mom sewed me a new body out of yellow and white checkered cloth because I wore the original cloth body out. That was a shirt with a vest, a big red tie that said MOE going down it, and checkered pants. Moe is still in our toy box somewhere, though some of the black is fading from his bangs—it's a creamy tan color underneath the black. I think I'll dig him out when we get back home.

Anyway, after we heard the Frito commercial, Mom picked up a big bag of Fritos at the gas station when Dad stopped for gas. When we got home, everybody had to try them, so we had our first bag during *Yogi Bear* when Yogi and Boo Boo drove the ranger crazy.

Danny loves Yogi—"Smarter than the average bear," Yogi used to say all the time. Danny likes to say, "Smarter than the average boy," when he is proud of himself for thinking he is clever. Danny had a Yogi Bear stuffed animal with his tiny green hat on top and a green tie; I had Huckleberry Hound Dog, he was blue with a red bow tie. They were about two feet tall. Both of them had super soft furry bodies that were nice to cuddle with and a pleasant rubbery smell to their faces. They got lost in one of our moves, or maybe Mom got rid of them. She does that sometimes to old toys, to make room for new toys, I guess, but I wish she wouldn't without asking first. Some toys are too precious to lose.

Mom opened the Fritos bag and gave us each a small bowlful. We started munching the salty corn chips as Yogi painted a redwood like a tunnel for the ranger to smash into with his jeep. Danny and me loved how Fritos tasted; Mom liked them too, but Dad couldn't get past the smell they have— he calls it a dirty sock smell. He's never touched them since.

"Mmm mmm," as Andy Griffith says; goose liver and Fritos go great together, almost as good as chocolate and popcorn. That's my favorite movie snack. Any kind of chocolate will do, but Raisinets or Goobers are the best. I eat a handful of popcorn and then pop in some Raisinets at the same time. The chocolate mixes with the popcorn in a special way that can't be beat.

Danny always likes Reeses Peanut Butter Cups with his popcorn. We used to go to the movies a lot in Germany. We couldn't watch TV because it was all in German—we tried once, it was a show about insects. A praying mantis was chewing on some kind of beetle, but we couldn't understand anything they said, so we turned it off. Besides, the movies were cheap on base; we would usually get two cartoons, a short—either the Three Stooges, Rocket Man, or Zorro—and a movie for thirty-five cents on matinee days.

One week we were super excited because they would show *King Kong vs. Godzilla* at the next matinee. We looked forward to it all week. Finally, it was Saturday. We bought our tickets, got our goodies, and took our seats. Danny was smiling from ear to ear. Before the movie was about to start, the movie guy came out—we saw him plenty of times before; he was a short man with a crew cut, and he climbed the steps up to the stage. He faced us with his hands on his hips.

"I'm sorry, boys and girls, but we won't be able to show *King Kong vs. Godzilla* today. The film did not arrive on the truck last night like it was supposed to, so we can't show it. However, we have a good movie in its place, *Tammy and the Doctor*."

Everyone started groaning and booing. Someone yelled out, "I want my money back!" Other kids began shouting the same thing, but the crew cut guy quickly cut them off.

"There will be no refunds. It's against our policy. You can either watch the movie we have, or you can leave." He walked off the stage as kids continued to boo, and they started showing previews.

Danny looked at me in disbelief. I couldn't believe it either. We were missing one of the greatest monster movies of all time, and they were making us watch *Tammy and the Doctor* instead. Debbie Reynolds as a lovesick nurse replacing the monster fight of the century. How could they do something so unfair? Why didn't they tell us before we bought our tickets? We had already paid for our popcorn, chocolate, Juicy Fruits and Coca Cola, so we stayed, even though we had already seen *Tammy and the Doctor* a few days before.

I was in shock all through the movie that we weren't watching Godzilla and King Kong slugging it out. It was such a letdown. I didn't enjoy my snacks as much as usual—even the icy Coca-Cola in my paper cup tasted flat. As we left the lobby, Danny told the crew cut guy we were never coming again, but he didn't pay any attention to Danny. He must have known we didn't have any other choice. Life can be so unfair, especially if you are a kid. If there had been any adults in the theater, it would have been a different story, I bet.

Sure enough, the very next Saturday, we were right back there watching *The Seven Faces of Dr. Lao*—which was a fantastic movie. Tony Randal played seven roles; one was Pan with his pipes; he had horns on his head like the devil and goat hoofs. The movie had super special effects, especially when he turned into a giant dragon with seven different heads at the end—it was during a storm, and dragon heads were thrashing every which way in the night sky. We loved it. I was surprised that Tony Randal was so good being the star; usually, he plays Rock Hudson's friend in a Doris Day movie.

God, she is beautiful with her silver-blonde hair, smiling face—which has a few perfectly placed freckles, and her voice can sound so sweet when she is happy about something. I always thought Rock Hudson was so lucky to be able to hug and kiss her.

Speaking of pretty faces, the first movie we went to when we moved to Germany was *In Search of the Castaways* with Haley Mills. We had to live in Bad Kissingen at first until an apartment on base opened up. When we got off the train, Dad hugged and kissed Mom for a long time, then he hugged and kissed us, too. He'd been missing us awful, he said.

We got in a cab that drove us to where we would live. Dad had found two rooms in a German landlady's guest house, close to one of those tube-shaped billboards that Germans put on sidewalks. You have to walk all the way around it to see all the ads, which seems strange to me. The landlady reminded me of Grandma T, who has bouncy dark hair like they wore in the nineteen fifties, but the German lady wasn't as skinny as Grandma T.

Grandma T was Mom's mother, and according to Mom, Grandma pretty much raised all seven kids by herself. Grandpap Tinnemeyer was in the Sea Bees during World War II. That was the best time Mom's family had; the checks came regularly, and things were peaceful, but Grandpap came back with a drinking problem after the war was over. He'd have a decent job for a while, and then his drinking would mess things up, and he'd be out of work till he found another one.

Mom said that she could tell by looking at his hair when he came home if he'd be mean that night. If his hair was out of place and not combed, trouble was coming in the door. Grandma kicked him out of the house finally, but that took years to happen. Grandma cleaned houses for people and managed to take care of seven kids somehow.

Grandma T always makes me think of the witch on *The Wizard of Oz*, not because she is mean or anything, but she looks similar, thin and dark-haired with a wart on her nose that reminds me of the witch's wart. The witch's wart shows her ugliness on the inside; Grandma's wart just shows she is Grandma, a kind human being who loves me. She wouldn't look right to me without her wart.

Grandma loves to play games more than anyone I ever met, and she's good at every game there is. Even if she plays something for the first time, she learns fast and usually wins. She never lets me win; I have to beat her fair and square, and she never says no to me if I ask her to play something. Maybe I'm so good at games now because Grandma makes me work so hard to beat her. If I do win, she always seems happy and congratulates me.

Uncle Johnny and Uncle Dale are the only kids—well, teenagers—still living at home with Grandma. Aunt Joyce, Aunt Doreen, Uncle Bill, Aunt Carol, and Mom all got married. Mom is the oldest and got married first.

Grandma, Uncle Johnny, and Uncle Dale live on top of a gas station by the railroad tracks in Parnassus. A car can drive right under their house and get gas. It's an old gas station that only has one pump with a bubble on top. Sometimes when we walk up the steps to their house, the gasoline smell is pretty strong, especially if somebody spilled some on the cement.

When we left Grandma's house one time, Uncle Johnny followed us on his bike. Uncle Johnny looks a lot like Lucas McCain in *The Rifleman*, except Uncle Johnny is fourteen or so—well, he was then, he's probably about sixteen now. He chased us for a few blocks before we started going up a big hill and were able to lose him. Me and Danny were looking out the back window and waving at him the whole time. I think

Uncle Johnny is super cool, and we look like we could be brothers, except he's bigger, and my ears stick out more than his do.

Grandma also has a black and white dog called Trixie, who is awfully sweet and well-behaved. Trixie likes to lay her head on Grandma's lap when she sits in her brown chair and plays games with me and Danny. Trixie is smart, too. She gets up and runs to the top of the steps whenever she needs to go outside, bouncing her tail against the stair poles. Grandma took Danny and me with her once when she walked Trixie; she didn't even need a leash because Trixie is so dependable and well-behaved—even if a cat was lazing about in someone's yard, Trixie wouldn't chase after it.

The German landlady never played games with us like Grandma T, of course, but she loved Danny and gave him a special German chocolate bar when we first moved in. The wrapper was white with little pictures of people moving about: walking, riding unicycles, or rowing boats with seated ladies holding parasols; silver foil covered the chocolate under the wrapper. Danny gave me a piece, so it didn't bother me much that I didn't get one, too. It tasted different than American chocolate, smoother and more chocolaty somehow, really delicious.

We had to share the bathroom in the hall with other guests, and the floors were cold like ice at night if you had to go pee. Sometimes it was occupied, and you had to decide whether to go back and try again later or wait with your bare feet growing numb. Number two was brutal with German toilet paper; it was gray and coarse with little bumps and would make you bleed if you used too much. Thankfully, when we moved on Post, the commissary sold beautiful soft American toilet paper, which feels like heaven compared to German paper.

Me and Danny shared a sofa bed in the kitchen, and Mom and Dad had a giant bed in the other room with a feather tick that puffed up as thick as stacked pillows. There was a wooden wardrobe closet you could hide in next to their bed that had a mirror on the door. (There was no key to lock it, and we could open it from the inside.) It got cold in those rooms, so sometimes, when Dad had already gone to work early in the morning, we all piled into the big bed under the feather tick—usually on the weekends when there was no school.

One night we braved the cold weather, and all four of us walked through Bad Kissingen to get to the theater on Post. *In Search of the Castaways* was pretty good, I think. I remember them being stuck in a giant tree with a leopard during a flood, and there was a terrible fire, but my eyes, ears, and heart were all full of Haley Mills. She was so beautiful with her blond hair in pigtails. I guess she was about thirteen or fourteen, and her voice with her British accent just made me want to listen to her forever. Haley Mills was always as smart (or smarter) than the adults she starred with, and when she smiled, I felt like an angel was smiling at me.

Later on, we saw her in *Moon Spinners,* where Haley Mills was hanging from a spinning windmill—it scared me awful that she might fall. In *Pollyanna,* she was trying on clothes in an expensive dress shop; she had on those long underclothes they wore in the early 1900s. *The Parent Trap* was incredible because she played twins in that one. I couldn't get enough of her. Danny didn't think Haley Mills was that special; I don't know what planet he was from, not to think she was gorgeous. My heart was tingling all through the movie.

After it was over, we bundled up in the lobby and walked down the hill into Bad Kissingen to the bridge, which had old-fashioned-looking lamp posts that were turning green like some statues do. Snowflakes were fluttering down on our faces and coats. Mom and Dad had just bought me a new salt and pepper gray coat in a store close to the puppet shop; it was warm with red silky sleeves on the inside that felt nice on my arms.

An inch of fresh snow covered the river's flat ice, but patches of the ice showed here and there. It looked so thick I bet people could walk across it—if they were crazy enough to try, but I didn't see any footprints. The lamplight reflecting off the ice and snow made the surrounding darkness seem deeper beyond the bridge. I watched snowflakes falling past the streetlight in a busy flurry; then they seemed to slow as they drifted down, falling noiselessly onto the growing layer of snow on the ground or disappearing on my coat.

The smell of the snow and the deep cold tingling the inside of my nose and lungs made me long for a cozy fireplace and some hot chocolate. (We never had a fireplace, but I always imagined sitting next to one would be the perfect place to read and sip steaming cocoa.)

Danny was dragging a frozen clacking stick along the bridge's stone railing, scraping off fresh snow, which sprinkled down to the river. Dad held Mom's arm and all our breaths came out like smoke. I almost expected our breaths to stay frozen in the air from the bitter cold, but they puffed away.

I grabbed handfuls of snow from the stone railing and lobbed snowballs into the night. They dropped down to splat softly and silently on the hard ice. Thinking about how freezing cold the water flowing under that ice must be made me shiver.

The frigid air seemed to pull beauty out of the glistening pebbled stone, the crisp white snow, the still silent river, the crunch of snow under our shoes, out of every speck of the world around me. I could feel the Mystery throbbing gently in my head and my chest; joy was deep inside me, leaking out into the night.

The Mystery just happens. When it hits, I feel my breath sucking in from my belly and a gentle knuckle-rubbing kind of feeling in my brain, a sweet twisting in my chest. Then after a while, it slips away, and my heart tries to chase after it, but it's gone, wherever the Mystery goes. Sometimes it lingers in the background for a while, like that night walking home in the snow, as I felt the beauty of everything and sensed a deep closeness between all four of us that felt strong, permanent, reassuring.

When we got home, Mom made us some steaming hot chocolate with tiny marshmallows floating on top. Even Dad had a cup, and he's more of a coffee person. I looked at the icicles hanging down outside of our kitchen window and thought about how nice it was to be inside our cozy rooms as my face, fingers, and toes tingled while they thawed out. After we finished drinking, we took a sponge bath by the kitchen sink and dove under the quilt on our bed. The next morning Mom cooked brown eggs and gave us slices of buttered German bread, real bread, not the soft puff we eat in America.

The first time I remember naming that feeling the Mystery was on a train somewhere between England and Germany. Dad had gone to Germany a couple months before the rest of us—that's the Army for you. We followed later on the Darby, a huge silver-white ocean liner. I was awed by the high thick waves constantly rising and falling everywhere, which along with the bright blue sky and the Darby, became our world after we left the Statue of Liberty behind.

Even when we were below deck, which is where we had to stay most of the time, we could always feel the waves rocking the ship, sometimes gently, sometimes not. It was better not to think of how deep the water was underneath the Darby, how many thousands of feet of cold blue-gray water were between us, and the giant squids and octopuses waiting near the bottom. Our ship, big as it was, was just a pebble compared to that ocean.

The dining room had dozens of tables and chairs bolted down, and the food was better than Mom's—until the storm came anyway. We had fun exploring the ship. There was a gift shop at the bottom of some spiral metal steps with all kinds of souvenirs, toys, and magazines that we would drool over. We liked looking out of the round porthole in our cabin at the waves bouncing up and down; it looked like the waves were waving at us sometimes—that must be how they got their name.

Danny and me had little metal cars that the boat guy had given us; mine was green, Danny's was yellow. I think he must have felt sorry because just Mom was taking care of us, or maybe it was because he thought Mom was pretty, and he wanted to make her smile and like him.

When the ship dipped down with my belly flipping a little, we'd let go, and the cars would zoom by themselves down the hallway below deck. I guess nobody came out of their doors because the boat was rocking so much. Soon, the ship's front

would tip up high, almost making us slide backwards as we sat on the floor, and the cars would come zipping back to us. Sometimes they made it to the end of the hall, and sometimes the bucking of the ship changed their direction halfway down or up.

A couple times, they crashed into the wall and got flipped upside down, so we had to climb up or scramble down to fetch them. After a while, though, the fun wore off, and we were lying in our bunks with a bucket nearby—even Mom needed a bucket later that night, and she hardly ever gets sick. It seemed to storm for days.

After we docked, we got on a train somehow in the night, and I was so hungry that my stomach hurt. There was no way I could go to sleep with such an empty belly. Mom talked to the train guy, and he came back shortly with baloney and mustard sandwiches while the train rocked and the night rushed black at the windows. It was our first time on a sleeping train. We were up way past our bedtime, and the sound of the train clacking outside was exciting and sleepy at the same time.

Danny was laughing in his upper berth about something when the train guy came into our compartment. The smell of the yellow mustard made my mouth water as I picked up half a sandwich. When I took my first ever bite of baloney and mustard on white bread, my heart took a leap, and I felt close to something that made me a little dizzy, not like from spinning, but from feeling happy fast and deep—the Mystery was in that sandwich. I never tasted anything so good.

Chapter IV

Lizard Catchers

"Do you want anything else, boys? Another sandwich? Some chips?"

"I'm good, Mom." I hand Mom the empty Yoo-Hoo bottle.

"Me too," says Danny. Danny takes out a little black and white puzzle; it's square and fits in the palm of your hand. By moving the white squares with black on them, down, up, or across a picture can be made; it takes a while, but it's fun. This one turns into a picture of Felix the Cat, who Danny loves to watch on TV.

Felix has a magic bag full of tricks. Whenever he needs something, he opens his bag, and out comes something magical, like an escalator so Felix can reach apples on a tree, or his bag turns into a canoe so he can cross a lake. Some mad professor is always trying to steal Felix's bag; once in a while, he manages to snatch it away, but he never succeeds in keeping it for long. Felix is just too smart for him.

Mom offers Dad an opened can of Pepsi, which he takes and sips as he turns the steering wheel to the right, and we pass by a motel that looks like the one in *Psycho* with Norman Bates—it's creepy looking, there's even a big house behind the motel, but it's not up a hill like in the movie. I'm glad we're driving straight through to Mulberry without spending the night at some motel like that.

Psycho was one of the creepiest and scariest movies I ever saw. The actress in the beginning who got slashed in the shower was so beautiful. I couldn't believe it when the knife kept going into her body over and over, and the blood kept dripping down the drain as she collapsed. They don't usually kill a big star like that so early in the movie, so I was shocked. It's been quite a while since I saw *Psycho*, but I still try to keep my eyes open in the shower, just in case.

Norman Bates was so creepy in the end, too, sitting in a chair, letting a fly land on his hand. He knew they were watching him through the one-way mirror. He was thinking in his mother's voice about how he wouldn't swat it, saying how they would see that he wouldn't even hurt a fly. That movie gave me nightmares for a while.

The Birds was another great movie by Alfred Hitchcock. We all saw that one together in Germany. The school scene was scary, where the birds chased the kids down the street pecking their hair, but the scene where they found the guy with his eyes pecked out next to a closet scared me the most; his black eye sockets were dripping blood. I jumped a little in my seat and grabbed Mom's arm—she looked as scared as me.

The ending was great, too. I could hardly breathe when the people walked out of their house, tiptoeing past the birds sitting on their porch, the ground, in trees, and on their car. I don't know why the birds were still then and not attacking; maybe because it was early in the morning, or maybe they were just gathering as many birds as they could before they went hunting for people to attack and peck, but it was eerie. There wasn't any sound in the theater at all till the people made it inside their car and then slowly drove away through thousands of birds. Mom looked at me when they were finally safe and smiled at me, like, thank God they escaped.

Mom is like me; she's not a big talker. We're better at listening. Dad and Danny talk the most. Danny got held back in first grade because he talked so much and didn't listen very good to the teacher. Mom and Dad kept going to teacher conferences, but the teacher couldn't get him to listen and be quiet; Danny didn't get it; he just liked to talk all the time. Dad was not happy at all with Danny for having to repeat first grade. The funny thing is, I found out later that Dad had to repeat first grade too, probably for the same thing, I bet.

When Danny was in first grade the first time, it was just me and Mom during the day. That was when we lived in Parnassus on Fourth Avenue—Parnassus is on one side of New Ken, Arnold is on the other side. They all three kind of blend together, with the railroad tracks going through them all until the tracks pass the glass factory and leave Arnold behind.

We lived in the upstairs of a green and white house shaped like a barn. There was a powder blue archway between the living room and the kitchen; the arch looked so thick and solid somehow that I enjoyed looking at it. I could lay on the couch watching TV, and when I turned my head to the right, I could see Mom through the arch putting food on the table at the same time. Our kitchen table was red and white metal with slippery cushioned chairs to match. A tall cupboard was against the wall. A white cake box with red roses and green leaves was always on top unless we were eating cake, of course.

73

I couldn't see the sink, stove, or refrigerator when I was lying down.

We had a swing-set outside and an inflatable wading pool that we loved to splash in. The landlords lived downstairs, Mr. and Mrs. McCutcheon. Mom would make me breakfast, usually scrambled or soft boiled eggs and toast, but sometimes I'd just eat a couple bowls of Sugar Pops, my favorite cereal. Then we would watch *Captain Kangaroo* and reruns of *I Love Lucy*.

Captain Kangaroo was a nice show to wake up to, with Mr. Moose, who loved talking, and Bunny Rabbit, who never spoke and was always searching for carrots. Also, sleepy Grandfather Clock, Dancing Bear, who just danced, the Captain, who always had carrots in his big pockets standing behind his counter, and Mr. Green Jeans, who was always happy and usually outside wearing overalls and a rounded flat hat. They also had a cartoon on the show every morning called *Tom Terrific and Mighty Manfred the Wonder Dog.*

Tom Terrific had a funny hat shaped like an upside-down funnel, and he was able to turn himself into different things like a dinosaur, a tree-house, or a trampoline, whatever he could imagine. It was way better than Felix's magic bag because Tom became everything and experienced it all himself; it wasn't just a bag that was magic; Tom was the magic.

The cartoon had a jingle at the beginning that I liked to sing along with: "I can be what I want to be and if you'd like to see, follow me; if you see a plane up high, a diesel train go roaring by, a bumblebee or a tree—it's me!" Tom turned into over a couple dozen things in each show; he really could be anything he wanted.

That's the ultimate superpower, almost power like God has, who creates everything there is. Maybe God turns himself into different things like Tom does just for fun and to see what it's like to be what he created. If I was God, I would. There are all kinds of things I'd like to be for a little while, like a monkey or an elephant, but most of all, I'd love to be a bird so I could fly, soaring high over the trees, and be able to sing so beautifully while I was diving and gliding through the air. I love birds. Maybe God does that, turns himself into stuff; he could even do it with everything at once if he wanted to; God can do anything.

Whoa, now my head is spinning, and I'm getting a chill up my spine. What if God's turned himself into everything in the universe already, and he's watching everything from inside of everything, playing hide and seek with himself. I think I twisted my head into a knot with what I just said; I can feel my head squeezing.

Jesus said the kingdom of heaven is within. I remember thinking like this before when I saw the reflection of the moon everywhere with Debbie. I couldn't quite grasp it then, but now I feel closer. It's connected to the Mystery.

The Mystery can only spring from one source: God. When I feel the Mystery moving in me or see it somehow in the beauty around me, it must be glimpses of God that I'm seeing or feeling. It's like I spy the sleeve of God hiding behind a tree for a second, but then when I look closer, there's nothing there, so I keep searching, the game continues, and in time the Mystery comes to me again—there's his sleeve until it slips away once more. Somehow I need to grab hold of God's sleeve and not let go so I can know for certain sure what God is all about and so I can always be with him. Someday, God, someday, you can't hide forever.

Anyway, Tom turned into all these amazing things, and he thought Manfred the Wonder Dog was great and helped him so much, but Manfred never did anything wonderful; he just seemed to be wondering what was going on all the time as he laid on his back or his side drowsing till Tom came by. I loved that cartoon and all the rest of Captain Kangaroo with its characters who had such a gentle way about them.

Mom loved Lucy. She must have seen some of those episodes five or ten times, but she still laughed loudly at every funny part. When Lucy and Ethel were gobbling chocolates on the conveyor belt because the chocolates were starting to go too fast for them to box, Mom got tears from laughing so hard. She also loved the episode where Lucy and Ethel were stomping on grapes in a big vat with their feet, then they slipped and fell, of course, and were covered all over with crushed grapes. Fred and Ricky were funny, too—Fred more than Ricky, but Lucy and Ethel were something. It was nice to laugh with Mom every morning and enjoy our time together.

After Lucy, Mom would clean the house, and I'd play with my stuffed chimpanzee Zippy, who wore overalls and a striped shirt, my red pistol that shot ping pong balls by squeezing the handle, my little cars or plastic animals. When the house was all tidy, we'd eat lunch, usually a can of Campbell's soup, a fried baloney sandwich with ketchup, or a tuna fish sandwich mixed with Miracle Whip and celery.

Then Mom would sit and watch her soap operas for most of the afternoon, and I would play with my toys until Danny came home. Those days just slowly went by as we did one nice thing after the other. I was still three, and I loved being with Mom; my world felt safe and complete—except for the shampoo day and the day I almost got killed.

Mom wanted to shampoo my hair one day. For some reason that I can't remember, I got mad and wouldn't let her wash it. I put up a big fuss by the bathtub and told her I was running away. I ran out of the house and went left past Danny's red brick school at the end of our street. I kept walking another half block or so up to the railroad tracks, which I was never to cross by myself, and then I stomped over them.

When I passed the newsstand on the left (Dad said it was called Ginny and Clyde's), the man at the window asked, "Where you going, Sonny?" I wondered if he was Ginny or Clyde, but he seemed nice, so I answered him.

"I'm running away."

"Hmm, it's a beautiful day for it, I guess, being so sunny and all, but hey, before you move on by, why don't you try one of these giant pretzels? I just got a new shipment, and you can let me know how fresh they are." He held up a salted pretzel log outside the window.

After I moved closer and grabbed the pretzel, he said, "Why don't you sit down while you eat and read something? Come on in; it's cooler in here anyway." His one eye kept twitching funny, and he smelled like cigar smoke. He had gray stubble on his face and funny glasses that looked like they were cut in half lengthwise. I found out later they're called bifocals.

He had me sit on an old stool and gave me a *Hot Stuff* comic to look at while I licked the big crystals of salt off the pretzel. It smelled funny in there, like some of the magazines had been in the racks for years. I could see that the place was kind of run-down, but I loved those long salty pretzels; the stool was comfortable; the comic had a cute red devil doing silly things, and I was enjoying myself, even though I just looked at the pictures to figure out the story. I forgot all about shampooing my hair and running away for the moment.

The man must have gone out because the next thing I knew, he came in the door with Mom right behind him. Mom must have been following me, and he found her coming. Mom had me put the comic down, but I got to keep the pretzel, which I finished on the way home. When Dad came home, he gave me a lecture about running away, and I remember crying and saying I was sorry, but he didn't take his belt off. He laughed about it with me later, after I was bigger.

The day I almost got killed wasn't funny at all, and it must have been the weekend because everybody was home. Dad was sipping coffee on the couch reading the comic section of the newspaper, and Danny was inside the kitchen helping Mom bake chocolate chip cookies. Mom promised she would save one of the mixer blades for me to lick later, so I went outside to play with my trucks.

There was an alley by the backyard, and I wasn't allowed to go near it. The neighbor girl saw me outside and rode her bike over to our yard through the alley. We decided to play together under the front porch. The porch had a green lattice kind of fence around the bottom, and we could crawl under there and play in the cool gray dirt. It was cozy under there, but we had to watch out for spiders. Daddy Long Legs were okay, though; we weren't afraid of them; I let them crawl over me, and they never bite, just a slight tickle from their long legs.

She was older than me, five or six, with long brown hair and a pretty smile, so I kind of followed what she wanted to do. After pushing my toy trucks for a bit and playing with a few roly-poly bugs we found crawling in the dirt, she wanted to ride bikes in the backyard instead. She had training wheels on her red bike, and I had a green plastic tank that I could sit on top of and pedal.

Dad often brings up a story about that tank when we are with our relatives, and it always embarrasses me, "Bobby was riding his tank on the sidewalk when one of the wheels fell off. A bigger boy, about six or seven, happened to be walking by, so he offered to help Bobby. When the boy bent down to pick up the wheel, Bobby punched him in his stomach. The boy looked shocked and left in a hurry rubbing his belly." Then Dad would burst out laughing. I don't remember doing that, but it must be true. For some reason, Dad seems proud when he tells that story; I feel bad I hit the kid for trying to help.

Anyway, this girl got bored riding in our yard and went into the alley, encouraging me to come. She left the gate open, so after a couple minutes, I followed her with my head down as I pedaled my tank into the alley. Luckily, the truck driver saw me out of his mirror just as I pedaled under his tractor-trailer truck. Dad told me later it was a moving van.

The truck jerked to a hissing clanging stop and shuddered; something smelled burnt. I lifted my head, frightened and confused by the noise, the darkness, and by metal being right over my head. The driver sounded scared when he bent down under the truck and saw me, "Are you all right, kid?" A giant smelly black wheel was about six inches away from crushing me.

Dad must have heard the truck wheels squeal; he was out of breath from running when he bent down with the truck driver and saw me next to the wheel. Dad pulled me and my tank out, making sure I wasn't hurt. Dad looked just as scared as the driver.

"I'm sorry, mister, he just went right under my truck. Thank God I saw him in my mirror. God, my hands are shaking." The truck driver had a blue cap on, his white T-shirt was tight over his big belly, and he was trying to light a cigarette.

Dad looked him in the eye and shook his hand. "Thanks for saving my son."

The truck driver seemed surprised, then he smiled at Dad and patted my shoulder.

"I'm just thankful the boy's okay."

Dad picked me up and hugged me tight for a minute before he took me inside. Mom squeezed me with tears in her eyes after Dad told her what happened. Then she sat me down and gave me some water. They both looked shaken. We all knew something terrible had just passed us by a whisker.

"Bobby," Danny says as he puts his Felix puzzle into his pocket.

"What?"

"If you could have any one of Superman's powers which one would you pick: super strength, super speed, x-ray vision, heat vision, invulnerability, super hearing, cold breath, or the power of flight?"

I don't even have to think for a second. "That's easy, flying; I've always wanted to be able to fly. I'd love to go up in the sky and fly with birds high above the Earth, go through the clouds. Who knows, I might bump into some angels up there and get to be friends. Angels would make the best friends, don't you think?"

"Angels? Do you think Superman has angel friends?" asks Danny.

"They don't have angels in comic books because they are afraid of mentioning anything about God, but angels are out there in real life."

"How do you know? Did you ever see an angel?"

"No, but that doesn't mean there aren't any."

"I hope there are angels, but you don't know for sure," says Danny.

"Look at it this way. Did you ever see God?"

"No, and neither have you."

"But is there a God?"

"Sure, everyone knows there's a God," Danny says.

"Well, what kind of God would he be without having angels?"

"I don't know."

"There you go. There must be angels then."

"What? You're twisting stuff up. Look, there probably are angels. I'm just saying you don't know; Superman doesn't have angel friends, and neither do you."

"OK, I'm just saying I know there are angels, and someday I'm going to see some and make friends with them. Now what superpower of Superman's would you pick?" I ask.

"When you see some angels, let me know, and I'll take a picture. As far as powers go, I'd pick the most obvious best choice, of course, which is invulnerability. That way, nothing or nobody could ever hurt me or kill me, and I could live forever."

"Wow, you're right, that would be fantastic, maybe even better than flying!"

"Maybe? Invulnerability is way better than flying. I won."

"Were we playing a game?" I ask.

"Sure, and I won."

"OK, if you say so, but the more I think about it, I'm sticking with flying. If you never die, how can you get to heaven?"

"The sky sure is pretty," Mom says. I look to her side of the car, and the sky is just everywhere. A great long cloud, black, and orange like a giant Gila monster's tail, is stretched across the sky, but the cloud isn't scary; it makes me feel like curling up and getting quiet. Night will be here in a while. I think about the Gila monster that Danny found last week. We were on our favorite lizard-catching hill.

It's just a big old hill covered with white rocks and boulders. We flip those rocks over quick when we're looking for lizards, not only because there may be a snake or a scorpion underneath, but because those rocks get hot baking in the sun all day.

Sometimes we do uncover scorpions; they are reddish-brown and about the size of my thumb. A scorpion backs up when the rock covering it disappears, their curved back tail cocked and ready to sting with sharp front pinchers raised high. I back away just as quick as they do. I've got nothing but respect for scorpions.

We saw a movie once called *The Black Scorpion* about a giant scorpion on the loose in Mexico or somewhere. It wasn't that great, but the stop motion animation was pretty good, and the scorpion looked deadly from a distance. The close-up of its face was so phony, though. Me and Danny looked at each other and laughed when we saw the face the first time. His tail could smash a truck, but the little scorpions here move like they know how to use their tails, too. They are nasty-looking, so we keep plenty of distance. Luckily there are a lot more lizards than scorpions under those rocks.

There's only one kind of lizard on that hill. They're all white, like the rocks, except for two black rings around their tail tips—which, if you grab them wrong, will pull off in your hand, and the lizard gets away. I don't miss many, though, as I'm probably the best lizard catcher in Texas, and since Texas has the best and the most lizards, I must be one of the world's greatest lizard catchers (the best ten-year-old one anyway).

That hill is a good hike from our house, but not far enough to pack a lunch. Usually, we rest under the shade tree at the bottom of the hill chewing juicy green weeds before we climb it. Then we walk around the white rocks, flipping them with our hands, ready to snatch lizard or to run like heck if there's a rattler coiled up.

A while ago, I was in a different part of town going to the library, where currently I am checking out dog books like *Rin Tin Tin, Big Red,* and *Old Yeller*—Danny is reading the *Oz* books; he found out there are a bunch of them, not just *The*

Wizard of Oz. He loves them and is trying to get me to read them, and they look great, but right now, I'm just into dogs.

Anyway, on my way to the library, I was looking for lizards in an open field when I lifted some cardboard, and there was a black, red, and gold coral snake—they are awful poisonous. I felt like one of those cartoon characters who leave a puff of swirling air behind because they move so crazy fast. I use a stick now to flip up stuff like paper or cardboard, but you have to use your hands to move a decent rock. I haven't found a rattler yet, though our neighbor saw one in the field behind our house. He said it was at least six feet long and as thick as his wrist.

We did find a baby rattlesnake recently in another field across the street from our house. They're digging stuff up with a bulldozer, and there's a big hole carved out. The deepest side filled up partly with water. We could see teeth marks of the bulldozer in the red clay. The yellow bulldozer is still there next to the hole; I guess they aren't worried about anybody trying to steal it. We thought about climbing up on it so we could pretend that we were digging more holes, but we didn't want to risk pushing a lever or something and having the thing start up and dig holes for real.

The hole is about four feet deep, and I noticed something curled up exposed from the clay being sheared away. I got real close and saw a rattle on the end of a baby snake; it was probably four inches or so curled up tight.

"Danny, come down here and look at this!" Danny slid down the other side of the hole and stood next to me in the wet, muddy bottom.

"Is that what I think it is?" said Danny.

"It's a baby rattlesnake, all right."

"Wow, look at him! He must be sleeping or hibernating or something. His rattle looks so cool. It would be neat to see him move or shake his rattle. Maybe we should dig it out with a stick," Danny said as he started looking around for one.

But then I got a creepy feeling shivering up my spine.

"Danny."

"What?"

"What does a baby usually have near it, watching it, making sure the baby is safe?"

"A mother!"

We backed away real slow and careful, scrambled up the cool, wet clay, and then ran like heck. Maybe the rattler our neighbor saw was the mother; the other field was just across the street. It's a good thing we did get away from that hole because later, someone told us that the poison from a baby rattlesnake is more deadly than an adult rattler's poison.

Luckily we never ran into a rattler amongst those white rocks, no snakes at all. Once we get to the top of the hill where the rocks start, we always visit our frog bush before we get to catching lizards. It's a scratchy bush next to a cactus at the edge of where the rocks end. Cute little green tree frogs live on the bush with their suction-cup toes that look so cool, like aliens from space might have on their fingers, except the alien's fingers would be bigger, of course, and certainly not cute.

The tree frogs are about the size of a quarter, and they can't really get away from us. Their green skin feels smooth, not bumpy at all like toad skin (they don't pee on you either, like toads do), and they have soft white bellies. We usually find a couple that we just pluck off the bush and play with for a few minutes. The tree frogs are so gentle they don't even try to hop out of our hands; their big eyes look up at us as trusting as puppies. They probably wonder what kind of bizarre giants we are. We always set them back down carefully so we can catch them again the next time we come.

Then we go after lizards. Danny usually carries the school satchel; he's older, but I'm faster, and I need my hands free. We try to walk quiet, so we don't let them know we're coming. Surprise is what we are after. The best time to get them is as soon as we lift the rock before they have a chance to run. Once they are on the move, it's a lot more work, but we can still scoop them up.

The third rock Danny lifted was gold; there was a beauty about seven inches long under there. Before he could blink, I was on him. That lizard was strong and fought hard to get free, thrashing his nice tail around and trying to squeeze through my fingers, but I had a good grip on him. The way I held him, he couldn't really scratch me, and these kinds of lizards don't bite; he felt great in my hand. It's a fine feeling to catch a lizard all right.

After we catch one, we admire its size for a bit, how cool the lines on its belly are, how the eyelids wrinkle up like a dinosaurs would. Then we put it in the satchel and go looking for more. We usually catch at least two or three of them.

When we finish for the day, we hold them all once more and compare them, which one's bigger or cooler looking. Then we find a good spot, unstrap the satchel and tip it over gently so they can crawl out, escape, and be free again. Beauty gets spoiled by cages. Those white lizards are the only kind we ever found on that hill until the other day.

Danny was a ways away, just poking around when he started hollering and pointing. "Bobby, get over here, hurry!" I rushed to him, clopping over the rocks. "That," Danny said, pointing down the hill a bit, "is an honest-to-goodness Gila monster!" Sure enough, it was. We had both admired the picture of the one in our *Golden Book Encyclopedia*, so we knew it was for real.

"What shall we do?" I asked.

"There's only one thing you can do with a monster."

"What's that?"

"You have to kill it so it won't hurt anybody."

Danny pointed to a big boulder just below us. We crept down the rocks as quiet as we could, scattering only a few small stones but breathing heavy. Danny's eyes were round and scared-looking, his wide loose lips chapped and caved in from the sun. We rested at the boulder. The monster hadn't moved; it was about ten feet away.

"It's not a very big one, is it?" I asked.

"No, I'd say it's only about five inches, but one bite, and you'd be dead like that," Danny whispered as he snapped his fingers softly under my nose. "And they would have to cut off your toe if he bit you because once they bite you, they never let go, ever!"

So we pushed and leaned and grunted on that boulder while the sun made my throat scratchy, and the Gila monster just lay there, lost in a lizard dream, I guess. Suddenly, we both slipped on the rocks and fell to our knees as the boulder broke free, rolling, bouncing, and crunching over rocks till it landed

smack on top of the monster and stopped. He had to be squashed flat. We grinned and looked at each other like we had just killed Godzilla.

But now, curled in the car, looking at the Gila monster cloud get darker, puffier, and more mysterious, my cheek pressing against the cool glass of the window as twilight takes over, I know that lizard was far from Godzilla. The poor thing never knew what hit him, bursting into the middle of its sunny lazy lizard thoughts.

Chapter V

Mortimer

At least it was over quick for the Gila monster; Mortimer wasn't so lucky. Mortimer was my pet box turtle. I caught him in the woods behind our duplex in Louisiana. Dad called it Lousyanna because of how sticky and buggy it always was there. We moved there after Germany, and it sure was different.

Dad was right about it being sticky. Afternoons were the worst. During summer vacation, I did most of my outside stuff in the mornings. At two or three, when it was the hottest and stickiest, I read in my bed. Mom let me use the small gray metal fan that we had, and I would lay right in front of it, reading as it swiveled back and forth from my head to my feet. I used to sneak downstairs and raid the freezer for popsicles; banana was my favorite, but in that heat, cherry, grape, and orange were just fine, too. After two or three, I would stop so I wouldn't get in trouble, but I could have eaten ten of them.

Those afternoons, in our first and (thankfully) only summer there, I read *Robinson Crusoe, Gulliver's Travels, 20,000 Leagues Under the Sea, Treasure Island, Journey to the Center of the Earth*; any adventure book I could find fascinated me. Sometimes I would take breaks, read comic books or go outside to ride my bike and feel the wind against me. Texas is hot too, but the heat never bothers me much in Texas; it's not so humid and uncomfortable somehow like in Louisiana, where even your lungs seem to sweat.

The mornings were fresh and cooler, so that was my time for catching lizards or fishing for crawdads. Usually, I went by myself, Danny stayed inside mostly, but sometimes I could get him to come out with me. Half a dozen small ponds were in the woods behind our duplex, with a packed-down mud path weaving through the trees from one pond to the next. The ponds were about as big as the inside of our car; the woods mostly pine trees.

When we walked past the last pond one day, Danny and me made a startling discovery. We heard something big splashing in the water, and when we bent over to look, there was a giant fish swimming in the pond. It was almost as big as one of Bozo's shoes. The only thing we could figure is that someone must have caught it fishing somewhere else and then put it in the small pond for some reason. There is no way a big fish like that could have grown up in such a tiny pool. We left it where it was, but when I passed that way a couple days later, the fish was gone. Life is full of little mysteries like that, you never find out how they happened, and life just keeps moving on to the next thing.

Pine lizards live in the pines. They have spiky scales, but not like horned toads in Texas with their sharp horns and spikes; it feels good to pet a pine lizard from his head to his tail, but the scales jab if you try to pet backwards. They are kind of silver and black, and they are hard to spot on pine bark.

One grab is all you get because if you miss, they run up the tree lickety-split.

Climbing a pine tree is not for me because they have hard, sticky sap oozing all over, and it takes forever to get it off your hands. There are also pine snakes that live in the trees as well. They look almost like a pine lizard, the same colors and similar scales, but they are snakes, and they can get big.

We saw one in the pine tree in our yard once. Me and Dad were catching with our orange football that I got for Christmas. Dad threw one really high by the tree, and when I looked up to catch the ball, I saw the snake; half its body was stretching up at a sharp angle to the branch above—they must have strong muscles to climb like that. I don't know if they bite or not because the only snakes I ever caught are little milk snakes, but I'd sure hate to run into a riled-up pine snake when I was climbing a tree and find out they have fangs or sharp teeth.

The only other kind of lizards I found in Louisiana are chameleons—that's what we call them, but their scientific name, according to our *Golden Book Encyclopedia,* is anoles. They are skinny, in different shades of green or brown, sometimes yellowish, depending what they are on or how they're feeling that day, I'm guessing. A few times, I've seen them brown when they are on green leaves, so it must be more than just what they are touching that changes their color. They have long snouts and white bellies. I usually find them in bushes.

Chameleons aren't as fast as pine lizards and are pretty easy to catch, but they like to bite. They open their mouths real wide, and their teeth are just little white bumps. If you are ready for it, their bites aren't bad, but a surprise bite smarts a bit. Since I'm so fast, I don't get surprised much. When chameleons are mad and their mouths wide open, a pouch puffs up under their throats, that's when they remind me of the dinosaurs we saw in *The Mysterious Island*, but I think they actually used real dressed up iguanas in that movie.

The day I found Mortimer, I was walking along the hard mud path, and sunlight was slanting through the pines, lighting up spider webs stretching between the trees or hanging on a branch. Sometimes I saw strands of web float up in the air when I looked straight up into the bright sky. For some reason, there seem to be tons of spiders in Louisiana; maybe they like the humid weather, or maybe it's because there are so many bugs everywhere to eat, which makes it sort of a spider heaven.

I crossed over the wooden plank that goes over some squishy black mud; it's the kind of smelly mud hat will suck your shoe off if you step in it by mistake. I learned that the hard way, my shoe stunk for days, and my sock was never the same. When I walked around a bend in the path past some bushes, I saw a beautiful box turtle sunning on the bank of a pond. He was black with gold lines highlighting each shell segment. He closed up tight when I grabbed him. It's interesting how the front and the back of the shell seal so perfectly, like two drawbridges shutting to protect a castle. It must be cozy in there.

After he got used to me, he opened up and crawled around my room. For some reason, the name Mortimer came to me when I played with him that first day. He was perfect, the most beautiful turtle I ever saw.

Once I saw a green snapping turtle in one of the ponds, he came up out of the water to snap at a dragonfly. The upper part of its mouth was a sharp beak pointing down; his head was just ugly, and his crusty green shell wasn't attractive either. I wouldn't be surprised the way he chomped that dragonfly up if he couldn't bite off a finger--if someone was dumb enough to get close to that wicked mouth.

Mortimer was just the opposite; not only was he the Cary Grant of turtles, he was also gentle and would never bite me, even when I was feeding him and my fingers were right next to his mouth. I fed him bits of mushrooms, carrots, and lunch meat for treats. I made him a home out of a cardboard box filled with a bowl of water, a nice flat rock he could stretch out on, and plenty of plants and dirt to mess around in. He seemed to like his home, but maybe that was just my imagination; he might have missed the woods and his pond.

Mortimer wasn't the first turtle I had. Danny and me had little turtle pets before when we lived on 4th Avenue. Mom called them painted turtles. They had delicate green and yellow designs on the bottom of their shells; the tops were like green shingles. Their necks were green with little red stripes on the side. They were about the size of an Oreo cookie, maybe a little bit bigger, and they had a turtle smell to them that smelled like the pet shop somehow. Mom bought a plastic turtle dish for them to live in. There was a place for water at the bottom and a hill with a plastic palm tree on top.

We loved those turtles and let them crawl all over our apartment—with us close by, of course. Danny called his turtle Groucho and mine was Harpo, after our two favorite Marx Brothers. I love how Harpo chases girls honking his horn and how beautifully he can play the harp like an angel. Danny thought Groucho was the funniest, especially when he walked with his hands behind his back, smoking a cigar and making funny comments about everyone.

There was one Groucho scene in particular that Danny loved. Groucho was sitting on a couch next to a fancy-dressed woman, and she kept telling Groucho to ". . . get closer my darling, closer, come closer." Then Groucho said, "If I get any closer, I'll come out the other side." Danny laughed and laughed at that one.

Soon after we got Groucho and Harpo, we were outside one day taking turns riding on a red motor scooter that Dad got from somewhere. It had a flat seat, and I held on tight to Dad from behind as the wind gusted all over me. We weren't wearing helmets. Dad zoomed down a hill with me, but the scooter barely made it back up on the way home. Dad didn't look too happy when he parked on our front lawn. He didn't have that scooter very long. Dad doesn't have the best luck at picking good cars or stuff.

When we went back in the house to get a drink, I passed by our turtle dish, so I stopped for a moment to play with Harpo—but he wasn't in his dish, neither was Groucho. That's when we realized our turtle dish had a problem; there wasn't a lid or top of any kind. Somehow Groucho and Harpo had crawled out of the dish; they weren't supposed to be able to do that. We all looked everywhere, under everything, but they must have crawled into a mouse hole or something because we never did find either one.

I made sure that Mortimer's box was too high for him to crawl out of. My room didn't have a door—it's the only place we ever lived that me and Danny had our own rooms, but I had one of those accordion gates about waist high that keep babies from getting hurt—the gate wasn't for me, though. When I came home from school one afternoon, the gate was wide open. My heart froze. I rushed in and found Mortimer's box drug out from under the dresser; it was all ripped up.

I knew right away that our mutt dog, Midgie, did it. I searched in the closet, behind the door, under my nightstand—that usually covered a lopsided pile of comics; I discovered a couple of popsicle sticks on top of a *Fantastic Four* comic, but no Mortimer. Where could he be?

Finally, I found him under my bed behind a sock. Relief changed to horror when I saw the back half of his shell chewed away. It looked like a half-eaten giant chocolate Easter egg, with red streaks and white chunks mixed in with the chocolate. It made me gag. Mortimer was still alive, and he had three legs so he could move slowly. I couldn't find the rest of him anywhere; Midgie must have swallowed it.

I put Mortimer in an old green ammo box that Dad had given us and took him out to the woods. I thought about finding a big rock and smashing what was left of him, so he wouldn't suffer. I picked up a heavy stone and raised it high, one hard throw would end his pain quick, but Mortimer seemed to turn back his head to look at me, so I tossed that rock into the weeds instead. Maybe he could live somehow— I knew that was almost impossible, but I just couldn't make myself crush him. I watched him slowly crawl away into some weeds at the edge of the woods.

97

After a moment, I climbed up my favorite tree and cried for a while. Images of Mortimer's mutilated shell kept going through my mind, and I imagined what it must have been like for poor Mortimer to have a vicious snapping dog gnawing and crunching on him with no one to save him. As I was wiping my nose, an awful thought popped into my head. If I hadn't captured Mortimer, he would still be a beautiful, healthy turtle swimming in cool water or baking on a hot rock. Midgie was the murderer, but I was her accomplice.

Midgie was no friend of mine after that. She had been so cute when we found her in the city pound with her black face and tan little body. She tried to crawl under the fence to us, so we picked her. It turns out that was her problem; she was always trying to get away.

We named her Midgie because she was so small, like a midget. As she got bigger, we realized she wasn't too bright. Midgie had to be chained up all the time, or else she would chase cars. That got annoying because she pooped everywhere in the backyard, and we couldn't keep up with scooping up all the poop; there was always poop hidden somewhere that got stuck in the treads of our tennis shoes. Even a stick couldn't get it all out, so we had to take soapy water and a scrub brush to the bottoms.

When Midgie was in the house, we had to be careful every time we opened a door, or she would slip outside between our legs and the screen door. Midgie was awful fast, and she could keep up with a car for a while before she fell behind. It took forever to catch her and get her back in the house.

We could only collar her when she was all exhausted and muddy, with her tongue hanging out from running around like a maniac. Sometimes she found dead things to roll in, and we had to wash her with special shampoo to take away the dead stink.

Midgie had her nice sides, though. Mom took a cute picture of her as a puppy sitting inside one of Dad's black army boots, her little black and tan face and wagging tail sticking out. She was adorable as a puppy with her fat little belly, snuggling up to us, licking our faces, and growling softly while chewing on our shoe strings—too bad she grew up. Even when she was older, though, she had nice brown eyes and could be gentle and quiet. Midgie love to be petted, especially to have her belly rubbed. She was in heaven then and would lay there all day, still as a statue with her belly up, if someone would keep petting her.

When we moved from Louisiana to Texas, we stopped for gas at some small town near the Louisiana state line, and Midgie bolted out of the car before I could stop her. She took off like she was running for her life. The last I saw of her, she was chasing a Buick around the corner a couple blocks away.

After the gas station guy filled the tank, Dad turned around and drove that way for a bit. Dad kept mumbling and cursing as he cruised the roads with our heads out the window, yelling, "Midgie! Midgie!" There was no sign of her anywhere on the empty streets. It felt like a bad dream as the sun started to get low, and so did Dad's patience. After a while, Dad said it was time to get going. I felt sorry for Midgie then, and I realized that I still cared for the stupid mutt even after what she did to Mortimer. It was a crummy day.

The car hits a big bump in the road and pops me up in the air. I'm glad I'm not drinking anything.

"Damn it! I just hit a God damn armadillo! The stupid thing ran right into the wheel. There wasn't a damn thing I could do."

Me and Danny turn around and look, but the twilight is making the road shadowy, and we don't see anything back there except the white circles of headlights glowing in the distance. A shiver goes up my back from knowing we ran over an animal. I feel bad for the armadillo.

Our next-door neighbors on Easy Street have a pet armadillo who roams around their yard behind the fence. They call her Abby, and we like to look at her walk along the metal fence and curl up into a ball sometimes; she seems medieval with her armor, but she is cute at the same time. Her long snout reminds me of Olive Oil's nose—wherever Olive went, her nose went first, just like Abby's nose does. It's too bad this one got run over; life is cold and hard sometimes.

The bump makes me realize that I need to go to the bathroom. Dad's not going to be happy if I make him stop, but he'll be even angrier if I make him pull over somewhere by the side of the road without any gas stations around; besides, that's so embarrassing. I had to do that once, and I kept worrying that someone would see me. I try an indirect approach.

"Maybe you should stop and check the wheel, Dad, and make sure it's not damaged; they do have armor after all," I suggest.

"That's not a bad idea, but the wheel sounds okay," Dad says.

"Why don't you stop anyway, Hon? We could all use a break for a few minutes to stretch our legs," Mom says.

"All right then, but just a short stop at the next gas station. We still have a long way to go."

"There's one up ahead, past the Pancake House," says Danny.

Dad pulls into an Esso station; there's a statue of the Esso tiger standing between a red Coke machine and tires stacked like a pyramid with little red, white and blue plastic flags fluttering in the breeze. The commercial on TV says, "Put a tiger in your tank." The tiger doesn't have a name that I know of. He looks a lot like Tony the Tiger from Frosted Flakes cereal. I wonder which one came first, who copied who.

Dad gets out, squats, and starts inspecting the wheel as I make a beeline for the restroom. Danny is right behind me.

"It feels GRRREAT to be out of the car, doesn't it," I laugh at Danny.

"Are you trying to sound like Tony the Tiger for some reason?" Danny asks as he gets the key from an older man listening to a transistor radio behind the counter—it sounds like a baseball game.

"I'm not trying, I did sound like Tony the Tiger, or you wouldn't have said Tony the Tiger," I answer. We walk outside, and Danny opens the white metal door on the side of the station. The restroom smells like one of those pine trees people hang from their rear-view mirrors. I never smelled a pine tree like that. I'm glad Dad doesn't hang one in our car; they stink; how can people like the smell?

"Ok, Mr. Smarty-Pants. Did you take a goofy pill or what?" Danny asks.

"No, I was just born this way; what's your excuse for being a Goober?"

"If I'm a Goober, you must be a Gomer, like Gomer Pyle," says Danny as we wash our hands with powdered soap like Borax; it's rough on my hands and smells as bad as it feels. No mirror, who cares how I look anyway?

"Gomer and Goober are cousins on the show, not brothers, but if they were brothers, it would mean that Dad was. . ."

"Sergeant Carter!" Danny finishes. It doesn't make any sense, of course, but there's no one else that fits besides Sergeant Carter.

Danny and me are laughing as we head back to the car, thinking about Dad being Sergeant Carter, who always gets made a fool of by Gomer. Dad kind of looks like Sergeant Carter a little bit; at least their bodies are similar, and they are both drill sergeants, but Dad doesn't have a crew cut, and he is more handsome; Sergeant Carter is all chin and neck.

"How's the tire, Dad?" I ask.

"It's fine, just a little blood under the fender; we must have smashed the poor booger."

As we get in the car, I see Mom walking out of the lady's room. She's wearing a yellow sweater over her blouse now. How can she be cold? Mom seems to get cold easy. Mom always takes a hot soak in the tub before she goes to bed. It doesn't matter how hot the day is; she puts in smelly powders and relaxes; she says, "I'm soaking the day's work away." Then she puts on her bathrobe, sticks pink curlers in her hair, and watches TV till very late.

I've woken up sometimes around midnight, and she is still curled up on the couch if Dad isn't home, on the easy chair if he is. She sits in the dark with just the flickering bluish glow of the television lighting up the room. Mom always waits for him to get home, even if it is really late, so Dad doesn't feel lonely about coming home to a house where everyone is sleeping. I imagine being a soldier's wife can be a bit lonely for her too, because Dad spends a lot of the day on base, or sometimes is on bivouac for a few days with his platoon.

They don't do much hugging or kissing in front of us, but Dad often says that Mom is the only woman in the world for him. Mom has a giant stack of letters that Dad wrote to her when Dad was in Germany by himself, waiting for us to come over. I snuck a peek at some once when I stumbled on them— I know I shouldn't have, but I was just so curious, and no one would ever know. I had been looking in Mom's closet for presents she might be hiding before Christmas. It surprised me how in every letter Dad wrote about missing Mom so badly. He wrote that he missed Danny and me too, but it sounded like he was dying without Mom. He also wrote about money and how he felt like he was letting Mom down because things were always tight. Then I heard Mom coming home from the store, so I put the letters away and got the heck out of there.

After Mom gets in the car, Dad checks his mirrors, then looks behind and pulls back out onto the highway. Dad told me one time that cars have a blind spot that the mirrors don't see, so if you are going to make a move like pulling out, changing lanes, or passing another car, you should always turn your head behind quickly to check the blind spot.

I notice that he always does that when he drives. Sometimes people give advice or tell you what you should be doing, but then they don't follow their own advice, not Dad—unless it's about smoking. He tells me and Danny he will kick our butts if we ever start smoking, yet he goes on puffing at least two packs a day. Dad says he started when he was young and dumb, and now he can't quit because they are addicting.

They started putting warning labels on cigarettes, saying they may be hazardous to people's health. Of course, they are horrible for you, how could breathing in hot smoke all the time be good for someone's health. I just can't figure out why it took them so long to admit that smoking hurts your body. I know it's about cigarette companies making money, but I mean, how could they get away with it for so long? Why didn't the government make them admit how horrible smoking was years ago? Sometimes I worry about Dad smoking so much, who knows what kind of damage he's doing to himself, yet smoking is such a part of his life, I can't imagine him ever quitting.

Once we get going again, it isn't long before we start leaving all the bright lights of restaurants and stores behind. After passing a couple final gas stations, we are heading out more into the country.

There is something about watching the world go by through a car window that makes you wonder about things—especially when daylight sinks and dark starts to creep around the edges. Your brain starts taking over for what your eyes can't see.

I wonder what kind of things Dad and Uncle Billy did together when they were kids? Did they even have comic books back then? They couldn't have been great lizard catchers like us because they grew up in PA, no lizards there, only salamanders. Anyone can catch salamanders; their first instinct when the rock hiding them moves away is just to freeze and hope they aren't seen.

Maybe they collected rubber and stuff to help with World War II? It's hard to imagine Dad being little and pulling a wagon. The youngest I can see Dad is in a picture where he has his hair combed like James Dean. His arms are still skinny before he got all his muscles, a pack of cigarettes is rolled up in the sleeve of his T-shirt, and he seems to be laughing about something.

Wait a minute, I remember one other picture where Dad is about Danny's age, and he's smiling and happy; he sure looked similar to how Danny does now. I wonder why he was smiling then; that was such a long time ago; if he happened to look at the photo now and tried to recall, he probably wouldn't remember. It's nice to know, though, that Dad was happy sometimes as a kid and not just getting hit in the head by Grandma Ludwizcak.

Photographs fascinate me because they show what life used to be like, a whole different world than now—especially black and white photos which are ultra-real—I mean, the world is not black and white, yet somehow black and white photos seem even more real to me than color pictures. Like when they show black and white film clips of the Nazis goose-stepping and saluting Hitler or Winston Churchill smoking a cigar—it's history, super real.

Photos also give a glimpse of how time keeps moving; relatives looking way younger back then makes it all seem so long ago. Everyone keeps moving on into the future, yet so gradually that people don't even seem aware of it; then they look at an old photo of themselves or others and wham, time pinches them.

Dad sure has been more quiet than usual. I wonder how close he and Uncle Billy were as kids. Come to think of it, Dad must be almost ten years older than Uncle Billy, so they couldn't have been as close as me and Danny. When Uncle Billy was learning how to walk, Dad was my age; they couldn't have had a lot in common. Also, if they were really close, Dad would have told us some funny stories about Uncle Billy, and I can't remember any, but they had to be a little close. How could you not be close to your brother?

Lights start to shine, here and there, from the houses that we rush by. I can see televisions on, but I can't make out what they are watching. People are sitting or walking past windows; people I've never seen before and who I'll never see again keep disappearing with the telephone poles that drop further and further behind in the gloom, till a new pole snaps past the window and drags my eyeballs along. It kind of gives me a lonely feeling.

Danny has his eyes closed, but I don't think he is sleeping yet. Mom and Dad are both quiet up front. Dad has the headlights on now, two searchlights cutting through the dark up ahead.

When we go around a curve, the lights shoot deep into the woods for a second, a ghostly snapshot of the forest. I wouldn't want to be way back in there. Trees look spooky at night, gnarled branches twisted and still. Who knows what could be hiding behind a trunk waiting for someone fool enough to walk by. I feel a shiver shake me quick and creepy, like the feeling I always get when we drive over a dead skunk, snake, raccoon—anything smashed and still on the road.

The trees end, and there's nothing but sky, deep empty space, on either side of the car. We're up high; the car seems like a plane for a moment, cutting through the night, stars are everywhere, even below—no, that's light on dark water. I can see waves sloshing around down there. Maybe we're flying through heaven, and that's God's bathtub down there—where he takes a bath at night when no one can see him.

He might be a giant; maybe he scrubs his back with a handful of stars, or maybe angels rub him clean with their wings full of water and soapsuds. I figure that God must be amazing if he can make beautiful angels. Someday, like I said, I'll manage to grab hold of his sleeve and not let go—until then, if God wants to hide himself in the night, fine—but I'd really love to be with angels and look at them. I don't think I'd ever get tired of looking at angels.

Suddenly, the moon breaks through a cloud, a silver horn shooting light into the puffy shadows below and the stars above. I can feel the Mystery tugging at my brain, trying to tell me something important as the beauty of the night seeps deep into my eyes, squeezes my heart, and takes away my breath. After a few long sweet moments, the Mystery somehow twists away into the night, out amongst stars that people have been looking at in wonder for thousands of years.

The water seems to be getting closer, and I can see brightness up ahead. The bridge is taking us into a city. My eyes shut out the glare and the concrete, and then the lids get comfortable and heavy resting on each other. I can smell Mom's Jergen's Lotion, and the humming of the rubber tires smacking the road seems to be pulling me somewhere. As the rushing of the car swallows me up, I wonder if lizards, turtles, and dogs go to heaven when they die.

Chapter VI

Belonging

It's dark when Mom wakes me up. "Get up, Bobby, we're here." The car isn't moving anymore, my belly is growling, gurgling, and my right hand seems to have fallen asleep from using it as a pillow; I can hardly bend my fingers. Mom is shuffling around in the front seat packing things up. Dad is already out of the car, opening up the trunk.

Danny is yawning and tying his shoes. His hair is all cockeyed, and when he turns to face me, I see a red crease across his left cheek from sleeping against the door. "Last one out's a rotten egg," he announces.

The dome light flicks on and helps me find my shoes under Mom's seat. Mom just bought them for me last week; they still have the clean rubbery new shoe smell of fresh tennis shoes. They are black and white P.F. Flyers, real cool, real comfortable. *Superman* ended up under the seat, too. Danny smirks at me as he steps out his door. I guess I'm a rotten egg.

"Let's go boys, it's late," says Dad. I hear crickets chirping as I scoot out of the car. A porch light is on in front of me. "Robert. Come here and help your brother." The light from the trunk is shining on Dad's face; he looks tired, puffy under his eyes. I can see the bump he always has on top of his left eyelid in the middle. He calls it a stye and says he can't feel it. It looks like a tiny boulder of flesh that could roll off his eyelid, but it never does. Dad puts a bag of something in my arms from the trunk. My cramped right hand can hardly grab it. "Careful now. Take it up to the porch."

Danny is already up there sitting on a porch swing, chains creaking spooky as he looks off into some shadowed bushes. Purple flowers shaped like little dog snouts are all over the bushes. After I drop off my bag by the swing, I walk to the porch railing and lift one to my nose. The flower snout feels like cool velvet as I gently squeeze it with my fingertips; it's made up of hundreds of tiny flowers, purple with lime green tracings; each little flower is unique, separate, yet part of this whole handful of beauty.

They are so delicate and soft, tickling my nose. I take a deep sweet breath that reminds me of the fresh smell of a baby's head. The night breeze ruffles my hair; a lone frog joins the crickets and the chains. Time leaves me alone as the beauty of it all soaks into me; the sweet fresh scent fills my nose; the Mystery thrills my heart and softly rubs my temples, the top of my head.

The screen door squeaks and slams, wood smacking wood behind me. As I turn, I see a bald man in a muscle-man T-shirt rush past us down the steps. He limps a little like Grandpa on *The Real McCoy's*, it's Uncle Chick. He grabs a suitcase out of Dad's hand and slaps him on the shoulder, then moves over to Mom and gives her a quick hug. Aunt Cora follows Uncle Chick down the steps in a flowered bathrobe and embraces Mom and Dad. Neither one of them see me and Danny on the porch as they hurry down to Mom and Dad.

111

"We were watching Johnny Carson on the back porch and didn't hear you all. So good to see you! How was your trip? Where are the boys?" Aunt Cora follows Mom's eyes and turns around, giving us a big smile. "My, my, how you've both grown since last year."

Aunt Cora has short graying black hair, black pointy glasses, and a smile that makes you feel like you're special to her. Before Mom can say anything, Aunt Cora is back up the steps squeezing me against her soft, plump body and kissing me on the cheek. I just let myself go and melt into her. I love Aunt Cora. She smells like bananas today. It's great to see her again and to feel her special hug. When she hugs me, she kind of caresses at the same time and rubs her hands over me like she's trying to remember what I feel like.

"Are you doing okay?" Aunt Cora asks me.

"I'm good; how are you?"

"Just fine, child, just fine, especially now that you boys are here. I've been looking forward to seeing you these last days."

After me, she hugs Danny too; then Aunt Cora goes back down the steps to talk with Mom and Dad. Aunt Cora is patting Mom's arm gently, and Mom is smiling back. Aunt Cora likes to touch people. Mom likes Aunt Cora, too. I heard her tell Dad last year that she would make a good grandmother because of how nice she was. Everyone has put their bags down. Dad is smoking a cigarette while he chats with Uncle Chick. Looks like they'll be gabbing for a while; adults can just talk forever when they see each other after a long time apart.

Sometimes as soon as I meet somebody, I know that we both like each other right away, there isn't any kind of awkward feeling. Aunt Cora was like that last year when we first met. She just opened her arms and smiled at me when I walked in her door, and we were hugging like we knew each other forever. With kids that happens all the time, I can usually tell right away if I'm going to be friends with another kid. With adults, that only seems to happen to me with women, not men. Women open up my heart somehow in a way men don't. I don't know why, but that's the way it is.

The first time I remember a woman, other than Mom, bursting open my heart was in Virginia. I was about four or so. Dad got stationed at Fort Belvoir, which is close to Washington D.C. Not long after we moved there, a friend of Dad's drove us to D.C. in his white convertible to see the street with all the cherry blossom trees.

It was great to feel the air blowing all over me as he drove; Danny was smiling too; no wonder dogs like to stick their heads out of windows so much—Midgie used to poke half her body out of our Dodge with the wind plastering her face and chest fur. Mom didn't like being in a convertible though, she was fighting a losing battle as she tried to hold down her blue babushka tightly with her hand, but her hair was still getting messed up. Dad had a hard time smoking as well; the wind kept blowing his ash if he wasn't careful, and he had to watch that the red and white seat didn't get burn marks in it.

The first thing we saw from a distance was the Washington Monument. It reminded me of a rocket ship pointing towards the clouds, waiting for its chance to erupt in giant clouds of smoke and lift off towards space. Back then, it was the tallest thing I ever saw. Danny kept pointing at it, saying, "Holy mackerel, willya, look at that! Wow!"

When we got to the city, the cherry trees weren't quite blooming yet, but they were still worth seeing. It was a warm sunny spring day, and all the buds were full of life and looked like they were about to pop; it felt like the whole world was just waiting till they burst open to share their beauty. When we pulled over to the side of the street for a moment, so Dad's friend could turn the car around, I could see that some of the buds were just starting to separate; we just missed by a few days, I guess.

Before we went home, we stopped off to see the Lincoln Memorial. We walked up about a hundred marble steps, and there was this giant man with a beard sitting in some kind of chair. Dad's friend pointed out that the chair's sides were actually books because Lincoln educated himself by using candles to read books at night. The statue was impressive, and I guess he should have scared me because he was so huge and I was only four, but he seemed to have a kind face, so I was just interested. I couldn't imagine how people could make such a gigantic statue out of stone; it looked so real, like he could just stand up one day and go for a walk along the river with his giant legs.

"That's President Lincoln. He was the greatest president this country has ever had," Dad said. He went on about other stuff I didn't understand at the time, but I went away feeling like I had just seen the statue of a king, someone who the world should be grateful to, who we should look up to, and try to be like.

Last year, in Mrs. Martinez's class, I read a biography of Abraham Lincoln for a book report. All I can say is his life's even more impressive than the Lincoln Memorial. God must have known that Lincoln was the perfect president for the Civil War. He was great, but it doesn't seem like he was a happy man. Professor Marvel described Aunt Em as careworn in *The Wizard of Oz;* that's how Abraham Lincoln looks in photographs, too, careworn. I guess he just had too much of a struggle trying to hold the country together, plus his wife seemed kind of mean or crazy. Then he got assassinated in a theater—what a shame. The president after Lincoln was so crummy he got impeached and kicked out of office. He messed the country up pretty bad before they got rid of him. Maybe he wasn't smart enough, or maybe his heart was black with greed and selfishness.

Dad's friend drove us back home from D.C. the same day. Mom and Dad seemed especially glad to get home. We lived off Post in the basement part of a house that was next to a two-lane highway. It was a busy road; the cars and trucks zooming by at night made me drowsy and helped me fall asleep.

Teresa was a little girl my age with short brown hair and brown eyes who lived upstairs. I thought she was pretty, and we liked being with each other. Sometimes we played together outside when Danny was at school—his second time in first grade. When we moved to Germany, Teresa's mom wrote to Mom a few times to let us know how Teresa was doing and that she missed us. I missed her, too.

One sunny morning we found a big ugly bug on the oak tree out front. Teresa and me had been collecting acorns at the bottom of the tree that had good caps on top; they sort of look like French berets on little brown heads without faces. We both shouted and ran away when we first saw the insect on the tree trunk, but as it didn't move, I crept back. It looked funny somehow, so I poked it with a stick, and then I could see it was just the empty shell of a giant insect. We were both amazed at how much it looked like a monster. The world is so full of strange creatures; God must have one heck of an imagination.

People create all kinds of things, from cute little toys to giant rocket ships, and they think they are all so clever to have thought of and made such great stuff, and I agree; I couldn't have thought of such things myself.

But when I look around at the world, the moon and space, the sun and trees, the ocean, animals, people, the light blue sky, everything that God has created and is making all the time, well, God's creations are just a different dimension of genius. God must smile at us when people feel proud about one of their inventions. Compared to what God makes, they are like first-grade drawings displayed next to Leonardo da Vinci's painting of *The Last* Supper—I love that painting.

Well, all four of us were supposed to visit one of Dad's army friends that night who lived nearby across the highway, but during that very afternoon, something scary happened by our house. A couple hundred yards behind our house in a big field there was a dump. I never thought much about it till after that day, when I started having nightmares about that dump sometimes.

There was a high bank coming down into our giant yard from the highway. A skinny tree that I once had a nice dream about was at the bottom of the bank. The tree was full of cute little yellow monkeys, the same color as those banana-flavored bubble-gum cigars that cost five cents, and I was just sitting next to the tree admiring their happy faces and how graceful they were swinging and scampering about.

I tried to pet one, but it was too high, so I climbed the tree and managed to stroke the soft yellow fur on the back of his hand before it climbed high above, chattering and pointing back at me—like I gave it the cooties or something. Then I woke up with a smile on my face, and I must have laughed because Danny asked me from the top bunk what was so funny down there. He was under the covers trying to read a comic—

he often did that before getting out of bed. I was happy all day from having that dream, and I used to think of those yellow monkeys for a while whenever I needed cheering up.

About fifty feet from the tree, we had a solid swing-set with metal poles cemented into the ground. Twenty feet from the swings was a round stone thing about two feet high and six feet across; Dad said there was a well underneath, but it had a hard cement cap on it, so I couldn't see the water.

I liked to sit on it and play sometimes. Well, that sunny afternoon, I was playing on top of it with Moe, my Three Stooges puppet, and Teresa was next to me with a couple of her Barbies—Moe was trying to make up his mind which one was prettier. Suddenly, I caught a glimpse of something running down the bank.

My heart froze up. A rat almost as big as our old alley cat, Buttons, headed across the grass right for our swing set. It was fat gray and hairless with a long ugly rat tail sticking out straight behind as it ran under one of the swings. Teresa screamed when she saw what I was staring at and ran over to the house, leaving her Barbies behind. I couldn't move as it ran closer.

The rat came within a few feet of the well, and I got a good look at its face; there was nothing human in it at all. The devil probably has a face like that. A creepy shiver tingled all over me as it went by. The rat was heading towards the dump.

A few weeks earlier, Teresa's dad drove his pick-up truck to the dump and threw a mattress, some bedsprings, and an old dresser on top of the giant pile of junk already there. Me, Danny, and Teresa got to sit in the cab—I was next to the black knobbed gear shift as we bounced across the field. It's exciting to drive in high grass without a road. It reminds me of John

Wayne in *Hatari* when they drove trucks through the African savanna trying to catch zebras and giraffes for zoos—they shouldn't have messed with that rhino though, he knocked over a truck and hurt the Indian's leg real bad.

That devil-faced rat and my earlier truck ride to the dump combined to give me an awful dream a few days later. Rats like the one I saw were crawling all over the garbage in the night. I was standing behind a tree, watching them slink about through the junk and the trash, and I was afraid they might see me. Thank God they never did, or I probably would have had a heart attack in my sleep. I've had that same dream many times.

Ever since then, I've been afraid of rats, way more than any other animal. Sometimes though, I have dreams about lions chasing me; they are scary too if they're not in a cage and are just roaming about in the open where they can get you. Lions are just too fast and strong; I feel helpless running from them. They never get me in my dreams, but the feeling that there is no way to stop them from catching me is terrifying.

Rats, though, just seem to be evil somehow. One of the most frightening movie scenes I ever saw was in *Lady and the Tramp*. This big black rat climbed up a gutter and humped its way through an open window. He crawled over the floor to a crib. A baby was all alone, sleeping peacefully and unprotected as the rat perched on top of the crib bars with his rat tail hanging down.

Just when it looked like the rat was going to crawl in with the baby, Tramp burst into the room barking and snarling and chased the rat away. The rat fought hard, but Tramp was a good-sized dog, so he finally killed it after getting a nasty rat bite. A cornered rat is no joke.

Uncle Johnny told us he used to take his BB gun down to the Allegheny River to shoot at the river rats near the glass factory; he said they were as big as cats there, too. He told us that when we flew back from Germany. Since we had been out of the country for three years, we stopped in PA to visit all our relatives first before we drove down to Louisiana, where Dad was stationed next. Dad had a few weeks of leave saved up.

On the plane ride back to the U.S., we flew on a Pan-Am jet, our first plane ride. Before we took off, we were waiting in the airport for a while eating banana splits that weren't as good as I imagined they would be—the bananas were too hard, when people started shouting that the Queen of England was in a motorcade outside.

We all rushed to the windows and looked out. She was sitting on the back of a convertible, waving to everyone. I guess queens don't have to worry about getting shot like presidents do. Because we were high up, I couldn't make out how pretty she was or if she was wearing a crown, but at least we got to see a real queen.

Me and Danny were wearing green Bavarian hats with short quail feathers (the kind yodelers wear). Mom and Dad got them for us as going home presents. We had souvenir pins from Bad Kissingen and the airport stuck in our hats. As we sat waiting, a super tall colored man walked by with a cute baby cupped in one hand; he had the most enormous hands I ever saw. Slobber bubbled out of the baby's lips as the man strolled through the dining hall, slowly lifting and lowering the baby to keep her happy like he was dribbling a ball that never touched the floor.

We were excited about going back to PA, but not so much about Louisiana, which we knew nothing about, and I felt sad about leaving Germany. It's not easy to leave a place where you have lived for so long, especially a beautiful place like Germany. The US doesn't have castles or cobble-stoned villages with crooked streets and little shops full of handmade toys, or candy stores with German chocolate and seashells full of hard golden honey candy to lick, or lazy green rivers with swans and pine trees reflecting deep into the water. And no German bread—ouch, that was a tough one. Germans bake the best bread in the world: heavy seeded brown moist chewy, perfect with German cheese or butter, fresh-baked every day— a smell I bet even angels must love; I was going to miss their bread forever.

On the plane ride, Danny got airsick next to me and had to use one of those bags. He was as pale as a ghost for a while, and I got to eat most of his meal when it came because looking at food made him cringe. All of the food had a funny taste to it like it had been in a box for a long time, but I was hungry, so I enjoyed it anyway. Danny turned his head away as I ate both meals.

After the plane landed, we caught a fat checkered cab to a hotel somewhere in New York. The cab driver had a hard time squeezing all our suitcases in the trunk. A sign on the back of the hotel door scared me because they were warning about burglars and double-locking the door to be safe, so it took me a while to get to sleep.

The next day we caught a train to Pittsburgh and got the heck out of New York. Dad and Mom didn't like it either, too big, too much traffic, but Danny thought the tall buildings were tremendous and kept saying, "Wow, look at that one!" They were pretty cool to look at, but I was glad to get on the train.

Grandma T's house was the first place we visited. Mom and Dad had bought a German cuckoo clock for her and one for Pap-Pap and Grandma Babe. She was happy to get the clock; she loved how the cuckoo came out of two little doors at the top of the hour. Green leaves bracketed the sides of the doors; cute little shingles were on the roof. The bottom of the chains had metal weights made to look like pine cones—I guess they pulled some kind of gears inside the clock somewhere.

Grandma and Mom and Dad drank coffee and talked about the trip and stuff. Grandma loves drinking coffee, anytime, anywhere. I heard her say once, "Yes, thank you, I never turn down an offer of coffee, black with one teaspoon of sugar, please."

Grandma said that Uncle Dale was out with his girlfriend. Uncle Dale has dark brown hair like Dad and an easy-going smile that shows how handsome he is. He is tall and lanky, but Dad said he carried himself well after watching Uncle Dale playing baseball.

A few days later, I saw that Uncle Dale had fat black dice with white spots hanging from his rearview mirror; the name Cindy was sewn on them in red longhand. Me and Danny got white sailor hats with our names in red longhand once at a carnival. They were cool, and we wore them everywhere for a while—I wonder what happened to those hats. I got a good long look at those dice from the back seat because Uncle Dale had trouble on Drey Street, a giant hill with roller-coaster-type dips. There is a red light at the top, and if you have to stop, it is very, very steep, especially scary if the car has a clutch and the driver isn't an expert at clutching. Unfortunately, we found out that Uncle Dale wasn't.

Danny and me were in the back when we had to stop at the light. Uncle Dale had just been driving around to show us his new car, an old black and white Plymouth with a red interior. It was sharp-looking with lots of chrome on the bumpers. Uncle Dale said he had just waxed it a few days before; the whole car looked shiny. It was old, though, so it only cost him two hundred dollars, which he had saved up from a part-time job he had cleaning a bakery after school and on Saturdays.

When the light turned green, the car started to drift backwards, way too far—my stomach was flipping before Uncle Dale slammed on the brakes. There was a red Pontiac right on our bumper. Uncle Dale knew he couldn't try again with the car that close; he'd back into the Pontiac for sure, so he motioned for the Pontiac to back up, but there was a car behind them. The light kept turning colors while the line behind us got longer and longer, people started to toot horns.

I was getting more and more scared because that hill is uncomfortably steep, gravity seemed to tug the back of my head, like how my head feels when a roller coaster clacks slowly up a steep track to the top, and I wished I was anywhere else but where I was. Danny was studying the floor mat, afraid to look.

Finally, the cars behind managed to back up a couple feet. The light turned green, and Uncle Dale eased up the clutch and stomped on the gas. We jerked up that hill, squealing rubber, and something smelled like it was burning. A big cloud of bluish smoke was in the air behind us. I promised myself that when I got older, I would never ever drive a car up Drey Street.

Uncle Dale couldn't drive a car with a clutch good, but he sure could pitch. He pitched for the Arnold Lions—that was his high school team's name, and he struck out eighteen batters in one game. He struck out fifteen the day we went to watch him with Dad and Mom. Uncle Dale was so impressive that the Pittsburgh Pirates came to watch him play. They thought he was good enough to offer him a chance to play in their farm system, where they develop players for a few years before they get a shot in the majors with the Pirates.

Uncle Dale thought hard about it but said no thanks. He had a good job lined up after high school in the aluminum fabrication shop where Uncle Bill worked, and he wanted to marry Cindy. Making a major league team was no easy thing, he said, and minor league pay wasn't much for starting a family.

But I'm guessing on top of that; he just didn't have the desire to do it. If he had really wanted to, he could have figured out a way to make it work with being married, but Uncle Dale must have known where he belonged. People were surprised he turned the Pirates down, but I kind of admired that he did what he wanted to, even if everybody else wanted him to play baseball, including me.

Before all the trouble on Drey Street and going to the baseball game later, we had a nice visit with Grandma that first day. While Grandma, Mom, and Dad drank coffee and gabbed in the kitchen, Uncle Johnny, me, and Danny played crazy eights in the living room with Trixie lying on top of the couch, looking down at us on the floor. She had sad brown eyes but no bad dog breath. That's when Uncle Johnny told us about shooting the river rats with his BB gun. He said they weren't easy to kill, and he went through a lot of BBs trying to kill one.

Well, after my fright from the devil-faced rat by the well had faded somewhat, and we had eaten a good supper of mashed potatoes, Salisbury steak, peas, corn on the cob, and biscuits, we went to visit the couple Dad knew across the highway. (Danny was the king of eating corn on the cob—he gobbled down eight of them once, and I was the biscuit king. I could eat as many as Mom would let me, and Mom knew how to bake them just right, golden brown on the outside and steaming white when they were cut open begging for butter to melt.)

This couple we visited didn't have any kids. I can't remember how the husband looked at all, but Sue was the wife, and she had me on her lap right away. She had short dark hair, pretty brown eyes, and a wide, warm smile that grabbed at my heart. It felt good to sit on her soft lap, and she had a sweet soap smell that reminded me of strawberry jelly. It seemed like I knew her for a long time even though we had just met, so I cuddled up and felt right at home with her.

I had my Lambchop puppet with me (Lambchop was a lamb puppet that Shari Lewis, a lady ventriloquist on TV, talked with), and I let Sue put it on. She had fun playing with it and having Lambchop kiss me and whisper in my ear.

All the adults were playing some kind of card game—Hearts, I think, drinking Pepsi, except the husband who had a golden bottle of beer—it smelled kind of like the sidewalk outside of the bar by Bongi's Market, except not nearly as overpowering.

We'd walk up to Bongi's to either get Chum-Gum, two sticks wrapped together with a mild cherry flavor, red licorice, or salted pretzel logs, all for a penny each. Danny usually got licorice, while I grabbed a pretzel unless I wasn't hungry, then I got Chum-Gum. Bongi's was up from the alley where I crashed my blue and white tricycle and hurt my chin. When we walked or pedaled by the bar next to Bongi's, it always smelled like someone had tossed a bucket of beer out, and it had soaked into the sidewalk all night.

All the bars in Arnold smell like that outside though, the smell must just ooze out the doors when people open them, and Arnold has tons of bars. I don't know if it's true or not, but Uncle Friday said that Arnold has the most bars and the most churches per capita in the world. When I asked, he said per capita means there are more bars and churches per person than anywhere else.

While they played cards, everyone ate pretzels, peanuts, and chips; I ate my share, too, as I watched. Danny was guzzling Pepsi—he had two bottles and was filling up on the peanuts. Danny loves peanuts, especially Planter's peanuts with the nut on the bag or can that wears a top hat and a monocle. Danny got a rubber figure of that peanut guy in a box of Cracker Jack once—or maybe from a can of peanuts. It was cool till he left it behind in a motel room on our car drive down to Louisiana from PA.

Dad and the husband were smoking a lot as they played cards; it seems like everybody in the Army smokes. I was next to Sue all night, and she couldn't keep her hands off me. My heart was full of her, and I wanted to stay longer when it got late, and we had to go. I just felt like we belonged together.

Mom and Dad were shocked because they always thought I was kind of shy. They often bring up the day I hid under the table from Aunt Joyce and Aunt Doreen when I was three. I remember looking out from under the table, wondering why everybody was making a fuss; I just didn't feel like being bothered by anyone that day—plus, I was in my pajamas, which is only for immediate family to see. Mom made me come out from under and say goodnight; then I went upstairs to bed. I heard people laughing as I went into our bedroom.

Well, I sure wasn't hiding from Sue. That same night I had a dream where I was looking all over for her through a big house full of hallways and shadowed rooms. Finally, I found Sue sitting in a white room rocking a chair, waiting for me. She held me for a long time, just rocking peacefully with my head on her breast. From time to time, for some months after our visit, I would dream of Sue sitting in that chair waiting for me till I eagerly crawled up and sank into her lap.

Once, while I was having the dream—the last time I can remember having it, I lifted my head to look at her, and she wasn't Sue anymore. Her hair was black and long enough to reach her waist; her arms were brown like a colored woman's skin, and her face was shining like a bright star; I couldn't really see what she looked like, but it felt like her love was washing over me, and the Mystery was squeezing me so good while she held me I almost started crying from how happy I felt. Then I woke up with sunlight poking through the window blinds onto my face. It's been years since then, but I still keep hoping I'll have another dream about that brown-skinned, long-haired lady, so far though she hasn't come back.

It isn't as fierce a hunger as I had for Sue, but Aunt Cora and I belong to each other, too. Last year when we visited Aunt Cora, something horrible happened. Me and Danny shared a big bed upstairs. I remember being excited about sleeping in a different room and super tired before falling asleep next to Danny. Mom woke me up by shaking my shoulder in the morning. "Bobby, get up; what did you do! I can't believe it!"

I opened my eyes and felt the cold, wet sheet under me. A hot flash of terror shot through me as I realized that I had wet the bed. Oh, God. Mom doesn't get mad easy, but she was red-faced, huffing and puffing about what a big mess it was and did I ruin the bed; how could she get it dry? Dad had murder in his eyes when he came in the room. Danny was worried that I might have gotten pee on his Yogi Bear pajamas. I felt so ashamed I almost cried—well, I might have leaked a tear or two.

It was a problem I'd had for years; now and then, it would just happen. I never knew I had peed until I'd wake up in the cold wet the next morning, the stinky sheet plastered against me. Mom hated cleaning it up and seeing all the stains on my mattress; nothing gets rid of the yellow-brown edges of pee stains. You could tell which mattress was mine or Danny's when we moved somewhere, and the moving men would carry it out into the bright sunshine where everyone could see it.

Mom had to have told Aunt Cora what I'd done to her bed, she couldn't hide something like that, but Aunt Cora never said a thing about it to me. I kept waiting for her to look at me in a disappointed way or with pity for how ashamed I must feel, but she never did. In fact, later that same day, Aunt Cora snuck me a few of her homemade chocolate chip cookies when we were alone in the kitchen and gave me her special hug. She knew what had happened all right, but she didn't care about her old bed—we belonged to each other, that's what mattered.

"My, it's so good to see you, boys, again!" Aunt Cora climbs back up the porch steps, with Dad, Mom, and Uncle Chick behind her lugging suitcases, and puts her arms around me and Danny; then Aunt Cora steers us all off the porch and into the house with our hands full of baggage. "Let's get some milk and banana bread in you before you're off to bed."

Chapter VII

Uncle Chick's Advice

The banana bread is as good as Grandma Babe's, moist with just the right amount of walnuts to crunch, and plenty of banana flavor. We're all having a piece around the dining table. Aunt Cora is pouring ice tea for Mom and Dad. Me and Danny and Uncle Chick are sipping cold milk that came out of a silver metal pitcher; beads of moisture are dripping down the sides onto a round burgundy placemat.

There is a china closet with blue and white dishes and cups against the wall that leads to the kitchen. I can see the corner of the stove through the doorway. The linoleum in the kitchen has black and white squares like a checkerboard. We used to have giant black and red checkers that we played on a foldable plastic mat. If we still had them, we could play checkers with them on their kitchen floor; that would be cool.

The dining table is round, and the wood is maple syrup brown. There is a circular turning thing in the middle of the table that can hold salt, pepper, sugar, milk, whatever is needed; it's fun to spin around. I turn it slowly and gently, so no one will make me stop. The Douglas family has one on their kitchen table, too—that's the family on *My Three Sons*. They don't have a mom—I think she died or something. They seem to get along okay without one, thanks to Uncle Charlie doing all the cooking, but I feel sorry for them. Not having a mother would be like having a black hole in your heart—nothing could ever fill up that hole—except maybe God.

My eyes go to Uncle Chick's hand, holding his cup. Uncle Chick is missing two fingers above the knuckles; they just end in rounded stumps. Last year when I first saw his fingers, I could hardly believe what I was seeing. Danny was looking, too. We were sitting on the couch getting ready to watch a *Star Trek* episode when Uncle Chick stuck his stubby fingers into a big bowl of Ruffles potato chips on the coffee table. Uncle Chick must have seen us staring at his hand.

"Oh, my fingers huh, they look sort of scary, don't they? I suppose I should tell you, boys, how it happened. Do you want to hear about it?" After we nodded our heads, Uncle Chick continued.

"I was eighteen when I first got out of high school, and a friend of mine got me a job in a mattress factory. They are probably safer nowadays, but back then, it was a hot, noisy, dusty place without very many safeguards. The factory was full of all kinds of machines making various mattress components.

"I was young, and they probably should have trained me more carefully, but the truth is it was my own fault. One day I was careless and wasn't paying enough attention to what I was doing. There was a girl with long brown hair that smelled like cinnamon rolls that I was thinking about; Rosalind was her name, who I was going to see that evening. The machine I operated didn't care that I was daydreaming; it was doing what it was made to even when my fingers got in the way of some gears. By the time I could shut off the machine, my fingers

131

were a bloody mess. The doctors did the best they could with what was left.

"It was a hard lesson, but I learned that life demands your attention at all times. Like that machine, life is going to do what it is made to do, whether you are aware or not, and if you're not, you better hope God is ready to pick up the slack. Don't forget that, boys, or you might lose more than your fingers."

I've thought about what Uncle Chick said since then, and more than a few times, I've seen people getting hurt by not paying attention, being unaware of something happening, or that was about to happen.

One incident at recess will stick in my mind forever. When Dad got stationed at Fort Polk in Louisiana, we moved into the nearby town of Leesville. Leesville Elementary had the best recess of all the schools I've ever been to; in fact, it's my favorite school ever. I couldn't wait for lunch because the food was so good all the time: hot cornbread every day, buttered black-eyed peas, rice with some kind of tan-colored beans that went together perfectly, hush-puppies, peach or sweet-potato pie for dessert.

Older women wearing black hair nets did all the cooking, then they would spoon out the food from big silver bins and plop it onto our trays. I always smiled my best smile as I was walking along the counter. I wanted them to know how much I enjoyed their cooking, so I'd comment about how delicious it smelled or looked, hoping, of course, that they might give me a heaping spoonful. Sometimes, if they had enough, we got to go back for seconds. The cornbread was especially good: moist and honey-sweet with a pat of butter smeared on top.

After lunch, we would have recess for a whole half hour. We also had two fifteen-minute recesses, one at ten and one at two. They had tetherball courts all over, swings, monkey bars, merry-go-rounds that we'd hop on after we got them zooming around—they even had candy machines outside of the classrooms on the outdoor hallways. We had our choice of Jolly Rancher sticks, Turkish Taffy (chocolate was better than vanilla), Chuckles, Boston Baked Beans, Red Hots, grape-flavored candy cane logs, Lemon Heads—all for only five cents apiece.

At the far edge of the playground, there were some woods. I used to sit on an old stump there while I ate my candy and thought about things. That was usually when I was hot and tired from playing tetherball or whatever. Other kids would come sometimes, and we would talk about stuff and mess around till the bell rang.

One day a kid from another class brought a penknife to school, and he and a couple other kids started playing mumbly peg with it by the stump. It was a game I liked to play myself at home with Danny or Jeffrey, our neighbor across the street.

Jeffrey had glasses and was a little chubby. I went in his house once while his mom was watching *Let's Make a Deal*. It's a fun show. I always enjoy looking at all the adults dressed up in goofy costumes making fools of themselves; they want to get Monty Hall's attention for a chance to win money or prizes. Jeffrey got us each a glass of grape Kool-Aid, and his mom told me to sit down as a contestant was about to pick either curtain number 1, 2, or 3. I was in heaven because she had an air-conditioner blasting, and it was so cool in there I couldn't believe it. The air even smelled and tasted cold. We just had fans at our house.

When we first moved to Texas, we went to Kelly and Cohen one day to look at air conditioners, but Dad and Mom ended up getting a water cooler instead because the air conditioners were too expensive. A water cooler is pretty crummy compared to an air conditioner, and it smells like rusty water.

Anyway, the object in mumbly peg is to drive a peg or stick into the ground with the part of the knife the blades come out of. You have to flip the knife from different positions. If the person you are playing can't make the knife stick in the ground like you did, you get to whack their peg into the ground with the knife. In the end, someone has to pull a peg out of the ground with their teeth. The deeper in the peg, the more dirt you get in your mouth.

I took my Lemon Heads and got the heck out of there when they started playing. I knew knives were trouble at school. It was a good thing I left because word got back to a teacher, and those kids got sent to Mr. Solomon, the principal. The area by the stump was off-limits for a while after that. Everybody gets punished sometimes when someone does something stupid. It stinks, and it's not fair, but being part of a group causes that, especially if it involves a group of kids.

I found that stump one Saturday morning after I decided to go on an adventure by myself. I was just walking alongside the gigantic power lines a few blocks from our duplex when I discovered a long stretch of fields that led to woods with a lot of swampy land. I decided to see what I could find if I kept going.

After a while, everything was still, and there was no sign of houses or people anywhere around. Soon I left the power lines behind, too. I followed a hard mud path into the shadows under the trees. Long shallow pools of water were all in a long curving line separated by stretches of mud, which gnats and mosquitos hovered and spiraled over like tiny cyclones. Greenish white moss was draped all over tree branches. I felt like Ponce de Leon looking for the fountain of youth as I went deeper into the woods. I got startled once by loud noise next to the path, but it only turned out to be a bird flapping and hopping about in some bushes.

I was walking along the bank looking down when I saw a clam lying there on top of some black mud. I had never found one before, so I climbed down the bank to pick it up. My hand got scratched from holding onto a hairy vine that kept me from falling in the thick mud, which I pretended was quicksand; one of my sneakers did get a little muddy, but I was just able to reach out and grab the clam.

It felt great to hold it. The clam was black and as big as my hand. I looked at it for a while, admiring the curved ridge lines on the shell; they reminded me of ripples in a pond, like when someone tosses a rock in the water, except the lines were closer together and a little bumpy. I tried to pry it open, maybe there was a pearl inside, but it stayed closed tight like a bank vault.

I thought about taking it home and getting a screwdriver to pry it open, but I might chip or damage its shell that way. There probably wasn't a pearl inside it anyway, and I couldn't do something like that to an animal after Mortimer, even if it was just a clam with no eyes or anything. It wasn't easy to give it up, though there isn't much you can do with a clam besides carry it around and show it off, but I climbed down again and set the clam back where I found it.

After I walked away, I felt good about leaving it. I walked on for about ten more minutes till I came out of the woods right into the clearing with the stump where I ate my candy during recess. I was amazed to find the playground and my school—it almost felt like I was in an episode of *The Twilight Zone,* where the bizarre is normal; I had no idea I was anywhere near our school.

I talked Danny into going with me the next day. I didn't tell him where it ended up, so he was just as surprised as I had been. It was a good hike, and Danny thought it was cool to find a secret way to school, so we went there from time to time. We never walked that way to school, though; we always took the bus.

I've always liked riding school buses, maybe because I had such a good experience with the first one I rode in. It was when we lived off base in Germany for the first couple months. The bus was small, maybe half the size of a regular bus. It was always cold and frosty outside in the mornings, but inside, the bus had a warm toasty kind of bus smell that I loved; I always sat in the back so I could smell it better.

Maybe the smell came from the heater or the exhaust fumes or just from the bus materials, I don't know, but I looked forward to it every morning. The bus bounced us around as we drove through tree-lined hills and curves, and the smell of the egg salad sandwiches in my lunch box mixed with the warm toasty smell of the bus. The sun would finally start yellowing the morning darkness as I looked eagerly out the window with Danny sitting next to me. I always looked forward to school in Germany.

I was so proud one day when I was the only one in class who could read a word that Mrs. Glass had tacked to the wall. The word was 'come.' She gave me a beautiful sticker of a speckled trout. I took it home and stuck it on my bed. We read stories about Dick and Jane and Spot. We also got to read Halloween stories of a cute ghost; the books were all black, orange, and white, with naked tree branches swaying in the night.

I loved learning how to read, and it was fun cutting out pumpkins and funny-looking turkeys that we got to take home. For Christmas, we made wreaths by gluing different kinds of uncooked macaroni noodles onto a ring of cardboard, then Mrs. Glass spray painted them all with gold paint. The paint stunk up the whole room. When she shook the cans, we could hear some kind of ball bouncing inside; then, she sprayed all our macaroni wreaths lying on newspapers in the back of the class. They looked great. Mom loved mine; in fact, she still takes it out of our Christmas decorations box every year and hangs it somewhere. It's a wonder only one of the macaroni noodles has gotten knocked off so far.

Unlike the bus in Germany, the bus in Leesville was big and crowded, and it didn't have such a great smell, but there were a couple of cute girls that I looked forward to seeing get on the bus every morning, who I could glance at on the way to school. One of them had black hair down to her shoulders and the prettiest dark brown freckles I ever saw covering her face, neck, and the soft tops of her ears. Usually, freckles are reddish or light brown, but hers were nice and round and a beautiful chocolate color. I heard her girlfriend call her Susan; she was a beauty all right, but a sixth-grader who probably couldn't be bothered by a fourth-grader, so I never talked to her, but I watched her secretly every day as we bounced our way to school.

Well, when the bell rang and recess was over, we would run from the stump or the tetherball poles, depending on where I was at the end of recess that day, to be back to class on time. Mrs. Martinez had shoulder-length reddish-brown hair, brown oval-shaped glasses over her bright green eyes, and like Wonder Woman, she had the body of a goddess. She was the most beautiful teacher I ever had, with a voice to match, and she would read us a ghost story every day when we came in from lunch recess and cooled down with our heads on our desks.

Some of them were really scary, like this creature with no legs and a Turkish upside-down cup hat, who would creep up on people somehow by shuffling his trunk over the floor and strangle them when they slept. He could even make his way up steps, and the person he was after in the story saw him coming up the stairs, looking up at him with a sinister smile on his face.

Mrs. Martinez said she was the great-great-great-great-great granddaughter of President John Adams—I'm not sure how many greats she said, but it was true all right. Mrs.

Martinez got all enthusiastic whenever she taught us about explorers like Magellan, De Soto, and Ponce de Leon. She would pace and bounce around the room, filling my mind with images of wooden sailing ships, stormy seas, and trail-blazing heroes. History was my favorite subject that year. I just loved watching her all day; class was never boring. The last day of school that year was especially painful because I knew I would never see her again. I watched the clock all day, and when three o'clock came, I knew that time had taken her away from me. That was one bus ride home I didn't enjoy.

Anyway, one day at recess, I was over at the tether ball courts where I usually played. I love tetherball; it's such a satisfying feeling to see the rope whip around the pole, knowing that your opponent can't stop the ball from thumping the hollow metal with a solid ping. I'm pretty good at tetherball, and I was giving the ball a solid smack when I saw something terrible about to happen at the swings next to us.

Tim, the biggest boy in my class and who reminded me of a smart Jethro from *The Beverly Hillbillies* with shorter hair, was swinging real high and hard. Edgar, a dopey kid with greasy blond hair, who used to gross us all out by licking the snot that always seemed to be dripping down to his upper lip, was walking behind the swings, oblivious to Tim swinging.

I opened my mouth to scream out Edgar's name, but it was too late. Tim was flying backwards at torpedo speed, and the swing rammed right into Edgar's head. He hit the ground instantly like an invisible truck ran over him. Kids nearby started screaming. I froze at first; then I walked over, afraid of what I might see. Mrs. Wedner ran to him and put her hand on her mouth; she looked ready to cry as she sent some boys to get Mr. Solomon.

When I got close enough, I could see the side of Edgar's head caved in from the edge of the swing, like when you press something into Silly Putty and get an impression. He was unconscious, and blood was all over his head, face, and neck. Most kids were turning away or hiding their faces, but I was fascinated by how still he was, almost like he was dead. He didn't die, though, but the last I saw of him was when the ambulance guys put him in the ambulance. Mrs. Martinez had us all make get-well cards for him, mostly decorated with flowers, but by the time Edgar recovered, school was about over for summer vacation, so he didn't bother to come back.

"Life demands your attention at all times . . . you better hope God is ready to pick up the slack." I guess God wasn't ready in Edgar's case. Uncle Chick's words went deep inside after seeing what not paying attention did to Edgar—I'm also real careful now when I'm playing around swings.

Uncle Chick is Dad's uncle, Pap-Pap Harvey's brother. They don't look that much alike because Uncle Chick has more meat on his bones, while Pap-Pap wears glasses and also has more hair on his head. As I reach across the table for another piece of banana bread, Uncle Chick turns his head, which is almost totally bald like Yul Brynner's, in an odd way to talk to Aunt Cora near the kitchen, and suddenly I'm reminded of the Banana-head monster.

I don't know why I called him the Banana-head monster—it really was shaped more like a lumpy potato now that I think about it, but I was four or five at the time in PA, and Banana-head is the name that came to me when I saw him.

Mom took Danny and me downtown to the Liberty Theater in New Kensington. Dad must have had the car at work because we were walking through downtown New Ken. On the way, we passed Ben Franklin's, which had rabbit feet hanging in the window display. They were dyed different colors, and Danny and me thought they were great. We begged Mom just to go inside and let us look at them. They were supposed to bring you good luck if you rubbed them, the salesman told us. Each foot had a silver cap on one end with a little ball chain we could swing on our fingers. Mom let us get one, mine was green, and Danny's was blue.

I was rubbing it all through the second movie because I was scared, but it didn't bring me any luck at all. It also started to bother me some days later that I could feel a bone through the fur at the bottom of the foot, which made me realize that someone had killed a bunny to get my foot. So I quit carrying that foot around; it probably got buried and lost at the bottom of our toy box or something.

The first movie was about aliens from outer space that landed by some cliffs and who looked almost like trees. It was confusing and not too scary, just strange; I don't remember much of it. The second movie was called *The Brain That Wouldn't Die*, and it was one of the most terrifying movies I ever saw. This pretty lady got her head chopped off in a car wreck. Her scientist boyfriend, who was driving the car, managed to walk back to his laboratory with her head wrapped in his suit jacket. Somehow he was able to keep her head alive on a table wrapped in bandages and hooked up to wires and bubbling tubes.

The scary part, though, was this monster behind a heavy, bolted door. It kept pounding at the door throughout the movie, and from time to time, the scientist would look at the monster through a slot that he slid over to peek in. Once, a big ugly hand tried to squeeze through and grab the scientist. The bandaged woman's head was able to communicate somehow with the monster behind the door. Her scientist boyfriend was trying to find a body for her somewhere—like Frankenstein, I guess, but she wanted to die and not live on a tabletop or get someone else's body, so she eventually got the monster to bust down the door. We finally got to see him when he burst out and started a fire by knocking glass beakers over.

He was huge. One eye was on his cheek, the other was on his forehead, with his bald head pointing up like a banana. When he snarled at the screen, I sprang out of my seat and ran up the black aisle of the movie theater, terrified. Mom found me hiding behind a red drape in the lobby. My shoes probably gave me away.

Danny thought it was funny, and later when he teased me about it, I pretended to laugh, too. But there was nothing funny at all about that Banana-head, and every once in a while, I still dream about him trying to break down our closet or cellar door to get me, and I wake up in the dark, sweaty, out of breath, lonely.

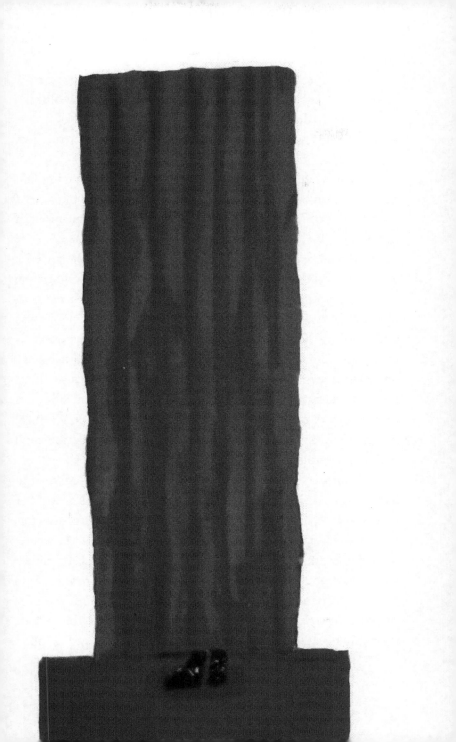

"I'll be picking up Harvey from the bus station tomorrow afternoon," says Uncle Chick. He takes a big swallow of milk.

"Isn't Babe with him?" Dad asks.

"No, Harvey said her legs are paining her too much to make such a long trip cramped in a bus."

I can see that Dad isn't happy about her not coming, but he doesn't say anything. Grandma Babe has puffy blue veins sticking out of her legs, and she stays in her easy chair most of the time.

"What about Joe and Joan? Can they make it?" Dad asks. That's Aunt Joan and Uncle Joe. I always thought it was strange that Mom and Aunt Joan should have the same first name—Uncle Billy and Uncle Bill, too. Uncle Joe is Italian with glasses and a strong hooked nose. I like him, but he doesn't talk as much as Aunt Joan, Dad's sister; she has short reddish hair, and Dad doesn't really like her. He claims it's because she is so fussy and particular about keeping her house clean. She puts plastic covers on top of her furniture and makes people take off their shoes before coming in. Dad complains that he can't feel comfortable in a place like that.

I think there must be more to it than that for Dad not to like his own sister. Maybe they fought all the time as kids or something. They have a boy, Joey, who is two years younger than me. He's a nice kid, a little short for his age, kind of quiet with glasses like his dad, but a smaller nose. We've only played with him a couple of times as we don't see them much. One time Aunt Joan took us bowling. It was the first time we ever bowled. My balls always seemed to curve into the gutter, probably because I'm left-handed, but Joey was pretty good.

They move around a lot, too, since Uncle Joe is in the Air Force. Joey seemed lonely, and he really liked playing with me and Danny. Most of the time, he has to play by himself. I'm glad I have Danny around to do things with; even though we fight sometimes, we always have each other to play with if no other kids are around.

"No, the Air Force gave Joe orders to go to Japan. They left the States last week by ship and are probably just about there, I imagine," Uncle Chick says.

"Japan! That's a great overseas tour. Lucky them," Dad says.

"How is Elva doing?" Mom asks.

"Oh, about how you would expect. She's taking it pretty hard. Poor Steve has his hands full," says Aunt Cora.

Elva is Grandma Ludwiczak's first name. Grandpap Steve is real quiet. He came from Poland, and he can speak English, but he lets Grandma do most of the talking. He just seems to let her take charge and stays in the background, letting her carry on as she wants. Grandpap Steve likes to eat and smoke and watch TV. He retired from Alcoa when they shut the plant down years ago in New Kensington. Grandpap Steve gave Mom an aluminum pot and six aluminum cups for Mom's wedding, I think. The short little metal cups keep drinks cool.

Mom said they used to have five movie theaters in Arnold and New Ken when the aluminum factory was operating full steam. There used to be freight trains running the tracks all the time back then. Across the Allegheny trains took people to Pittsburgh every day to work, too—I imagine them all in the trains wearing Humphrey Bogart hats like they did back then.

Business was good everywhere; now things are slowing down, only two theaters are left, and one is only for adults.

"We'll be going over to see them late tomorrow morning," Dad says.

"Well, you let me know what time you'll be wanting to get up, and I'll have breakfast ready for you. But we'd best get these boys to bed." Aunt Cora nods at Danny, whose eyelids are droopy.

As I'm lying in bed waiting for sleep, my body still feels like it's rocking and spinning a little from the long car ride, but God, it feels great to be able to lay down flat and stretch out for a change. I didn't realize I was so stiff and sore from being crunched up in the car until I laid down. Danny is in bed too, but it's plenty big, and he sleeps on his side, which takes up less space. Danny does snore sometimes (though he always denies that he does), especially when he is really tired, but I don't mind, though; listening to it kind of relaxes me.

It's great to see Aunt Cora and Uncle Chick again and to be back in their house. They both make me feel safe somehow like I do around Grandma Babe and Pap-Pap. It's real comfortable being in the same room as before, like I was just away for a little while, and now I'm back, almost as if it's my own room. I remember how the mattress feels, firm yet springy, and how the tree swaying in the breeze sends shadows onto the wall.

I'm happy about seeing Pap-Pap tomorrow. It's great to have three grandfathers, but Pap-Pap has always been my favorite. He was married to Grandma Ludwiczak once, but when Dad was in high school, Pap-Pap went away. Grandma, Dad, Uncle Billy, Aunt Joan, Aunt Elaine—Pap-Pap just left them all one day. I don't know all the details; if he let them know he was leaving or not, he must have, I guess, or Grandma might have sent the police looking for a missing person.

Some months later, he came back from Kansas with Grandma Babe. One day Dad just saw both of them get out of a car in New Ken, smiling and wearing cowboy hats. Dad turned his back and walked away because he was so upset. I don't think Pap-Pap saw Dad; at least Dad didn't think so because he was down the street a bit, and Dad was trying to hide so they wouldn't see him. Back then, people didn't get divorced as often as they do now, so it was kind of scandalous. Dad was definitely embarrassed and angry about it.

I don't think Dad ever forgave Grandma Babe, though he seems to have forgiven Pap-Pap. It's hard to understand how Pap-Pap could just up and leave like that, but it's not hard to understand why he left. She's my grandma and all, but I wouldn't want to be married to her either.

I'm glad we don't have to travel far tomorrow; my butt is a little sore from sitting so long. It's a good thing I always sleep on my side, too. The room is nice and dark; Danny is breathing deeply, already sleeping next to me; he'll probably be snoring soon. Light from a car passing by fans across the wall. The soft pillow is cool, the blue blanket cozy. Suddenly I realize how tired I am, and my heavy body starts to sink away.

Chapter VIII

Colored Only

Me, Danny, and Uncle Chick are sitting on the cement steps leading up to their house. Big maple trees are spaced along the sidewalk next to the street. My belly is happy, full of mounds of scrambled eggs, bacon, Aunt Cora's hot blueberry muffins, home-fried potatoes, fresh-squeezed orange juice, and cinnamon topped oatmeal. No wonder Uncle Chick has his round belly eating like that all the time.

Aunt Cora was hovering around the table, scooping food onto my plate and filling me up with orange juice when it got low. She kept offering this and that to all of us; I must have had three or four blueberry muffins. I made scrambled eggs sandwiches out of them with dripping butter—boy, did that taste great together.

That breakfast is like a beautiful painting that keeps coming back into my thoughts after looking at it. It's a sunny morning with birds singing in the trees. I see a blue jay hopping sideways along the telephone wire that connects to Uncle Chick's house. Mom and Dad are upstairs, still getting ready to go. Danny is smiling as slanted rays of sunlight are peeking through the trees at us; some of the lit-up leaves waving and wiggling look like slices of green light. Uncle Chick is whittling a fat stick that he picked up from the sidewalk; he just seems to be shaving off all the bark, so it's smooth and white.

Uncle Chick points with his penknife to a plump gray squirrel climbing up the tree in front of us, his puffy tail curled up like a question mark. The squirrel circles around a big knot as we watch it climb high up into the leafy part. A minute later, we hear a bird going on a rampage. The squirrel comes running down the trunk, and a bird is right behind it, chirping like crazy. She chases the squirrel up the next tree; the squirrel runs out on a branch as far as it can before it leaps out in space over to another tree, with the bird still after him as mad as heck.

Uncle Chick is laughing and slapping his knee, "That squirrel must have gotten too close to that sparrow's nest up there. She probably has her babies in it. Nothing's as fierce as a mother protecting her children, even if it is a sparrow. A mother's love is the strongest love of all. Listen to her giving it to him." We can still hear the bird scolding the squirrel further down the street.

"Danny. Bobby. We're leaving now," Dad calls out from the porch. We walk over to the porch steps to say goodbye to Uncle Chick and Aunt Cora, who came out with Mom and Dad. The sun is lighting up the purple flowers in the bush; they must love their morning bath of sunlight. Suddenly, a hummingbird is hovering over a purple flower snout with his long bill poking inside. He is greenish and sparkling blue with his wings an almost invisible blur. Uncle Chick puts his hand on the step railing, and the hummingbird takes off like a flying saucer, gone up in an instant.

Mom has a big bowl of something covered with aluminum foil. Aunt Cora is wearing a pink blouse and black pants with white pockets. The color combination reminds me of Black Jack candy: soft licorice-flavored chews that taste great but get stuck in your teeth. I haven't had those in a while.

"You tell Elva to hang in there, and we'll see her tonight," says Aunt Cora. She gives my hand a squeeze and my eyes a sweet smile as I get in the car. Uncle Chick waves and then heads back into the house, probably for another cup of coffee. I kind of wish I was staying with them for the day. Dad backs up down the driveway, and when he looks over the seat, I see that he has a small piece of toilet paper on his neck with a red spot in the middle; he cut himself shaving again.

Grandma Ludwiczak lives on the other side of Mulberry—a short drive from Aunt Cora's. Danny laughs whenever someone says Mulberry, and he starts whistling the tune from the *Andy Griffith Show*. Andy is such a calm father. He always explains things real clearly and carefully to Opie, so Opie can make a good choice. He never loses his temper or uses a belt on Opie. It was the same with Ward Cleaver on *Leave It to Beaver* and Mr. Douglas on *My Three Sons*. All those TV fathers are perfect dads, but I don't think real life is like that—Dad's sure not. He tries to be like them, but he can't; he has too much temper and a lot of pressure from earning a living, I think. Those TV dads don't have to worry about money; they all have good jobs that pay well.

Barney Fife, Andy's deputy, was funny with his wide eyes and big Adam's apple poking out of his uniform; he always stretched his neck funny when life didn't go how he planned it. He was the one who made that show such a good comedy. Andy and Opie gave the show its heart, though; I often had a warm feeling about life being just fine after I watched the show.

Mulberry is much smaller than Mayberry, though; they don't even have a sheriff or a barbershop like Floyd's. There isn't much in town at all. There's a boarded-up bank that Jesse James is supposed to have robbed in the old days, so it's pretty special if you believe it happened. The bank is so old-looking it could have been around back then, I guess.

Across the street is the general store where they sell hot-dog-shaped bubble gum that is blazing hot and gum made to look like cigarettes—when you blow on one end, a puff of white stuff comes out like smoke. Each cigarette is a different color and flavor, but banana is my favorite. They also have every kind of Adam Brother's gum there is—those are the guys with the old-fashioned big beards on the label. Orange and grape are the best; they really wake up your mouth.

The store sells everything else you could want, from bread and milk to clothes and grass seeds. There are no other stores close by, so it's all squished into one. Houses are spaced far apart on either side of the road once we pass the store.

The last time we visited, Grandma Ludwiczak lived in a nice red house with a shady front yard, but she moved since then. Dad told us earlier, "Your Grandma can't stay in one place more than a year or so before she gets restless. After a while, she starts complaining about this and that. Finally, after listening to her bellyaching enough, Grandpap Steve gets worn down and moves her again to keep her quiet, sometimes just across town, sometimes back to PA or back to Kansas. She's gone back and forth between Kansas and PA so much that no one has any idea how many times she's moved."

I know Dad must love Grandma Ludwiczak, she's his mom after all, but he never has anything nice to say about her. When he mentions her, we usually get the frying pan story.

"She could be mean sometimes. Once, when I came home late for supper after football practice—the coach made us run extra laps because no one could block that day; she called me over to her and whacked me on my ear with the frying pan. It was stainless steel, and she wasn't bunting; she was going for a grand slam. When she got mad at me, she'd strike me hard on the side of my head with her right hand or whatever was handy. That's why I can't hear so well out of my left ear." Grandma's arms are flabby but meaty, and when she was younger, she must have packed a wallop—I feel bad for Dad when he was a kid.

Dad does hit us with his belt from time to time, but it's not very often, and only when we do something really bad. The threat of the belt usually changes our behavior, and when he does use his belt, it doesn't last but three or four whacks. Dad always says it hurts him more than it does us, looking sad and running his hand through his hair, but my butt isn't buying that. At least he doesn't damage our hearing like Grandma did him.

Last year, Grandma Ludwiczak had gone on a rant while watching the news. We had just finished watching *Superman*— "faster than a speeding bullet, and more powerful than a locomotive." Superman almost got killed because some crooks trapped him in a hideout with kryptonite, but Jimmy Olsen came by and moved it away. (That would never have happened to Wonder Woman.) George Reeves made a good Superman once you got used to him; at first, he didn't seem handsome or muscular enough to me, but he had a way of smiling as Clark Kent that made me like him, and he was all about saving people when he took off his glasses.

Mom said George Reeves had committed suicide by shooting himself in the head for some reason. Danny's theory is that really some nut killed him to show how tough he was and was bragging about it to his buddies—"Hey guys, I killed the Man of Steel." Whatever happened, it's pretty sad that he is dead. Well, after Jimmy, Lois and Clark finished teasing each other at the end of the show like they usually do, the news started, and there was a protest with some colored people somewhere.

Grandma wasn't happy about it. "What the hell do those niggers want? Who do they think they are, marching in the streets and waving signs? They ought to ship all their black butts back to Africa if they don't like our country. If they had spears and grass skirts instead of signs, they'd look like cannibals with those fat lips and white eyes and teeth—do you call that hair? They're getting might uppity lately if you ask me. While we're getting rid of low lifes, let's ship all the chinks, spics, dagos, and commies out with them and clean up our country. They aren't the kind who belong in America."

Dad took us aside, later, "Your Grandma doesn't really mean what she said; you guys just chalk that up to an old woman being crabby because she has so many aches and pains from her operation. And don't ever let me catch you talking like that, do you hear?"

Dad was wrong, though; I heard the meanness in her voice; she meant what she said. Talking that way was natural to her; she expected everybody else to feel that way, too. I wonder what made her so bitter about people who were different from her. How does that happen to a person? Kids of all different colors will get along just fine playing together in a sandbox; no toddler cares about another kid's skin color. Sadly, that changes for people like Grandma when they get older. She would have fit right in if she lived in Leesville.

The first time me and Danny walked to the movie theater in Leesville, we got quite a shock. On the way there, we walked on top of a waist-high cement wall next to a fence. Through the fence was a reform school that we always stared at. We never saw any kids on the grass fields in front or anywhere. They must have had them locked up tight all the time. We could see that the windows had thick metal screens, which made me feel sorry for the kids stuck in there, but who knows what sort of things they did. Maybe they were gang members like in *West Side Story,* and they stabbed people.

All four of us saw that movie in Germany. Mom loved it; Dad endured it; I'm not sure what Danny thought, but I was fascinated by all the dancing, and the singing was tremendous. When this man started singing a song called "Maria." I felt my heart squeezing from the beauty of the sound and the lovely face of the woman he was singing to. The Mystery was twisting through me, filling me with an ache to be like the singer, to dance happily in the night, to shout out with joy, and to love Maria or someone else as pretty with all my heart. That night

I fell asleep with the name Maria echoing in my mind and her beautiful face floating in and out of the dark.

The next morning at breakfast, I told everyone that I knew what I wanted to be when I grew up.

"What's that, son?" Dad asked, with a fork full of scrambled eggs halfway to his mouth.

"It was great how they danced in the movie last night. I'm going to be a dancer. I'd love to be able to dance like that."

He almost choked on his eggs. "A dancer? Really? Are you going to wear dresses, too?" Dad asked.

I never mentioned dancing again.

Well, the theater in Leesville was downtown, not far from a goldfish pond by city hall that we usually stopped at. It was cooling somehow to watch the long fat fish appear and disappear as they swam around the dark water. The girl in the ticket booth that first day had red hair and green eyes that matched her soft fuzzy sweater. She had a gold chain with a tiny cross on it. I guess she saw me admiring the cross resting on top of her sweater because she smiled at me without showing her teeth—she had a cute dimple. Danny had to push me along because I wanted to keep looking at her.

Inside, the smell of fresh pickles was even stronger than the smell of popcorn. That was new to us, pickles at a theater. They were floating in a big jar with the lid off. The pickle juice scent was all through the lobby, and it made my mouth water. I bought one. The lady stuck it inside a white paper wrapper with a smiling cartoon pickle tattooed on it, but the pickle didn't taste nearly as good as it smelled, so I gave it to Danny later. I still had a box of Red Hots and a Zero candy bar to go with my popcorn—a great combination that always satisfies. The shock, though, was a white sign with purple letters at the bottom of the steps to the balcony, "COLORED ONLY."

Danny and me just looked at each other like we couldn't believe what we were seeing. It took a second for me to understand that all the colored people had to sit in the balcony, and all the whites had to sit downstairs. What sort of people lived here? Why do they feel that way about colored people?

A colored girl with a red-dotted white dress skipped up the balcony steps, shaking a Good n' Plenty box. She was about six. She was smiling about something; maybe she was pretending to be a train driver like Choo Choo Charlie in the commercial. Her stiff pigtails bounced up the steps. It didn't make her feel bad to have to sit up there, but it made me feel like I was watching a friend get picked on in school.

We found some seats to the side that were nice and cool in the dark. Every face I could see in the audience was white. All the people waiting took it as normal that colored people weren't allowed to sit next to them. I don't want something like that to ever seem normal to me. The balcony seats were way up near the ceiling; it must have been hot up there. It wasn't fair because there were plenty of empty seats below.

No wonder there are so many colored people marching in the streets protesting about how white people treat them. I would too. In history class, they taught us how President Lincoln abolished slavery and what a good thing that was, but there is still stuff like this balcony law going on—I found out later that Leesville had separate drinking fountains by the courthouse, one for whites, one for colored people. There must be other mean things happening that I haven't heard about.

I can't believe that President Lincoln would approve of colored and white people made to sit separate like this. We visited his statue at the Lincoln Memorial long ago. What if President Lincoln's soul could see out of the statue's eyes, if he could witness the protests of the colored people marching in Washington, D.C.? He might wonder what happened; how could so many people die or lose an arm or a leg fighting against slavery in the Civil War, and colored people still be treated horribly a hundred years later? I don't think he'd be too happy about it, maybe tears would leak out of the statue's eyes if they could, or maybe he'd get up on those long stone legs and join the protesters as they marched.

Now that I think about it, I don't remember any colored people being on the *Andy Griffith Show*. Mayberry was somewhere in the South; how come only white people starred in the show? I know a lot of colored people live in the South. Maybe they had some colored people on the show, but I sure don't remember any. Life might feel just fine after you watched the show, and you were white like me, but now I'm thinking that maybe colored people didn't feel quite so fine after watching it. Why should colored people have a warm feeling about a show that pretended they weren't even around?

Mrs. Budzelack told me once, "Bobby, there is one rule to follow above all others. It's called the Golden Rule for a reason because following it makes a person rich in their heart. It says, 'Treat other people the way you would like to be treated.' You'll see if you watch and listen carefully that the people who live by that rule are the happiest, and those that break it are often miserable, bitter, and lonely. Don't be one of those."

Mrs. Budzelack had told me that after she saw me arguing outside with another boy at recess. We both wanted the same spot in line for some dumb reason, and we had pushed each other a little when Mrs. Budzelack came outside to the playground to pick us up. I was embarrassed when I saw her looking at us, and even more so when she pulled me aside and talked to me, but I never forgot what she said. She had a way of making me look at myself and try to be better.

I guess the people of Leesville forgot about the Golden Rule, or maybe they thought it didn't apply to colored people for some reason. In the Army, there are lots of colored people. It's taken for granted that colored people and white people work, go to school and sit in the movies together. It doesn't matter what part of the world you're in; all Army bases treat colored people equally. That's how life is supposed to be; separating people in movie theaters or at fountains is not.

Carl Williams was colored, and he was my best friend for a while when we lived on base in Germany. He had a dragon robot with a round flat tail that shot ping pong balls. I would take our robot, The Great Garloo, over to his apartment, which was right down the hill from us, and we would have monster battles.

Garloo was cooler than Carl's robot. Garloo has light green spikes going down the middle of his head, darker green scales covering the rest of his body, a leopard loincloth like Tarzan wore, and brown sandals. His open-mouthed smile shows his strong white teeth and a red tongue. Garloo can

open and close his mighty arms together so his green foam-padded hands can pick things up; he's also able to bend over and move forward and backwards. Me and Danny love Garloo, even after one arm got broken off somehow in Texas.

Neither Carl's dragon nor Garloo ever really lost a battle; we each thought our robot was the best and didn't want ours losing, so we just had them fight each other for a while; then we'd have them gang up on some unsuspecting cowboys and Indians riding plastic horses that Carl had. They always got slaughtered, of course.

Carl's house had a different smell to it than our house. I liked it, though; the smell reminded me of fresh roasted nuts in Murphy's 5 and 10 store back in New Ken. I remember noticing Carl's hands because his palms and fingernails were different colors from the rest of him, and the wrinkles around his knuckles and by his thumb looked really wrinkly. The bottoms of his feet were a different color, too. We always had fun playing together, and we never fought about stuff. His mother was nice to me too and always offered me Kool-Aid or Hawaiian Punch. Once, she gave us chocolate cake with really thick vanilla frosting and red and green sprinkles—it wasn't even anybody's birthday.

I had to do number two in their bathroom once. I didn't want to, but there was no choice. At someone else's house, I'm always afraid I'll put too much paper in, and the toilet will overflow. Different toilets might not be able to take as much paper as you are used to using and then look out.

That happened to me once at Aunt Joyce's house, in their upstairs bathroom; God, that was embarrassing. She even had shaggy green carpet on the bathroom floor—what a mess that was. Aunt Joyce wasn't mad at me, though. She told me not to worry about it; maybe she saw how upset I was about doing it. I still appreciate her being so nice about something so embarrassing.

I remember going at Carl's because the night before, I had swallowed a green cat's eye marble by mistake, and I had been wondering if something bad was going to happen to me because of it. I was relieved when I looked in the bowl at what came out—like I always do—and there was my marble sitting on top. I happily flushed it down. No way was I trying to get it out of the toilet. The same thing happened to me when I was five or so with a dime, except I never saw the dime come out. You'd think I'd learn not to put dumb things in my mouth.

Carl sat next to me in Mrs. Schrader's 2nd-grade class. She was tall with big horse-type teeth and short blond hair. I was in love with her like most of my teachers, even though she once put tape on my mouth.

David sat to my right; Carl sat to my left. David had brown hair, big brown eyes, and he usually had a closed-lipped smile that looked like he knew a secret about something. He had invited me and Danny to his birthday party to play Pin the Tail on the Donkey and other fun games, like dropping clothespins into a plastic milk bottle. That's harder than it sounds. Walter won that game, but we all had fun trying.

David and me were chatting away in class. Mrs. Schrader warned us twice, but we kept on talking while we were cutting out our pilgrim ship parts and gluing them together with white paste. I couldn't believe it when she put a big piece of masking tape over each of our mouths. I tried to pull off the tape, and then Mrs. Schrader got mad and put a second piece of tape on my mouth. She gave David another piece, too, because he was giggling at me.

Carl never got in trouble. He was kind of quiet in class like I usually was, and he had a soft way of talking; maybe that's why we got along so well. When Carl looked over at me with the big X of tape on my mouth, I could tell he felt bad for me. For some reason, it was after she had taped my mouth that I really fell in love with Mrs. Schrader and thought she was beautiful; even with those teeth, she had a pretty smile, and she liked how well I could read.

Danny had a colored friend from his class called Hoary. The back of his head was shaped like a kidney bean. I didn't like him at first because he seemed a little mean. One day though, Danny convinced me to come with him to Hoary's room in a nearby apartment building. He had a whole dresser drawer full of monster magazines like *Eerie* and *Creepy* and ones that had pictures of great monsters from famous monster movies.

Hoary let us look through his magazines all afternoon. We oohed and aahed over pictures of Dracula—both Bela Lugosi and Christopher Lee (who is scarier by far than Lugosi)—Wolfman, Frankenstein, the Mummy, the Creature from the Black Lagoon, and giant monsters like Gorgo, Godzilla, and King Kong.

We were also thrilled by pictures of cool monsters we had never seen before, like the monster from *20 Million Miles to Earth*, the giant who lost one of his eyes in *The Amazing Colossal Man,* and a huge demon that was super with dripping fangs. I really liked Hoary after that day. We even got the idea from him to make a monster scrapbook. Hoary had an extra copy of one of his magazines, so he let us have it to get started with. We made the scrapbook cover out of thin, gold spray-painted plywood—we still have it somewhere, I think.

My favorite colored person ever is Mrs. Mingo. It makes me disgusted and really mad to think that she would have to sit in the balcony seats, too. Me and Danny were in the Cub Scouts for a while in Germany, and Mrs. Mingo was our den mother. She was beautiful, and I liked to look at her and see her smile, especially when she smiled back at me.

Once she organized a taffy pull for our den. I thought the taffy would be different colors, like in a box of saltwater taffy we got for Christmas, but the taffy we made was all the same clear golden color. The taffy tasted great, though, and it was fun to make and eat with our sticky hands.

She also had us make kites for one of our projects. We got little kits with balsam wood sticks, but we had to make the rest. Mom gave us a yellow cloth, and then she drew Bugs Bunny, Yosemite Sam, the Tasmanian Devil, and Daffy Duck on it; it looked great because Mom can really draw. Dad helped us put it all together. All four of us were in the field behind our apartment building for its maiden flight. We all cheered when it took off flying high. All the cartoon characters were visible from the ground as they swayed back and forth in the blue sky, the tail swirling about like a red Chinese dragon with bow ties.

Mrs. Mingo invited me and Danny to her apartment on base for lunch one day. Her husband was a Lieutenant, but he wasn't home—he would have to sit up in the balcony, too. Maybe he even ended up fighting in Vietnam like Uncle Billy, but the people of Leesville wouldn't care about him risking his life for our country—he's colored, up to the balcony he goes.

What happens to people to make them hate like that? They pretend it's not hate and try to justify what they do against colored people—that what they think is normal, the way things should be—but they're wrong. Hate isn't normal; it's all so sad. I'm sure God expects us to be better than that.

I can't imagine Mrs. Mingo hating anybody. Mrs. Mingo's hair reminded me of Sophia Loren's hairstyle (who is the most beautiful woman in the world—well, her, Elizabeth Taylor, and Doris Day are all at the top, but Sophia Loren squeezes my heart the most). Mrs. Mingo always wore pretty flowered dresses and high heels. If Danny wasn't with me that day in her

163

apartment, I might have done something crazy, like put my head on her lap. Well, I wouldn't have, but I would've wanted to, that's for sure.

She made us a salad with purple cabbage, walnuts, and raisins sprinkled in. We also had corn beef sandwiches and freshly squeezed lemonade. I never saw purple cabbage before or had eaten corned beef, but it tasted delicious, especially with Mrs. Mingo sitting next to me smelling like fresh flowers.

Mrs. Mingo taught Kindergarten at our school, and one day she let me visit her class. I wasn't in the cub scouts yet, but I had gotten to know her when she had recess duty on the playground and organized Red Rover games. (The following year, when I was in second grade, she asked me to join the cub scouts.) She was so pretty I was drawn to her like a magnet, and I could tell she liked me. It was near the end of first grade, and I could read really good, so she asked me to read to her class during my visit.

Since we couldn't watch German TV, we went to the library on base all the time to get books. There was also a shuffleboard table near the library entrance that me and Danny used to play with. I liked the feel of the heavy pucks, with red or green circles on top of the silver metal, and how they slid down the long saw-dust-covered table. I was pretty good at playing, and surprisingly Danny wasn't bad either; once though my fingers got hit by a puck, boy did that smart!

The first book I checked out was a riddle book with a picture of a Red Rock Eater on the white cover. I remember feeling super excited when I used my new library card and carried the book home like a treasure. Later, my favorite books were about Baba Yaga with her chicken leg house and King

Arthur and his Knights of the Round Table. I tried to check out *Don Quixote* one day because a knight was holding a lance on the cover, but the librarian wouldn't let me. She said I wasn't old enough—what did she know—I could've read it; she should've let me try instead of being a mean witch.

That day in her class, Mrs. Mingo let me read *Curious George* to some of her students, then we went on a walking field trip around the school by the fence. I got to walk right behind her. Every movement of her body fascinated me; she walked careful like how a deer steps, even the way she turned her head was pretty as she pointed out plants, flowers, and butterflies while the morning sun made us warm and lit up spider webs on the leaves and streams of floating dust.

Then there was the night of the banquet for pee-wee league baseball—and the leagues for bigger kids, too. It was an award dinner for all the baseball players. Everyone on our team was to get a BK letter that stood for Bad Kissingen. The pitcher on our team was even supposed to get a trophy. He pitched with a first baseman's glove—I think it was his dad's old glove. He got teased for it by other teams, but his pitching shut them up.

Dad was training somewhere, and Mom was at home with Danny, who was sick with the measles, so I had to go all by myself. I had the measles the week before, and it was great. I had a slight fever, was tired, smelled a little funny, had an odd taste in my mouth, and red spots were all over me, but they didn't itch, so it really wasn't bad at all.

I got to miss school for a week, so I stayed in bed all day and read comics. There were some cool ones about robots in the future that had kind of taken over the Earth. Good robots were helping humans fight the evil robots. I also had a stack of Green Lantern and Turok Son of Stone comics that Danny borrowed from Terry Macintosh, our neighbor friend, across the hall.

Turok was an Indian who lived in the time of dinosaurs and cavemen somehow. He had a younger sidekick called Ander, who Turok ended up rescuing a lot. With a knife, bow and arrows, and brains, Turok managed to defeat and kill dinosaurs who tried to eat them—Turok and Ander also ate the dinosaurs they killed, which they called honkers—I guess they made loud honking noises.

Green Lantern was cool as well and could use his ring to make giant green hammers or anything he could think of to fight aliens in space—he could use his ring to fly in space, too. His ring was a lot like Felix's magic bag, but of course, he fought supervillains with it, and he had to charge it up with his green lantern—Tom Terrific still had the best power of all.

From time to time, Mom would bring me toast and sugared tea with milk in it or some soup and a grilled cheese sandwich. I got to eat in bed with a tray and stay in my pajamas all day. Mom put the record player in our room so I could listen to Babar the Elephant's adventures. Sometimes I'd play with my dinosaurs and animals in the mountains and valleys of my soft blankets, or I'd just close my eyes and feel the sunlight on my eyelids while I imagined stuff. I was in no hurry to go back to school.

I must have given the measles to Danny, so Mom couldn't come to the banquet; I felt so out of place and lonely when I noticed all the other kids had their parents with them. Mrs. Mingo was there because her husband was one of the coaches, and she probably saw me looking lost because that's how I felt. She made me sit right next to her, and she clapped for me when I was handed my letter. The letter was purple with a white border around the edge and cool with the K a little lower than the B. I loved it. I still have it tucked away in a special spot on my bookshelf next to my Bible.

Mrs. Mingo was lovely that night; I felt lucky and privileged to be sitting next to her. She had little blue locomotives on her butter-colored dress, and she made sure that I got helpings of everything. Mrs. Mingo showed me how to place my napkin and helped me cut up my piece of meat. She offered to walk me home, but I said I would be fine by myself—I didn't want to make her leave early. Mrs. Mingo gave me a big hug as I was standing by her seat; her pretty neck smelled like flowers from heaven.

No matter how nice she was, though, Grandma wouldn't like Mrs. Mingo, neither would the people of Leesville. I don't understand why. Is it just because colored people look different? Are they afraid of colored people for some reason, like them being harder to see in the dark? Don't they know that the Mystery is for everybody and that we are all part of it somehow? Did Jesus care about skin color? I don't think so.

Painfully, I remember the colored boy at the swings. The swings were between two apartment buildings on Post in Germany, near where we used to play marbles. We'd make a big circle in the dirt and try to knock each other's marbles out of the ring with our shooter marble. If we did, we got to keep the other person's marble. I usually won more than I lost.

A colored boy wearing a green shirt and yellow pants was on the swings with his sister, who wore a nice blue dress with yellow ribbons in her hair—they looked like clothes people wear to church. He was about five, and she was probably three—I was around seven at the time. He was swinging high, and for some reason, I started to tease him—maybe I wanted his swing, I can't remember. He was chewing gum, and when he chewed, his jaw muscles and his temple muscles were very clear and strong looking.

"You chew like a horse. The way you chew reminds me of Mr. Ed; he chews like that when Wilbur gives him an apple. I never saw a human being chew like that. Are you a human being or a horse? Do you smell like a horse, too? I can't get over how much you look like Mr. Ed when you chomp away."

I went on like that for a bit, and I could see that he was getting more and more upset. At first, he was just mad; then, he got tears in his eyes. All the while, his little sister was watching her big brother getting made fun of; she looked like she was thinking of punching me, but she had tears in her eyes, too. At supper that night, I started to feel awful crummy for teasing him, and my food didn't go down so good.

I got what I deserved, though, just a couple days later. It's funny how life gets back at you right away sometimes when you misbehave. Maybe it's God's way of trying to teach us lessons while our memories are still fresh and full of what we did wrong. I was on another set of swings near our first apartment, not far from the sandbox where I lost Charley— my monkey puppet, when I got picked on, too. (That sure was an unlucky playground for me.)

There was a big teenager with dark hair combed like Ricky Nelson's by the swings, one of his friends was nearby. The teenager had a thick stick with black gooey tar on the end of it. He laughed with his friend, and then he poked the stick into my butt while I was swinging. He managed to do it again before I could get off the swing. I was crying pretty hard as I ran home. Mom just hugged me and tried to soothe me. I wanted her to go yell at him, but she didn't. It made me realize that sometimes things can happen in the world that no one could really help me with, not even Mom or Dad; I felt miserable and lonely that evening.

Well, that teenager, Grandma, the Leesville people, and (I'm ashamed to say) me all had a meanness in us towards other people because they were different. From what I've seen so far, most people, even nice ones, seem to have a small mean something in them that can pop out sometimes and be ugly. Not everybody, but a lot do. If a person isn't careful, that meanness might grow huge and make someone do something awful; they could even become a criminal or a murderer.

That's a scary thought, but I'm worried it could be true. I don't want that to happen to me, but to stomp out the meanness before it can spread, I need something solid and strong to hold onto—most people do, I bet. For me, it's beauty, the Mystery. Other people might hold onto Jesus or truth or who knows what, but my hunch is if people don't cling tight onto something good, they could end up like Grandma Ludwiczak or someone way worse, an evil president like Hitler.

Chapter IX

The Tick

"This place takes the cake," Dad mutters as the car stops in front of a rounded silver trailer in a lot empty of everything but grass and patches of sandy dirt. Dad looks at Mom. "Nineteen feet. How can a 250-pound woman and a grown man live in a nineteen-foot trailer?" There's no driveway, so Dad just parks the car in the grass next to Grandma's root beer-colored Ford pick-up truck.

Grandma Ludwiczak and Grandpap Steve are sitting on green lawn chairs in front of the trailer door. I'm surprised she can fit in that chair. She is bawling when she gets up to hold Dad. Grandma is barely five feet tall, but she is huge, twice as wide as Grandpap Steve, and he isn't skinny. Grandma has curly gray hair down to the back of her neck. When she is crying or wants to be nice, her face is soft-looking, but when she's riled up about something, she can get scary.

Danny is looking around—for a place to hide, I'm sure, but there is no escape for either of us. After a quick hug of Grandpap Steve, we wait our turn behind Mom. Danny positions himself, so I have to go first—rascal. Grandma scoops and swallows me up into her, and I can feel her pumpkin-colored dress is damp from crying. She smells like old clothes. I feel sorry for her; she must really miss Uncle Billy.

In a couple minutes, Grandma controls herself, brushes off her dress, and looks around for Grandpap Steve, who is coming out of the trailer with two more lawn chairs. After he sets them down, Mom asks Grandpap to show her the refrigerator so she can put her macaroni salad in it.

"Yeah, we had a good trip; at least we didn't run into a storm like we did last time," Dad says to Grandma.

Last year's storm was a doozy, all right. We were about halfway through Oklahoma when Dad picked up tornado warnings on the radio. He hushed Danny and me up, and we heard a news bulletin about a tornado being sighted close by. Dad had turned on the radio because the sky had gotten awful dark real quick, and the giant clouds up there were scary looking. The only tornado I ever saw was on *The Wizard of Oz*, which was super cool looking, so after we heard the scratchy radio alert, I was nervous but excited at the same time.

We started to hear thunder in the distance, and every minute or so, a big jagged lightning bolt would crack open the darkness with a blast of light. Danny looked at me with his worried look, but I could tell he was excited, too. Rain began to drizzle down, and the wind was picking up, gaining momentum quickly; tree branches started swaying and bouncing.

Suddenly, the whole sky in front of us, stretching as wide as we could see, erupted in white light as at least a dozen giant lightning bolts struck down from the heavens at once. I never imagined lightning could be so frightening yet beautiful at the same time. All of our mouths were open in shock; then the rain came down harder than I've ever seen.

Dad pulled over quick onto a dirt road by the highway and stopped the car. There was no way to see; the wipers did nothing as the water came down with the force of a fire hose. It sounded like hail, but it was just rain smacking the car like thousands of hard little BBs. We could feel the wind rocking the car. Mom grabbed Dad's hand.

Then a terrible sound moved closer, reminding me of *The War of the Worlds*, when the three space ships rose from the pit, right before they started shooting rays that disintegrated tanks. This whistling rushing roar smothered every other sound around and in the car; we all knew it was the tornado; nothing else could make such a loud horrid sound. I wondered if our car was going to get pulled into the sky like Dorothy's house or maybe just thrown against a tree.

Danny looked like he was watching a ghost outside the window; my stomach was flipping, Mom's face seemed startled and frozen like someone had just snuck up quiet and whispered "boo" in her ear, even Dad looked worried. A few minutes later, though, the Martian ship sound started to fade, and the wind began to ease up; shortly, the rain was just a steady shower, and we could see again.

Water was all over the roads, tree branches were scattered about, and a lot of leaves got knocked down, but there wasn't any major damage near us. Dad smoked a cigarette and waited another five minutes or so before he started driving again. When we were younger, Mom and Dad told us angels caused thunder by having bowling matches. God must have decided to join the angels that night, and he had to have been on a roll throwing powerful strikes every time.

When Mom and Grandpap come back out from the trailer, everyone sits down. Danny moves over and sits on the trailer steps, and I sit next to him. Grandma is okay now and talking about how much they enjoy their new trailer.

Grandma's feet are bare, and the bottoms are black, cracked, and hard-looking. They remind me of the skin of the Charcoal Man, except his skin looked black, cracked, and rocky all over his large body. Whenever he touched someone, they turned black like him and died.

We watched that movie in Germany when we lived off base in the German Lady's guest house. I can't remember the movie's name; just that it was kind of slow, suspenseful and awful scary—one slight touch and people died a gruesome painful death. He always seemed to find people when they were walking alone or resting somewhere with their eyes closed, like this pretty lady at the seashore was doing.

The Charcoal Man was like death itself, walking about looking for unsuspecting victims who never saw it coming. When we walked home from the movie, I kept looking into the shadows imagining that he might pop out and grab us as we walked past his dark hiding place between two buildings or from behind a thick tree or a stone wall. Even Dad couldn't stop the Charcoal Man.

That night I had a nightmare where I was walking along a beach. Someone was reading a newspaper as they laid down on a lounge chair. When I walked by, the newspaper yanked down, and the Charcoal Man was smiling all evil at me. I sat

173

up in bed sweaty and surprised he hadn't grabbed me and that I was still alive.

Who knows, maybe the Charcoal Man reached out from behind a jungle bush and touched Uncle Billy right before that sniper fired; he can probably make himself invisible if he wants to sneak up on someone.

The bottom of Grandma's feet would have looked right at home on the bottom of the Charcoal Man's feet. The last time we visited Grandma, I commented about how black and hard-looking her feet were, and she told me she could walk over rocks and glass and not feel a thing. She was driving their old pick-up through Mulberry at the time, and her black-bottomed bare feet could barely reach the pedals with her toes.

Me, Danny, and Grandma were in the truck cab going to the general store for some calamine lotion. Chiggers had slipped up inside our socks and made our ankles into a banquet, and Grandma claimed calamine lotion soothed the itching better than anything. I hoped she knew what she was talking about.

The truck had a clutch pedal, and she had to scooch up close to the steering wheel to reach the pedal and press it down; every time she did, she let out a little grunt because her belly was pressing hard into the steering wheel. Whenever she reached for the pedal, I couldn't help but wince and hold my breath a little, half-expecting her toes to fall short or slip off to the side. She must have muscles in her toes to push down the pedals with her toe tips. I just wanted to get out of the truck before she missed a pedal and ran into a wall or something.

After we made it to her driveway, we went inside
Grandma's red tar-papered house—the outside walls look like
fake bricks as thick as roof shingles, and me and Danny sat on
the living room floor. Mom used a tissue to rub calamine
lotion into our bites. It looked like Pepto Bismol, all pinkish,
but it smelled different, stronger, and went on nice and cool.

Grandma brought out some iced tea in a red plastic pitcher for everybody; it was wet and cold but too lemony for my taste.

Grandpap Steve turned on the TV, and we watched *The Mickey Mouse Club*. The kids wore these big black Mickey Mouse ears and told us what their names were all the time. An adult was wearing the ears too—Jimmy was his name, he just looked like a goof with those ears. There was one worth watching, though: she was Annette, a brunette who was beautiful with her big dark eyes. She had a little bow between her mouse ears, and her name was on her shirt. The mouse ears looked perfect on her. She wasn't as pretty as Haley Mills, but she was close, especially when she smiled and showed her lovely teeth as she laughed for no good reason. By the end of the show, I realized that the calamine lotion did help; Grandma was right.

"Superman is on next if you boys want to watch it," said Grandpap.

"You bet we do!" Danny said, a little too loudly. Everybody looked at him a little surprised, but not me; Danny loves Superman. Danny smiled sheepishly, but he wasn't really embarrassed; he just thought it was funny, too. Danny doesn't get embarrassed easy. He did, though, on that same trip the very next day.

I was in Grandma's kitchen getting a glass of water out of the spigot when Danny came to the bathroom next to the kitchen. He looked to be in a hurry, and he didn't bother to check. I was draining my glass looking at Danny when he opened the door to the bathroom. I guess I should have warned Danny, but to be honest, I was thinking about the stew we had eaten at the state fair the night before—it was the best stew I ever tasted, and an Indian with a full-feathered headdress was passing out the bowls—Mom let me buy two helpings, a bowl was a quarter. It was a cool summer night, and the hot stew warmed my whole body. Thinking about that stew made me forget that someone was already in the bathroom. Danny sure should've knocked first.

Grandma was sitting down on the toilet with the door wide open as Danny just stared at her. God, she looked so big on that tiny toilet. I almost choked on my water, and Danny looked so embarrassed I thought his red ears would burn off. Grandma looked just as embarrassed as Danny, "Shut the door!" Grandma shouted. After he slammed it closed, I made my getaway outside for a while, where I had a nice long laugh. Sometimes you can learn a lesson from someone else's mistake; I always make sure I knock now before I open any bathroom door.

Grandpap Steve is sitting in his lawn chair next to the trailer, rolling a cigarette from his tobacco pouch. He rolls with his tobacco-stained thumbs, and amazingly the cigarette comes out just as round and smooth as Dad's Pall Malls, except for a little tobacco sticking out of the end. He hands it to Dad, who takes it and then bends over to Grandpap Steve's lighter. Dad takes a deep puff and blows out a beauty of a smoke ring. He nods his head and smiles at Grandpap—Dad's pretending he likes it. I know because I've heard him say before that Grandpap's tobacco tastes stale and harsh.

Grandma is talking to Mom, who is squinting from the sun and trying to smile. Mom has never said anything bad about Grandma like Dad has, but I can tell Mom isn't as relaxed around Grandma as she is with Aunt Cora.

I can see Grandma's old red house from here, down the road a bit on the other side. There's a cool creek that runs along the edge of her backyard. I sure like her old place better. Maybe Dad will let us go for a while. I try to catch Dad's eye, but he is talking to Grandpap Steve about the hot weather. I decide to take a chance, so I walk over to Dad and wait for him to notice me.

Finally, Dad glances at me, and I try out a smile. "Could we walk over to the creek for a while, Dad?"

I can see he is about to say no, but then he smiles, "Get out of here, but when I call, you better come. Don't make me come looking for you. You got that, Daniel?" Danny nods as he hurries over, and we scoot out of there before Dad changes his mind.

"Good going," Danny whispers as we take off in a fast walk.

The end of town is only a few blocks away. It feels good to be walking. We pass Grandma's old house; we'll go to the creek later. The sun is nice and hot on my chest and face, and the tar covering the road cracks is already getting squishy and bubbly—lizards like this kind of weather. I better keep my eyes open; maybe I'll spot one sunning on a rock or being lazy on a bush. I haven't found any lizards in Kansas yet, but they must have some kind of lizards; it gets hot enough here for lizards, that's for sure.

"There it is," says Danny.

I look up and see the green and white sign under a big shady tree.

"I'm the Flash, and I'll beat you there!" I holler at Danny.

"I'm Superman; you don't have a chance!" Danny shouts.

I feel like the Flash as I listen to little black tar bubbles popping from my black and white P.F. Flyers. The Man of Steel is behind me; trees bend backward as he zooms past them. We are racing across the world, over water even because we're too fast to sink, straight up and down mountains, through the jungle startling lions and monkeys, across giant sand dunes, flashing like lightning, shattering the sound barrier, down the stretch on a highway, and there it is, the finish line.

WELCOME TO MISSOURI, the sign tells me as I flash past it first. When I can finally slow enough to turn around, I see Superman stretched out under the shade tree. Someone must mow the grass that Danny is laying on; it's only two or three inches high and soft looking.

"Now we know once and for all who the fastest man alive is," I tell Danny when I get back to him. Danny is chewing on a weed and has his arms under his head for a pillow.

"I would've won, of course," Danny says, "but I had to stop a space capsule that was out of control from crashing into a volcano. That slowed me up a bit."

"Well . . . while you were doing that, I was stopping a bank robbery in Montana, putting out a fire in Yosemite National Park, and rescuing a baby in a runaway baby carriage," I snap back.

"You know Superman is faster."

"I knooow nuthinggg," I say, trying to sound like Sergeant Schultz on *Hogan's Heroes*, as I walk back to the sign. Schultz and Colonel Klink are the funniest ones on the show. Hogan and his heroes are funny as well, but the Nazis really make us laugh. Twenty years ago, there was nothing funny at all about Nazis; it's strange how time changes things.

I put a foot on each side of the sign. I'm in two states at once. I feel huge, like the giant made of bronze in *Jason and the Argonauts*, when he had one massive foot on each side of the rocky bay, watching the ship sailing between his muscular legs. Then he picked up the ship and shook it, flinging men to their deaths hundreds of feet below. Casually, he tossed the broken ship into the water and walked away.

"Quit banging that stupid sign, Bobby. I'm contemplating."

"Excuuuse me, Mr. Brainiac. Hey, do you want to walk over to the creek and look for tadpoles and frogs, or would you rather just lay there and get covered with chigger bites?"

Danny's weed falls out of his mouth and sticks to his chin. "Damn," he mutters as he hops to his feet, "I forgot about those devils."

"Your butt's going to be chigger bite city," I laugh.

"Your butt's going to be black and blue once I kick it."

Thinking about getting bitten by bugs reminds me of the day of the tick. I woke up one morning—we lived in Leesville at the time, and I felt something funny and a bit painful in my private parts. I walked down the hall to the bathroom and checked things out down there. There was something black on my scrotum, and when I looked closer, I could see tiny black legs. It was a tick! I wanted to scream, but I just stared in horror as its little legs wiggled occasionally.

Midgie got them all the time, so I knew what it was all right. She had little black ones like this devil, and she also had big fat tan ones. Maybe the fat ones are the little black ones that are stretched full of blood. I don't know, but they are beyond creepy, and now I had one; it was a disgusting dirty feeling.

Now I knew how Humphrey Bogart felt in *The African Queen*. They were trying to get close enough to this Nazi warship to blow it up with a torpedo attached to his old boat, but first, they had to sneak up on it, so he shut the engine off so they wouldn't alert the Nazis. His boat, The African Queen, was in the shallow dark water of a small swampy river that led to the lake where the warship patrolled.

Humphrey Bogart was wading in the water pulling his boat with a long cable, and when he got out to rest, he discovered all these black leeches under his shirt and pants. He shuddered all over as Katherine Hepburn poured salt on the leeches, and he ripped them off. Then he had to climb off the boat, get back into the water and keep towing his boat. Going back in must have been the worst part, knowing they were going to stick to him again but having no choice. I felt like shuddering myself; the tick was sucking my blood too, the little devil.

How did I get it? Where had the tick come from? It wasn't from Midgie; she didn't sleep with me anymore or even get in my room, not after Mortimer. I had been over in Saladonia's backyard the day before making a fort out of pine needles. Maybe it crawled out from some of the needles or a pine cone.

Sal was Mexican, and his family lived in a brown adobe-looking house, not far from the reform school, with a great wide porch on three sides of the house. We used to roller skate back and forth over the smooth cement. Even when it was raining, the porch stayed pretty dry. It was also a great place to play Monopoly on a rainy day, and Louisiana had plenty of those.

It seemed a strange coincidence that the only Mexican-looking house I ever saw in Leesville had Mexicans living in it who had moved there the year before. I wondered why that was. Did Sal's family want a house like that, or was it all they could get? Leesville people don't like colored people; maybe they don't like Mexicans either because their skin is brown too, though lighter than colored people.

Sal was real friendly, and he invited me inside his house a lot. His mom often had flour covering her hands and arms as she made enchiladas, tortillas, and other great-tasting Mexican food. She rolled out and kneaded a bunch at once on a big table dusted with flour in their living room.

She made sure I got to try everything too, especially when she found out that I had never eaten that kind of food before; it all tasted doughy and beany and delicious, though sometimes it was spicy hot. We'd play inside or out on the porch and still be able to smell the dough baking and the beans bubbling till she was ready for us to eat.

Sal's mom was pretty with long black hair and a crucifix that hung from a silver chain between her breasts. Once when I came in, she was sitting on the couch with the baby at her breast. The baby seemed to be in heaven as he sucked away with his eyes closed. I wonder what that must be like. Mothers are like Earth angels tenderly caring for babies and small children, always watching out and filling them with love or, in this case, milk and love both. Sal's mom smiled at me when she saw me looking at the baby snug against her brown breast. They had pictures of Jesus scattered throughout the house and Mary with a red heart on her chest. I always felt real comfortable in Sal's home.

Since it had rained the night before, we decided it was a good day to make a fort—the mud would be softer for packing. Sal's yard had plenty of pine trees with brown dried-up pine needles scattered all over. There were wheelbarrows full of needles piled up under the trees from needles falling year after year. We used beaten-up plywood, cardboard, and branches; then we covered it all over with pine needles and mud.

We peeked out and pretended we were camouflaged commandos and that no one could suspect our presence. Sal's little brother came by looking for us, and we lobbed our pine cone hand grenades out the windows at him. We caught him totally by surprise as he blew up into smithereens. Then we let him come inside and play with us; his name was Jose.

Sal and Jose told me a story once. They slept with the window open when they lived in Mexico because it was always so hot there, even at night. One night Sal heard a strange noise and woke up to see a huge vampire bat perched on Jose's bed, ready to bite his neck. Sal threw his pillow at the bat, and it flew out the window. That was quick thinking from Sal; I don't know if I would've done as well. I might have just screamed or something. He said the bats usually just suck on cows. They sure looked like they were telling the truth, and I never knew Sal for one who made up stories to impress people.

After a while, when no one else passed by who we could ambush, Sal went to his room and got his Parcheesi game, and all three of us played it in the fort till I had to go home for supper.

The tick probably got on me from carrying those pine needles around or from lying inside our fort so long. Then it probably crawled up my pant leg during the rest of the day to end up where it was. That was a creepy thought. It must have been in me all night sucking my blood.

I tried to get the tick out for about ten minutes or so. Danny started banging on the bathroom door because he needed to do his business. I didn't want to tell anybody, but I couldn't budge that bug, and I began to panic. What might happen if it just went right on digging in? Would it disappear inside and start damaging stuff? What if it was a pregnant tick and had babies in there? That really scared me. I had to go downstairs and tell Dad. I was too embarrassed to tell Mom, of course.

Dad was on the couch drinking coffee and eating some powdered sugar donuts—I like the chocolate ones that are yellowish inside better. He hadn't shaved yet or combed his hair; it was not a good time to bring him a problem. I could hear Mom out in the kitchen rattling pots. Danny was flushing the toilet upstairs. I sat on the other end of the couch from Dad, but I didn't know how to start, so I just sat there thinking.

"Good morning. What's the matter? You look like you just lost your best friend."

"Uh, you see, somehow I uh, got a tick stuck in my body somewhere."

"A tick?"

"Yeah, a little black one."

184

"A tick. Great. Let me see it, Robert. Where is it?"

"Well, uh, it's in my private parts."

"You're kidding, right? No, I can see that you're not. Okaaay. . . let's go upstairs to the bathroom, and I'll take a look at it. I can't even enjoy a damn cup of coffee around here."

God, I was so embarrassed because Dad never saw me down there since I was a baby, I guess. Danny peeked his head out of our room into the hallway, wondering what was going on because he could hear Dad huffing and puffing. I closed the bathroom door behind us. After I pulled my pants down and showed Dad where it was, he sat down on the toilet seat.

"Damn it, Robert, how did you get a god damn tick down here?" Well, after some painful yanking, his luck was no better than mine. "Jesus Christ, how the hell can I get that little shit out of there? I'm not getting anywhere; maybe your mom can get it."

"Uh, Dad, can we not have Mom try? This is a guy thing, don't you think?"

Dad looked like he was about to yell at me, but then he nodded his head. "OK, let's not bother her, she probably couldn't get it either, but this isn't good. We can't let that tick stay in there, and I can't get the damn thing out. We'll have to go to the dispensary on base and see a doctor. There's no way around it. Get dressed; we'd best go now before it digs in deeper."

It was a creepy feeling knowing it was down there as we drove to Fort Polk. Dad was puffing on one cigarette after another, but he didn't seem to be angry anymore. He had quickly shaved, showered, and finished his coffee, so he was in a better mood. I wasn't looking forward to the doctor's visit, but I didn't want that tick in me any longer. I could feel my heart racing from the fear of getting naked in front of a doctor. I hoped he didn't have any nurses peeking around.

"Don't worry, Bobby, the doctor will have it out in no time. It will be over before you know it." After Dad parked, we went to the front desk where Dad filled out some papers on a clipboard, then we sat down on green cushioned chairs, and Dad flipped through a copy of Life magazine that had a black and white rocket ship lifting off on the cover.

When they called my name out in the lobby, I felt a hot shock flash through me. Dad walked with me as we followed the nurse to the doctor's office. She was carrying a brown clipboard, and she was wearing cloudy white stockings on her shapely legs. She had brown hair, red fingernails, and in spite of a large brown mole by her right temple, she was kind of pretty, but she looked at me funny like something was amusing.

Dad explained the problem to the doctor, who had me lay down on the table and pull down my pants. The fluorescent light above me was glaring right into my eyes. The doctor reminded me of that annoying neighbor on *Leave It to Beaver*, Lumpy's dad, who was balding with glasses and a long nose. At least the nurse left, but it was still awful. The doctor grabbed a pair of sharp-looking silver tweezers and bent over me.

"That's a place I've never seen one before. How did you manage that? Never mind, just stay still, and try not to move, OK? This won't hurt a bit."

After nodding weakly, I grabbed the edges of the table, and he started to yank and pinch me down there with the tweezers. I had to bite my lips a couple times from it smarting

186

some. "That's too bad; the head is still in deep; only part of it came out. We'll have to use ether on it. Now don't worry, it won't hurt, but it will feel cold when I put it on." He opened the lid to a can and poured some onto a cotton ball. It smelled kind of like rubbing alcohol, but way worse, like if I took a big giant whiff, it would knock me out cold. I already felt a little dizzy from the smell. Then he dabbed it on—boy, it was cold all right!

"Hold still now . . . here . . . it . . . comes; that's all of it this time. Let me just clean things up, and you are as good as new." He handed Dad a tube of something. "Have him put some of this antiseptic gel on it for a few days, and that's it. Wasn't so bad was it?" he asked, looking at me over his glasses.

He had to be kidding.

When I turned around after pulling up my pants, I saw that the nurse didn't leave after all. She gave me a little smile, like, of course, she was still here.

Chapter X

Creeks and Ponds

Danny catches up to me by Grandma's old red house. I put my finger to my lips so he'll be quiet. After sneaking through the yard along the hedges—who knows who lives there now—we climb down the bank next to a wobbly wooden bridge. The bridge has faded chipped red paint and is full of splinters; it crosses from Grandma's back yard to an open field. I got a wicked splinter from that bridge last year right in the web between two fingers—Mom had a heck of a time getting that one out with her needle. Maybe this used to be a farm or something, and the bridge led to a barn that disintegrated a long time ago.

The creek water below the bridge looks kind of rusty, and some of the rocks are stained an ugly orange. "The water didn't look like this last year, did it?" I ask.

"It's because there's too much metal in the water. Maybe someone dumped a car or something further up the creek since we were here last, and that's turning the water cruddy," Danny says.

Last year we came to the creek with Darla and Lenny, Aunt Elaine's two oldest—Darla is one year younger than me, and Lenny a year less than her. We had been visiting Aunt Elaine in her old gray house down the road. All the floors were wood that had worn down so much they just looked gray, like

189

an old wooden fence outside. Everyone was barefoot, and Aunt Elaine held a crying baby while five beagle pups were skittering all over the floor. I felt like I was visiting relatives of the *Beverly Hillbillies* or *Li'l Abner*.

Aunt Elaine was dressed more like Granny than Daisy Mae, though: Aunt Elaine's black hair was in a ponytail, and she had on a long, dull brown dress that was so old-fashioned it almost touched the floor. Dad said she belonged to some kind of church that frowned on wearing comfortable clothes. That sounded pretty strange to me. She was a little bit taller than Grandma Ludwiczak, with pointy black glasses similar to Aunt Cora's, except pointier. She seemed to squint even with her glasses on—maybe they didn't work so well.

Aunt Elaine has a kind smile, and she's always nice to me and Danny, telling us how handsome and well-behaved we are. I like her, but I felt a little sorry for her; she seemed so different from my earlier memories of her with her doll collection. There was something worn down and tired-looking about her, from her four kids, I guess, and her husband, Leonard, who was kind of a deadbeat, Dad said.

Leonard has wavy blondish hair like Mom's and mine, big teeth, and blue eyes. He's also strong-looking, I guess because lifting weights is one of his favorite things to do. He wanted Dad to lift weights with him earlier, but Dad said, "No thanks, I get all the exercise I need from working." Dad said Leonard was stuck on himself, and he couldn't hold down a decent job; he always seemed to be looking for work. Dad couldn't stand him. Leonard was leaning back in his chair, scratching his belly and bragging about his fine beagle pups, how they would make such good hunting dogs that he could sell one day.

Darla came over to me and smiled, "How'd you like to take a walk down to the creek?

"How far is it?" I asked.

"It's right down by Grandma's house, not far at all."

"Would that be all right, Mom?" Danny asked. I could tell he was eager to get outside away from the pups under our feet. We had petted them for a while, but they were getting too excited and started to leak a little pee when they got rubbed. Danny had new P.F. Flyers like me, and he probably didn't want them peed on. I was real careful myself, shuffling about, avoiding puppies rubbing and sniffing at my shoes.

"All right, that's fine, isn't it, Hon?" Mom said.

"Sure, sure." Dad was sitting on a hard wooden chair listening to Leonard, and I could tell he was getting a bit irritated.

"Come on then," Darla said as she led us out of the house. She took us past the dog house, where the beagle pups' mother was sleeping in the bare dirt; her chain must have rubbed away all the grass in front of her flat-roofed dog house. Flies were buzzing around some chunks of dog food left on a tin plate; I could see the can lines on one crusty chunk. Darla took us into the woods on the edge of their yard.

Darla is pretty and kind of quiet, but when she does talk, she's worth listening to, and her voice is clear and strong, not so soft like some girls who you can hardly hear sometimes. She has light golden-brown hair down past her shoulders, bright blue eyes, and a sweet shy smile that I enjoy looking at. Darla is a tomboy, too, and can climb over rocks and stuff real smooth-like. She can also pick out a good path that is comfortable and sensible to follow—not just anyone can do that.

Lenny has a crew-cut, blue eyes, and a white scar line above his left eye that makes his eyebrow look odd—whatever happened, he's lucky he didn't get his eye poked out. He doesn't talk much either, but he and Danny seem to get along good together.

After about five minutes of following Darla through trees, broken-down fences, and a flat field full of purple thistles, we came to a big blackberry bush. Darla turned around and smiled at us, "Let's take a blackberry break."

As we gathered around the bush, she picked a big ripe blackberry, "Open wide now," she said as she popped it in my mouth. God, it burst apart with one gentle bite. They were perfect, big black sweet, and oozing juice as soon as we picked them. It didn't take long before we had purple stains on our hands; everybody had purple tongues, too. Lenny even had purple around his lips. I got a few scratches on my arms from the thorns on the bush, but it was worth getting scratched for such delicious juicy treasure.

Once we picked off all the easy ones to reach, we licked our fingers and trailed after Darla. I was right behind her because I liked to watch the graceful way she moved. She has strong, smooth pretty legs that look like they are used to climbing and running. Every couple minutes, she would push her hair back behind her right ear.

It wasn't long before I could see the back of Grandma's house through a clearing in the woods. She had an old rusted wringer washing machine sitting behind her house for some reason.

Danny and me had been playing with Grandma's rusted machine one day, turning the crank, pretending it was a medieval torture contraption like in *The Pit and the Pendulum* when Danny's belt got stuck in the wringer. We both had these skinny Indian belts made of blue, red, black, and white beads; they were cool looking, but the beads kept popping out over time. We had a heck of a time getting Danny's belt out; he lost a good chunk of beads, which made Danny say a curse word. I'm just glad it wasn't one of our fingers or something. We stopped playing with the wringer after that. Mom didn't notice Danny's messed-up belt.

Mom got one of those wringer washing machines after moving to Texas and finally having a decent basement. Basements were impossible in Louisiana because most of the houses are up on blocks; the ground under the houses is just too wet for basements. Mom seems to like her wringer machine, but it looks like a lot of work to me. I'm sure she would have been happier with one of the newer kind where everything works automatically, but Mom said those kind were too expensive.

Darla led us down the bank to the creek and showed us a pool that was full of darting minnows. You could see the rocks at the bottom—so, there wasn't any rusty color last year. Come to think of it, when Danny and me passed through the back yard to the bridge, I didn't see that old wringer machine. The new people who lived there must have thrown it away. Maybe they tossed it in up the creek somewhere. We should check later and see if we can find that washer. The water was definitely clear when Darla took us last year. I remember seeing a crayfish swimming backward over the pebble-covered bottom.

It was the first time I had ever seen one swimming, and I was amazed at how it swam backwards and how fast it flapped through the clear water with its tail—I used to fish for them in muddy water where I couldn't see them. Back home, we also found some small holes—about the size of a Vanilla Wafer—near where the baby rattlesnake was. We wanted to find out what made the holes, so Danny and me dug them up with Dad's foxhole shovel. After a foot or two, water filled up the holes, and we found crayfish poking their antenna heads out. It was amazing! I tried to snatch the crayfish out that me and Darla saw swimming backwards, but it tucked itself under a big rock at the bottom, and I couldn't get to it.

It's incredible what things hide in creeks and ponds. Last month Danny, Ernie, and me were exploring a pond by Ernie's house. Ernie is a tall, handsome kid with dark hair, freckles, and a happy smile in my class, who I admire. Everybody just likes Ernie for some reason and wants to play with him. I asked him if he'd like to play sometime after school, and he invited me over.

The next time I brought Danny because I wanted him to see the pond by Ernie's house. The pond is about as big as our school auditorium. There are cattails everywhere at one end of the pond and lily pads close to the shore. Trees surround the whole pond and keep it secret; it's at the dead-end of Ernie's street (all the houses are newer one-story ranch-style homes with big picture windows in front), and no one seems to go there.

While we were looking at the still green water, I got the idea of building a raft so we could paddle across the pond. Danny was doubtful, but Ernie liked the idea, so we started to collect sticks. Ernie went to his house to get some twine, a knife, and a hand saw. Fifteen minutes later, we began to put the sticks together. We also found a few stray boards at a nearby construction site where they were building a new house.

After working for a while, the sun started to get awful hot, gnats kept buzzing around us, and we realized the job was taking a lot longer than we figured. "I don't know if we can get it all done in one day," I said.

"How about if we only make it big enough so we can all hold onto it with our legs in the water, instead of big enough so that we can sit on it? Then we can just kick our legs to the other side," Ernie said.

"That would save a lot of time, but I don't know if I'd be comfortable doing that," Danny said.

"I think it would be fine; let's give it a try; c'mon, what could go wrong. As long as we hold on and don't let go, we'll be okay," I said. Inside though, I was nervous about it too, because I can't swim hardly at all, but I didn't want to seem chicken in front of Ernie.

"All right," said Danny, "but let's just leave it about this size, and you and Ernie can try it sooner; it's starting to get close to supper. I'll be the lookout from the shore just in case anything goes wrong. Besides, I'm really not crazy about getting all wet."

"If that's how you feel about it, fine by me. How is that with you, Bobby?" Ernie said.

"OK, let's finish it up, and then we'll go."

We got back to work, but when I looked up a few minutes later, I saw something in the pond that chilled my bones.

"What the heck is that?" I shouted

They followed my pointing finger about fifty feet out from the shore.

"Where?" asked Danny.

"Right there coming closer, don't you see the eyes?" I asked.

"Goodness Gracious! Those look like alligator eyes!" Ernie said.

Two big eyes were poking out of the water a couple of inches. They definitely looked like alligator eyes. We could only see the eyes slowly coming towards us. The green water hid what those unblinking eyes belonged to.

"How can it be an alligator? This is a pond. Alligators live in swamps or the Everglades with Flipper, not in a Texas pond," said Danny.

"What else could those eyes belong to besides an alligator or a crocodile, and there aren't any crocodiles in America," Ernie said.

"Maybe someone had a pet alligator, and when it got too big, they turned it loose in this pond," I said. I was thinking of an episode on *Leave It to Beaver* when Wally and Beaver bought a baby alligator at a pet store without Mr. and Mrs. Cleaver knowing about it. They kept it in the bathtub for a while, but it kept getting bigger, and eventually, their parents found out—probably because they were starting to stink from not taking a bath. Mr. Cleaver made them take it to an alligator farm or a zoo after giving Wally and Beaver a good lecture.

The guy they gave the alligator to—it was the actor who played Uncle Joe on *Petticoat Junction*, said it happens all the time that people buy baby alligators because they are so cute and make fascinating pets. Then they get bigger, of course, and people don't know what to do with them.

I also heard stories of people in New York City flushing baby alligators down the toilet when they get too big. The sewers in New York were supposed to be full of alligators crawling around in the pipes. I'm not sure that's true, but they do sell baby alligators in pet stores, so someone must be buying them, and they've got to get rid of them somewhere.

The eyes were about twenty feet away now and still drifting our way.

"One thing I know for sure is there's not any way in the world I'm going in the water with those eyeballs out there," said Ernie.

"Me neither, in fact, I'm thinking that maybe it's time to be getting home. It is almost supper time, and I'm not sure I want to be here if that alligator gets any closer," I said.

As soon as I said that, we all started getting our stuff together as quick as we could. We left our unfinished raft lying there. When I looked back, I could see that the eyes were about ten feet from the shore.

Ernie's dad laughed when we told him what we saw.

"An alligator! You gotta be kidding me. What you probably saw was a big old bullfrog."

I didn't argue with him—it's usually a waste of time to try and change an adult's opinion once they've made up their mind about something, especially if you're just a kid in their eyes. But I knew that creature couldn't have been a bullfrog. If it had eyes that big, it had to be a frog the size of a German Shepard.

There wasn't anything as exciting as an alligator in the creek Darla led us to, but I experienced something way better and not scary at all. In fact, it was probably the best thing that happened on our trip last year.

Danny and Lenny wandered down the creek hopping from rock to rock, while Darla and I stayed put on the big flat stone and watched minnows flashing like living light over the pebbled bottom of the pool. It felt good to sit next to her; I didn't feel like going anywhere right then.

I guess Darla was allowed to wear comfortable clothes until she got older because she was wearing purple shorts and a matching purple halter top with white trim. Her clothes showed how pretty her brown legs and her round, smooth shoulders were. She had a few cute freckles on her nose. I thought about reaching over and holding her hand, then before I knew it, somehow I was.

Her hand felt warm and soft pulsing together with mine. She gave me her sweet smile. I scooted over closer to her, and we leaned against each other with the rock warm under us. A mockingbird was singing a happy song in a bush across the creek. The water was gurgling and tinkling as it flowed over the rocks. Warm sunlight soaking and tingling into my arms and legs almost felt alive, and my heart was twisting pleasantly. The Mystery seemed to slow time to a stop as I felt her tender hand and her smooth leg up against mine.

Under the sounds of the creek and the mockingbird, I could hear Darla's soft breath as her head rested against me.

The scent of blackberries lingered around her, and I felt a bit dizzy from wanting something to happen, but I didn't know what that something was.

Too soon, Danny and Lenny started to head back, so I slowly slid away and stood up. Darla gave me a look like we shared a secret now, as if we belonged to each other in a different way than before, and I guess we did. Danny and Lenny came back watching their feet on the wet rocks, so they didn't notice anything when they joined us.

I'm hoping to see her again soon. Probably at the funeral tomorrow, though it might be hard to get some time alone together.

Danny is down the creek a bit, leaning against a willow tree as he flips pebbles into the water. I'm looking down at the same pool we saw the minnows and the crawdad in last year.

I used to fish for crawdads in Louisiana, in the ponds where I found Mortimer. My favorite pond was the shadiest one, with a small hill behind me and pine trees on two sides. The dry mud path was on the other side of the pond from where I fished.

The hard-packed mud on the bank would be cool on my belly as I dangled my string in the muddy brown water. Danny didn't like to fish at all, so I usually went by myself. I enjoy fishing as long as nothing gets hurt, and fishing for crawdads was almost as satisfying as catching lizards. I could feel the weight of the baloney on the end of the string as I tugged the string up and down and then lazily side to side. Too fast, and the crawdads will stay away, but bobbing the baloney around gently gets their attention. I don't think they can smell baloney because I never found a nose on one, but they sure do love baloney once they taste it.

Sooner or later, I'd feel the extra weight of a crawdad jerking at the baloney. The trick is to wait a bit and let the crawdad get a good mouthful of baloney; then he'll get greedy and hold on tight with his fat pincher—not too long, though, or all the baloney will be in his belly, and it will swim away. At just the right moment, I pull the string up, not too fast, or the water will knock him off, not too slow, or the crawdad will figure out what's going on, and he'll let go when he sees me. It takes a smooth, just-the-right-speed-pull. Catching crawdads is definitely an art. I bet some people might use a net, but where is the skill or challenge in that? Besides, we didn't have a net.

When he breaks the surface, I have to be ready to grab him on the back as his pinchers wave in the air, searching for my fingers. I'd let him keep the baloney after I plopped him in my bucket. Their long antennas can move in opposite directions, black BB eyeballs stick out, and they have mouths that look like monster mouths, opening from side to side instead of up and down, really ugly—I don't know how people can eat them, yuck.

I'd let them crawl around, scraping the metal bucket with their claws until I was done fishing for the day, then I'd drop them one by one back into the pond. I don't keep anything that I catch anymore for very long.

Danny comes stepping over some rocks and pokes my shoe with a stick. "Hey, are you thinking what I'm thinking?"

"What's that?"

"That it's about time to eat. Aren't you hungry?"

"Not really, maybe in a bit, what time is it?

"It's time to eat."

"Did you see any tadpoles or frogs down the creek?"

"No, but I think I saw a water moccasin swimming on top of the water."

"What? Where?"

"Right behind you, look out!"

Halfway through turning around, I try to stop, but my reflexes are too quick.

"Got you! You thought there really was one, didn't you?"

"You're so funny."

"I know, and I'm hungry, too."

"OK, yeah, all right, Hungry, let's go see about lunch before you try to be funny again and before Dad calls us. We'll surprise him for a change."

"Superman will surprise him first," Danny boasts as he takes off.

"No way!" But he probably will. Somehow I don't feel so fast this time.

Grandpap Steve and Dad are smoking and grilling hot dogs and hamburgers on a small grill outside. The hamburger grease is spattering into the charcoal. Only one hot dog fell into the coals that I can see. Everyone else has moved inside the trailer as the sun is taking over out here.

"How was the creek?" Dad asks.

"It's getting polluted from something that's making the rocks turn orange," Danny says.

"That's too bad; maybe sulfur is getting in the water somehow. Are you boys hungry?" Dad says.

"I am now," I say.

"I was hungry first," Danny says, then he starts laughing. He can be strange sometimes.

Dad looks at Danny funny, then he smiles, "OK, you can be the first one to go inside and wash up. We'll be in shortly."

Mom is spooning out her special macaroni salad and heating some cans of pork and beans on the stove. Grandma is sitting on a stool, telling Mom about a bunion she has on her foot. She has the crusty black bottom turned so that Mom can peer down at the bunion while she stirs the beans.

A portable black and white TV is on the counter, and shortly we somehow all scrunch in there with our paper plates full of beans, macaroni salad, hot dogs, and hamburgers. French's mustard and onions are on my hot dog; pickle relish, Miracle Whip, and a thick juicy slice of tomato is on my burger.

A small fan is whirling, but it just blows warm air around as we watch an old episode of *The Lone Ranger*. Grandpap Steve mixes his beans and macaroni. He always slops everything he eats together. Dad thinks that's a disgusting habit, but he never says anything to Grandpap Steve, of course—just us later. It doesn't bother me, though; I always dip my meat in my mashed potatoes and my peas too sometimes, so why pick on Grandpap? All the food ends up mixed in our bellies anyway.

I'm enjoying my food and the show, even though Grandpap Steve's knobby elbow keeps poking my side from time to time. Danny is smooched up next to Grandma in her orange dress; her upper arm is almost as wide as Danny's chest; he looks like Ichabod Crane next to a giant pumpkin. Mom and Dad are sitting by the counter on long stools. It's a good episode where the Lone Ranger disguises himself as an old man with a beard in order to trap the bad guys.

It's funny that the only time you ever get a glimpse of what the Lone Ranger looks like behind his mask is when he's in disguise. It's also odd that the Lone Ranger has a mask, like a bad guy.

Crooks in cartoons have masks like his; it's a wonder he doesn't get shot by some sheriff. Why does he wear a mask anyway?

Tonto always looks cool with his headband and his Indian clothes like Davey Crockett's or Daniel Boone's. Tonto never gets to be the star of an episode, though; he helps, sometimes he even saves the Lone Ranger's life, but the Lone Ranger still gets most of the glory. "Yes, Kemosabe." Tonto always calls the Lone Ranger that; I wonder what it means?

I just had a scary thought. We're all eating pork and beans, smushed together in this tiny trailer. We need to get out of here before someone lets loose with bean gas. I know from prior experience that Grandpap Steve's gas is by far the worst; God, look at him shoveling in those beans.

Thankfully, Dad has to go with Uncle Chick to pick up Pap-Pap at the bus station in a while, so maybe we'll escape before the inevitable. We finish our meal shortly before the Lone Ranger rides off, leaving the people he has helped scratching their heads, saying, "Who was that masked man?" (They say that after every show.)

After we clean up from lunch, Dad says, "Mom, we have to go now so we can pick up Harvey; we'll be back later."

"All right then, thanks for coming," says Grandma. We shuffle around the cramped room so Grandma can get to us one by one for another squishy teary hug. Grandpap Steve wisely stays put and waves goodbye to everybody.

"Do you guys have everything?" Dad asks.

"Yes, Kemosabe," I answer.

Dad gives me one of his, are you crazy looks, then he bursts out laughing. Danny is laughing, too. Mom has a smirk on her face like she is wondering what kind of strange people she has as a family. Grandma and Grandpap have no idea what we're laughing about.

"We'll pick you up around 6'oclock, Mom," Dad says to Grandma.

"Okay, Bobby." That's what Grandma calls Dad. We have the same name, but I'm not a junior. Dad said he couldn't do that to one of his kids—have him called junior. It confuses people sometimes, though, because they expect me to be a junior since Dad and me have the same name. I'm thankful he didn't label me as a junior though, I'd hate to be called junior or Bobby junior, but I would have liked a different name of my own better, like Benjamin or Alexander, something a little cooler sounding.

After we climb in the car, and I get scorched by the hot car seat, Danny asks Mom, "What's happening at six o'clock?"

"Your Dad and I are taking your grandparents to the funeral home for the viewing," Mom says.

"Do we have to get all dressed up?" Danny asks.

"No, your Dad and I think you and Bobby can stay at Aunt Cora's and watch TV while we go. It's enough if you guys go tomorrow for the funeral."

"You had better behave while we're gone," Dad adds, giving us a quick blast of his eyeball, then Dad pulls out onto the road for our short drive to Aunt Cora's.

Danny and I exchange looks. We hit the jackpot! Alone with the TV, and since it's a Wednesday, that means *Lost in Space* is on. Will Robinson is my hero because he is so smart and brave; he's only twelve or so, but he has way more courage than Dr. Smith, who's a cowardly buffoon we enjoy laughing at. We love the robot, too. Danny heard there's supposed to be a midget actor inside the robot.

Last week's episode ended with Will and Dr. Smith attacked by a monster that looked like a huge gorilla with long fangs, horns on his head, and spikes on his back—really scary looking. They always end the show with a cliff-hanger like *Batman* does. "Same bat time, same bat channel." Batman is on tomorrow night, but I doubt if we'll get to see it with the funeral and all.

I can't wait to see the monster and how they escape from it. We can stretch out on the couch, well one of us can, the other gets Uncle Chick's easy chair, but both are great. Plus we'll have plenty of snacks. Aunt Cora and Uncle Chick have Ruffles, pretzels, Bugles, homemade peanut butter cookies she was baking earlier, and Dad's Root Beer, the foamiest root beer in the world—I saw a case next to the fridge. My, oh my, it will be heaven in Mulberry tonight!

Chapter XI

Pap-Pap

The first time I wore a suit jacket and tie was when we lived in Germany. It was Christmas Eve, and Dad took me to the church on base to listen to the choir sing Christmas carols. Dad loves all the old Christmas songs; he says they are one of the best things about the Christmas season. We never went to church before, so I was a bit surprised when he suggested we should go.

The church was next to a parking lot that had been the site of the Halloween Fair. They had a Horror House, which was a big tent overflowing with the strong, sharp smell of canvas inside—a smell I love. They blindfolded Danny and me and led us from one table to another as they had us touch creepy things like floating eyeballs and intestines—I think they were really olives and spaghetti, fun stuff like that. We shuddered when they stuck our trembling hands in and told us what horrible stuff it was supposed to be, but we loved it.

I saw Julie coming out of the tent after us. Julie was in my first-grade class, and she had pretty blonde hair that she always pulled up, showing the back of her neck. She sat in front of me, so I got to admire the fine blonde hairs swirling down her long beautiful neck every day in class. Julie came out with her face scrunched up like she just found an icky spider in her shoe; her dad laughed as he came out of the tent behind her.

They also had a ghost pond with little white ghost ducks floating by in a foot-wide stream of water. (I think they had painted little yellow ducks white and then given them black eyeballs. I could see the thick white brush strokes, and some of the eyeballs dripped black.) For ten cents, we were allowed to pick a ghost duck out of the water. The number taped on the ghost duck's belly determined what your prize was. Everybody got something.

I was lucky and got a Baba Looey piggy bank made out of soft brown rubber. Baba Looey is a burro with a yellow Mexican sombrero that his big ears poke through and a yellow kerchief around his neck; it was great; I never won such a big prize at a carnival or fair before. Usually, I got some cheap junk that fell apart after a day or two, like a pinwheel or something.

We already had Pepe, a giant yellow pig bank, who has his name written in red on his pig belly. Me and Danny open Pepe up and count from time to time—last count before the fair was fourteen dollars, and seven Marks—Marks is German money that has cool looking coins and bills with strange German faces or plants on them. I just used Baba Looey as a stuffed animal to play with, not a bank, since Pepe was already our bank. Danny got some Chinese handcuffs that were fun to get your fingers stuck in.

Someone was also selling orange pumpkin cookies at a table for five cents; they were moist and delicious—the icing's orange flavor reminded me of the orange feeling I get tickling my spine sometimes. It's hard to explain, but my back gets this tingling sensation up my spine that feels orange somehow, not very often, just once in a while, and I haven't figured out why or what it is. I asked Danny once if he ever got such a feeling, and he looked at me like I was crazy, so I keep quiet about it now.

The Halloween carnival was the last time I was next to the church, though I looked at the church every time we went to the commissary, which is just across the street. I don't remember why Mom and Danny didn't come to hear the choir. It was just me and Dad. We were all dressed up, Dad smelling like Old Spice with his hair slicked down neat. He said I looked sharp, and I felt so proud to be with him in church. The choir sang "Silent Night" while I sat close to Dad.

Silent Night was also the song that my first-grade class sang in the Christmas program a couple days before we went to church. Every school class got to go on the movie theater stage; our parents were in the audience, at least Mom was. We had some red and white paper costumes that we put our heads through. Mrs. Glass had black hair, glasses and was one of my least favorite teachers ever, even though she was pretty. Early in the year, she sent me to the vice principal's office for something I did that I can't remember—it was that unimportant.

He was big with brown hair, a white short-sleeved shirt, a skinny black tie, and he sat me down in his office across from him. He was mean to me, so I kicked him in the shin and ran outside to the playground where the rest of the kids were having recess. I knew I was in really hot water; I felt panicky like I was in some kind of nightmare. I was running all over from one clump of kids to another, desperately trying to find Danny for some reason—not that he could have done anything.

Pretty soon, a big hand grabbed mine and led me back to the school building. Kids were looking at me getting pulled along. After we were back in his office, he gave me a stern talking to and made me brush the dirt off his pant leg. I hated having to do that. He took me back to class, and I had to apologize to Mrs. Glass. I remember looking at her pretty legs and black shoes. I can't recall what I said, but she lifted my chin, gave me half a smile, and told me to go put my head down on the desk until we went outside to get the rest of the class.

For the concert, Mrs. Glass made me and my girlfriend, Heidi pretend to sing when the other kids sang. Mrs. Glass said we couldn't carry a tune and we should just move our mouths; no one would know the difference.

Heidi's mom was German, and her dad was in the Army. Heidi had beautiful blond hair done up in fancy braids, and she was pretty. Her clothes looked different from the other girls in class, more old-fashioned kind of with lots of flower patterns.

We liked to sit next to each other when we could, and when we went on our field trip to the fire station, we held hands walking there and back. That was when we realized we were in love. On the way back, the sun was high and bright. We saw some giant German bumble bees, bigger than a thumb, flying by a hedge. They are scary big, way bigger than the fat black and yellow ones in the US, but they don't ever bother anybody. Heidi's hand felt soft, and she had a pleasant clean smell like a fresh bowl of fruit. She had a pretty smile with a dimple on one side. I didn't want our walk back to school to ever end. I spent a lot of time looking and thinking about her during class after that. Sometimes we smiled at each other from across the room.

Well, we were both embarrassed as we stood next to each other on stage, hidden in the middle of the class, moving our mouths with no sound coming out, but we took some comfort in enduring our shame together. We couldn't hold hands, but we stood real close, and we gave each other a big smile when it was all over. Unfortunately, after first grade ended, I never saw Heidi again. Her dad probably got transferred somewhere else—that happens a lot with Army kids, you get to know them, then one of you has to move to some other Army base.

Listening to "Silent Night" being sung in the church was amazing compared to how our class sang it. Pictures of Jesus, Mary, and some holy saints were hanging around the church walls, and a giant cross with Jesus on it was near the front of the church. He had red blood painted on his palms and feet; his crown of thorns looked sharp and painful.

We sat on hard wooden pews with flat blue cushions behind our backs. I gazed at the stained glass windows, which had scattered pictures of Jesus and other holy people glowing in different colors. The windows were thick blue, red, yellow, and purple sparkling glass that stretched up to the roof, which was so high up that I wondered if God was up there listening to the music, too.

The men and women singing sounded like angels pouring out their hearts to heaven. When their voices sang out the words, "Siiilent night, hoooly night, all is calm, all is bright, round yon virrrgin Mother and child," the music sucked in my belly, and I felt the Mystery moving through me. I leaned my head against Dad's big arm and surrendered as my heart leapt, and the choir voices echoed like bells.

When the choir finished, it was late; usually, I was in bed by that time. Dad walked home with me under a night sky that had a sliver of a moon like a toenail clipped off. There weren't that many stars across the cloudy blackness; the only constellation I could make out was the Big Dipper, whose upside-down handle was pointing towards home.

"Silent Night" was the song still going in my head, and the night did feel holy like it really was waiting silently and eagerly for Jesus' birthday to come. Dad and me were both quiet, listening to our inner music. I'm sure the song in Dad's head was "The Little Drummer Boy." That was Dad's favorite Christmas Carol, and when they sang it in church, he gave me a big smile, and his eyes seemed to shine a little brighter. Every once in a while as we walked, I could hear Dad mutter softly, ". . . pa rum pum pum pum."

This is my second time in a suit jacket and tie. I'm sitting next to Dad again, but there isn't any singing happening now— only talking and crying. Grandma Ludwiczak has a black dress on and a black hat shaped like a fat pill. Her hands are in her lap, and I can see that she never turns her head away from Uncle Billy's face poking out of the casket. She is sitting between Grandpap Steve and Pap-Pap right in front of me, and just when I think Grandma is going to stop crying, the preacher says something else that gets her to cry some more.

Me and Danny were excited to see Pap-Pap yesterday when Dad and Uncle Chick brought him home to Aunt Cora's. He popped out of our car with a big smile on his face as we ran down to him from the porch. "I'm so happy to see you, by crackey," Pap-Pap said, giving me a tight hug and a kiss on my forehead. Dad said Pap-Pap was on the bus traveling for over twenty hours, but he seemed just as cheerful and full of energy as always. He pulled out half a roll of spearmint Certs and gave it to me. "Share these with Danny." I peeled one out and pressed it into Danny's hand. Spearmint is the best Certs' flavor, though the fruit flavor is good, too.

Pap-Pap looks the same as always. The hair he has left is white and sticks up funny from his head, and his black glasses slide down his nose a little—which is one of the most handsome noses I've ever seen. He has high cheekbones like all the Gambles do. Pap-Pap is an inch or so shorter than Dad and lean, but his arms have muscles from working in his upholstery shop for so long. Dad told us he's worked there over forty years, and he learned upholstering from his dad, Great Grandpap Gamble, who lived into his 90's. I hope Pap-Pap does, too.

Dad said they used to have a shop on 3rd Avenue by the Allegheny River before moving up the hill into Valley Heights, which is still part of New Ken. Dad said they moved after Alcoa shut down, business started to slow, and Great Grandpap passed away.

By moving into Valley Heights, they got more business from Lower Burrell, which was just down the other side of the hill. There was a shopping center there with a giant new store called K-Mart. Grandma Babe loved it because it was so close, and everything was cheap. They had a motorized fire engine and an elephant in front of the store that Pap-Pap and Grandma Babe gave us dimes to ride on once.

One day down on 3rd avenue, Mom and me and Danny were on our way to Jenick's Market when we walked by a red brick building with a big storefront window. Mom said that was where the old upholstery shop used to be. We looked inside at the dust, cobwebs, and pieces of stray wood lying about. There was no way to tell what kind of business it used to be, but it was just around the corner from the abandoned Alcoa plant.

When cars cross the Allegheny River on the New Ken Bridge, they pass a sign, "Welcome to New Kensington—the Aluminum Capital of the World." Someone should take the sign down now, but it's easy to see that it used to be true. The Alcoa plant is a series of massive connected factories and warehouses made out of billions of red bricks; it's so long and huge it stretches through most of New Ken and Arnold.

They must have put it right next to the river so that barges could transport the enormous quantities of materials they needed to make aluminum and also so they could dump whatever polluted gunk they needed to into the river. I don't know for sure that they did that, but back then, people weren't as concerned about clear water as they were about making money, so my guess is they poured all kinds of yucky stuff into the river. Mom said the Allegheny had a lot more pollution when she was a kid, and that's scary because it isn't that clean looking now.

Fireman's Park, which is right around the corner from Ricky's house, is just a small park with green grass, a fireman statue, park benches, shade trees, and a nice view of the river. There is also a dirt road we walk down that takes us right to the water. People can take boats down there. You can walk along the shore for a couple hundred yards and watch the waves lap against the shore. Uncle Friday told us he fishes down there sometimes. When a motorboat speeds by, the waves smack even harder. There are usually ugly purple, yellowish, and greenish foamy bubbles sloshing around the rocky shore. Some kind of chemicals are still getting dumped in from somewhere, even though Alcoa is no longer around.

I don't know why Alcoa moved somewhere else, but now all the buildings are huge empty husks of brick and cement taking up block after block of space. It's like a giant ghost town with nothing ever going on, except dust accumulating and birds flying over. They left everything behind; it doesn't seem fair that they should just be able to leave it there forever. Dad said no one will ever tear it all down because it would be too expensive.

I imagine after a thousand years, the plant will probably be the last thing left in the valley, like the Pyramids in Egypt remind us of the Egyptians, the plant will show what our time was like to people in the future. Egypt left something great behind; I'm not sure what people in the future will think of this humungous ghost town of red brick.

Great Grandpap Gamble's upholstery shop isn't the only empty storefront you can stare into on a walk; there are quite a few scattered around Arnold and New Ken. Some have lettered signs of faded paint on the windows, some don't, but they all look full of dust and kind of ghostly like their life got sucked away by time. Even the corner grocery stores that used to be on almost every block have shut down one by one—there's only a handful left.

I never got to meet Great Grandpap Gamble before he passed away. His wife, Grandma Gamble, is still alive, though, living with Aunt Nellie and Uncle No-No near Pittsburgh. Aunt Nellie is Pap-Pap's sister. Mom said I used to say "no-no" to Uncle No-No whenever he wanted to hug me, so that's how he got his name. Uncle No-No has really long ears, thin black hair, and big glasses. I can tell he likes me from the few times I've seen him. I like him too. He tells corny jokes and likes to tease, but he is gentle and kind. I think his real name is Henry.

Grandma Gamble has short hair and hardly talks anymore. Somehow her face reminds me of Popeye, but there is nothing funny about how she must be feeling sitting so helpless all the time. Aunt Nellie brings her trays of food as Grandma Gamble sits in her wheelchair watching TV or looks out the back window at the Allegheny River flowing by—it's wider near Pittsburgh than in New Ken.

They have a house right by the riverbank, but the bank is high like in Arnold and New Ken, so they never get flooded. There's a giant willow in their back yard with wooden chairs next to it for watching the river; every so often, speed boats pulling water skiers or monstrous barges filled with mountains of coal or sand pass by. The barges slosh giant waves against the shore. To the right of the willow, past a series of arched steel bridges, skyscrapers are poking high into the sky. Dad stays away from Pittsburgh as much as he can; he doesn't like cities because the traffic is so bad, and he complains about the knuckleheads who put up the confusing street signs in Pittsburgh.

Pap-Pap is Grandma Gamble's son, now that I think of it. It's strange to think of him as being somebody's son because he's so old himself. He doesn't act old, though; he plays wiffle ball with me, and he gets around pretty good catching the ball and pitching. He still pushes his lawnmower over his yard, which takes him almost an hour, and he'd rather walk two blocks up the hill to the IGA and carry the groceries back than take his car; he says he needs the exercise.

Dad says Pap-Pap has a heavy foot when he drives—he does like to drive fast with the window down. From time to time, he'll just burst out singing. He's his own radio. He also walks the dogs all the time up and down the hills of Valley Heights. It's funny that he's so active, and Grandma is just the opposite and likes to sit in her chair so much and hardly goes anywhere.

They enjoy a lot of the same things though: singing country songs together—sometimes Pap-Pap brings out his guitar and Grandma her ukulele, and they sing us a tune or two; watching wrestling and thinking it's great and not fake, and of course loving animals so much and taking care of them all. Neither one ever complains about all the work involved in keeping their pets as happy as they can. Most of all, though, they are both cheerful and happy people who care about others.

Pap-Pap works hard out in his shop, too. I used to watch him work when we visited sometimes. We have to walk through the shop to get to the rest of the house where Pap-

Pap and Grandma Babe live. He'd have half a dozen tacks in his mouth, and he'd take them from his mouth as he went zipping along, tapping them into a couch or a chair raised up on wooden horses, with a skinny-looking hammer. Then he'd load up his mouth with more tacks and keep going.

Above his head, rolls of material poke down from ceiling straps. Next to the horse by the window is a green machine with a wheel. Pap-Pap lets us turn the wheel when he isn't using it—I think it is for putting buttons on. It makes a good ship wheel for a paddleboat like they had on the river in *Huckleberry Finn*. Huck was on a raft with his friend Jim, the runaway slave, but they passed those paddleboats as they went downriver. *Tom Sawyer* was a fun adventure story, but *Huckleberry Finn* is something different, one of the best books I ever read, and the Mystery is practically oozing out of it.

Next to where Pap-Pap works is the door to the basement where they have a giant brown jigsaw machine taller than Pap-Pap, lumber, and some other machines they use; Pap-Pap also has his garage down there. Two gray wooden doors swing open out into the back yard by his pear tree, which has hard little green pears, and the grassy driveway that empties into the alley.

His basement has a unique musty smell of sawdust, wood, old rolls of cloth, and sagging furniture, which I never smelled anywhere else. If I was blindfolded and transported to Pap-Pap's basement, like they do in *Star Trek*, I'd know where I was instantly just by the familiar pleasant dank smell.

To get through the shop into their house, we have to get by Uncle Clarence, who works at the big table with the old

black Singer sewing machine; it's near the screen door to Pap-Pap's living room. They're partners—The Gamble Brothers. Their ad in the yellow pages says: "You don't gamble when you have work done by Gamble."

Uncle Clarence does most of the cutting and sewing. He wears a cap on his bald head most of the time—the kind they wore in the twenties like Babe Ruth and Jimmy Cagney. Uncle Clarence's way of showing affection is to give us what he calls an ear bore, where he sticks his knuckle in our ear and wiggles it around, or a Chinese knuckle rub, where he rubs his knuckles over the top of our head.

He always smiles good-naturedly when he does it, so I can't get mad at him, but I try hard to avoid his hand. Uncle Clarence and Aunt Evelynn have a beautiful red brick house about a block away. Dad sometimes wonders why he has a much nicer house than Pap-Pap does.

Dad says it like he thinks that Uncle Clarence might be cheating Pap-Pap, but I'm sure that's not true. Uncle Clarence can be annoying with his busy fingers, but he is a good honest man. You can just tell by spending a little time with him that he would never do anything like cheat his brother. I don't know why Dad thinks stuff like that sometimes.

The outside of Pap-Pap's house has large brown-gray blocks of stone, not cinder blocks, though; these are old fashioned somehow and bumpy with ivy up the sides of the house, and the roof is flat. Two big shop windows let people see them working on furniture as they walk by or pause at the stop sign on the corner. Sometimes people will toot their horns and wave at Pap-Pap and Uncle Clarence. They are both pretty friendly, and a lot of people know them. The square rusted door of an old coal chute is next to a gray wooden porch with four steps that lead to the front door.

After you get safely through the shop, and the screen door bangs, the living room and dining room are one big long room. Windows are all along the left side, facing a side street. The dining room, which is behind the living room, has a window seat covered with litter boxes.

On the other side of the dining table against the wall is a giant bookshelf, an old roll-top desk, and a long dresser that Pap-Pap covered in green leather with big brass tacks. The dresser is full of photo albums. Grandma has a Polaroid that she loves to take pictures with, mostly of cats and dogs, but she takes pictures of us too, and anybody else whenever they get visitors.

Grandma's easy chair is by the windows and the couch; Pap-Pap's chair is by the wall across from the couch. Both chairs face the TV towards the shop. There is a bronze-colored horse lamp with a clock on top of the TV that's always been there. You can tell it's a cowboy's horse because it has a handsome-looking Western saddle and stirrups—no cowboy, though. A door sealed up tight is to the right of the TV. There must have been steps there once; if someone stepped through it now, they would drop twenty feet to the grassy bank below.

Their bedroom, the spare room, and the bathroom are to the right, on the other side of the walls. The kitchen is behind the back wall of the dining room, and through the doorway to the right of the old refrigerator is the sunroom where a handful of cats, bowls of cat food, and litter boxes are. At the end of the room, gray outside steps lead down to the backyard.

I know their house better than any of the ones we've ever lived in because we never stay in one place that long. We've moved so many times because the Army transfers Dad to different bases every year or so—except for Germany, where we stayed for three years, but even there, we had to move three times.

The one place in our family that never changes is Pap-Pap's house; it's always there, and it's always pretty much the same. When we travel, especially if we go somewhere new or far away, I take comfort in thinking about their home and them being the same kind people who love us and who always will.

After we say hi and Pap-Pap says howdy and gives us a big hug, Pap-Pap usually pulls out Certs to share, and at some point in our visits, he always gives me and Danny a dime apiece so we can walk up to Frank's Market and buy candy or a comic.

The store, which has white aluminum siding and sits in the middle of the street, almost looks like a house, except for the KOOL cigarette sign with a cute penguin on the screen door. It's cool, comfortably shady, and dimly lit inside, a nice break on a hot day. The floors are cement, and there is a great candy smell from all the shelves of sweets they have. Two big racks of comics are by the candy. Milk, eggs, butter, and meats are in the refrigerated shelves against the walls; cans, bread, and snacks are in the middle with detergents further to the back. Frank is a nice man with round glasses and thinning black hair who loves Pap-Pap, and whenever we go with Pap-Pap to the store, he always says, "Hey, Harvey, happy to see you, how you doing? Brought your grandsons along, I see."

Once, I came back to Pap-Pap's with a comic called *Journey into Mystery*. This doctor—Dr. Don Blake saw some rocky-looking space invaders and overheard them talking about taking over the Earth. He wanted to warn the nearby villagers, but the space invaders heard him move and chased him. Luckily they were big and slow, so Dr. Blake escaped for the moment and ended up in a deep cave. He found a cane which he tried to pry aside a boulder with so he could escape. When the cane hit the rock, he transformed into Thor, the God of Thunder, with his magic hammer. The hammer had words on it saying, "Whosoever holds this hammer, if he be worthy, shall possess the power of THOR."

222

I wonder what made Dr. Blake worthy. It must be because he helped people by being a doctor and by trying to warn the villagers about the rocky-skinned invaders. That must mean anybody worthy could become a God—if they found a magic stick, of course. Maybe real life is like that, too? Maybe helping people is what we're supposed to do to be worthy of becoming like God, of going to heaven? I bet you don't have to be a doctor or try to save people though, most of us aren't heroes; maybe as long as we try to help where we can and do our best, God will let us in heaven to be with him? I'm hoping so anyway.

Chapter XII

Grandma Babe

I'm so used to seeing Pap-Pap smiling and laughing, or out of the blue just starting to sing some made-up country song, that it gives me an uncomfortable feeling to glance over and see him looking so sad. He looks little sitting next to Grandma Ludwiczak. He pats one of her hands, and I think about them being married before and about Uncle Billy being their son.

Pap-Pap never had any kids with Grandma Babe. She's my favorite grandmother. Grandma Babe is even shorter than Grandma Ludwiczak, and she is a little plump but not really fat. She always wears what she calls moo-moos; they are loose-fitting dresses with flower patterns that fall to her knees and have openings for her head and arms to pop out of.

Grandma Babe doesn't seem to care much how she looks. Grandma told me once that she is more concerned with what she thinks and how she feels than what other people think of her. I've never seen her wear make-up or lipstick or any of those kinds of things. She combs her silver-grey hair straight back and lets it hang down to her shoulders. If she goes out, which isn't often, she slips on one of her three wigs, so she doesn't have to fuss with her hair. It's easy to see they are wigs, but Grandma isn't trying to fool anybody, "They're just convenient, and my hair's done in a jiffy."

Grandma has lively sky blue eyes, and she's always smiling, well, most of the time; Grandma Babe's smile reminds me of a laughing Buddha statue I saw in a garden. You can't help but smile back because her whole face is a smile, and her nose kind of gets even flatter than it usually is and scrunched up funny.

When she's not smiling, it's usually because one of her pets is "ailing," as she says. That's when she takes them to see Dr. Blair over in Lower Burrell; Grandma must be his best customer. There always seem to be at least a few of them taking some kind of medicine from Dr. Blair or going there to get shots that pets need to have. Sometimes they even get cancer or leukemia like people do. It's sad to see them get skinnier and skinnier till they run out of life and just lay around. Eventually, Grandma has them put to sleep.

Grandma Babe loves animals more than anyone I've known. She had twenty-two cats at last count and five dogs. I can never keep track of all their different names, and they change from time to time. New cats come in, and old cats go out. Pap-Pap has buried quite a few cats and dogs in their back yard. If someone were ever to dig up their yard, there might be questions about all the skeletons they'd find.

Dad always fusses on the ride over to their house about the smell we were about to enter; Mom never says anything about it, she's too polite, and it never bothers me much; I'm just happy to see them. Danny's usually stuffy or blowing his nose anyway, and Pap-Pap can hardly smell at all, so it doesn't bother him either. They try to keep the litter boxes as clean as possible, but it's a lot of poop raking and litter changing.

Grandma doesn't let any of their cats go outside. She says that it's too dangerous for them and that cats are happy and content being inside all the time. They don't need to go outside like dogs and people do. She might be right, Buttons sure had a dangerous life outside in the alley, but I've watched some of her cats sitting next to the windows looking out; they look real interested in what's going on out there. I bet some of them would like to get on the other side and check things out, chase a bird or a butterfly.

Grandma loves all her pets like people, but she has some that she talks about the most, who I think are her favorites. Molly is a white Persian over twenty years old who just sheds white fur all the time and never leaves her own private box, which is on a little table under the big pocket watch; there is always white fur floating around her. Molly is like a queen; she will only eat a small metal tea saucer full of fresh uncooked liver, lapping at it with her pink tongue. Other cats have their special plates of food scattered around too, but Molly demands the best, or she just won't eat, Grandma says.

Smokey Joe is a gorgeous grey and silver Persian over twenty pounds who bolts into their bedroom and hides if any guest enters the house. Every once in a while, Grandma will pull him out to show us how beautiful and how much bigger he is since the last time we visited. He has the softest fur I ever felt when Grandma holds him for us to pet and make a fuss over. Pat was a chubby white and black tabby who died that Grandma often mentions and shows us pictures of. She always looks a little sad when she talks about Pat.

Her favorite dog, probably her favorite pet ever, was Teddy; he was a brown chow who she has a big picture of next to the giant gold pocket watch on the back dining room wall. A large photograph of Grandma's mother is on the other side of the watch; she has a wide flat hat, bobbed hair, and 1920s clothes. I've seen those pictures so much; I can see both Teddy sitting up with his tongue hanging out and Grandma's mother smiling, as clear in my mind as anybody I've known in my life. Maybe it's because there is just one picture of them frozen forever in time; with living people, their expressions change all the time, depending on what they are feeling or doing.

Grandma Babe likes to tell us stories about how loyal and loving Teddy was in Kansas. It was best not to approach Grandma too fast if Teddy was around, he was very protective, and chows look like small bears. Her first husband had to be mighty careful how he talked to Grandma because he had a loud, deep voice, and if Teddy suspected he was being mean to Grandma, Teddy would get all growly and scare her husband. He didn't care for Teddy so much, which might have something to do with the marriage ending. I can't imagine Grandma being married to someone who didn't love animals or at least like them. She said chows were one-person dogs who gave all their love to one person only; of course, that person was Grandma, Teddy lived for her.

Grandma Babe even had Pap-Pap build a cat hotel beneath the back steps, where she puts out dry cat food, water, and spare beds with little throw rugs for the stray cats in the neighborhood. I've seen cats strolling in and out of there when we play in the yard. Pap-Pap doesn't mind building stuff like that for her because he loves animals too, but once, Pap-Pap told me, "Cats are dandy critters, and I love them to pieces, but confidentially, I like dogs just a wee bit more. Dogs need more attention and love like people do."

Grandma overheard Pap-Pap. She smiled at me, "Don't you listen to him, Bobby. Cats need just as much love and attention as dogs do. They don't slobber all over you like a dog does, but inside they are hoping that someone comes by and scratches their head or makes a fuss over how beautiful they are." There is usually a cat or two curled up close to Grandma or on her lap as she sits in her chair; they must be able to sense how much she loves them.

Dad says it's a good thing that Pap-Pap is an upholsterer so he can fix up the furniture that the cats claw to pieces all the time, sharpening their claws. Usually, though, Pap-Pap lets the chairs and the couch stay shredded for a long time with the stuffing spilling out before he fixes them. Once they are really bad, he will repair them; until then, he doesn't seem to mind how raggedy they look, and Grandma doesn't either.

Grandma thinks declawing a cat is one of the worst things that cats have done to them by people. Sometimes she takes in a stray cat that is missing its claws, "It breaks my heart to see them trying to sharpen claws that aren't there anymore, but more importantly, cats can't grip surfaces right without claws. Sometimes they fall when they try to jump onto something, or they might bump into a piece of furniture or a wall because they can't stop so quickly after they run across the floor."

She's also a proud member of the Animal Protectors. They have their meetings above a motorcycle shop in Tarentum, which is just down from K-Mart across the Tarentum Bridge. One evening, me, Danny and Mom went with Grandma Babe to a meeting because she wanted us to come. There was an overhead fan spinning, but it was hot, the folding chairs were hard, and it was really boring with people talking to Madam Secretary and Madam Treasurer about money and stuff. Most of the people were older, so I guess they didn't mind it being so boring, but it was one of the longest hours of my life.

Grandma doesn't only care about pets. She has what she calls her 'hot line' where she talks on the phone to lonely old people who live nearby, trying to cheer them up. Sometimes she reads them some of the poems she writes. Grandma must know that helping people is important to get to heaven, but she also knows that we need to help animals. She told me once that animals have souls like people do and go to heaven like us. I sure hope she's right.

Once, we were over at their house, and an episode of *The Twilight Zone* was on. It was a terrifying one about a monastery. A traveler asked for shelter during a tremendous thunderstorm. The head of the order (the actor was in a lot of old scary movies, he played Dracula once wearing a top hat— Mom would know his name) who had a long beard, was reluctant to let the traveler in, but he did because the storm was so fierce. As a monk led the traveler to his room, they passed by a door with a small shepherd's crook used to bar it from the outside.

He was curious, but the monk wouldn't tell him who was in that room or how a small crook like that could keep a prisoner from breaking out, just that he should keep away from it. Later, an awful howling noise kept him from sleeping, so he went back to the barred door. The man inside claimed he was being held prisoner by these crazy monks, and could the traveler please let him out.

The traveler talked to the head monk, who told him that the man in the cell was the Devil, and he was making the howling noise. It had taken them a long time to catch the Devil, and the whole purpose of their order was to keep him from escaping into the world again. The traveler thought the monk must be insane to believe that, so he didn't believe him, and eventually, he snuck over and let the prisoner out. Once he was free, the prisoner grew horns and laughed in the traveler's face because the prisoner really was the Devil, and the traveler had let the Devil loose upon the world.

I've always had kind of a fascination about the Devil. In Germany, I had a devil puppet. It was all red except for black tips on his red horns, black eyes, and a pointy black goatee. I had fun scaring the other puppets and selected toys with it, but its rubber head smelled great, so at night I liked to cuddle with it by my face, especially after I lost Charley.

I also dressed up as the Devil one Halloween in Germany. The devil mask I wore had a blue tint to the face but bright red horns. Danny and me trick-or-treated through the apartment buildings on Post, and the people who lived in one apartment left out a giant bowl of candy for kids to help themselves with. We had big pillowcases so I could fit the whole bowl in there with no problem, and I *was* the Devil that night. The temptation was strong to take more than my fair share.

Danny looked at me, "What do you think, how much should we take?"

There's a cartoon with Donald Duck where he has an angel Donald on one shoulder and a devil Donald on the other. They are both trying to convince Donald to act a certain way, and Donald is looking from one to the other, trying to decide who to listen to. I felt that way for a few seconds, not sure what I was going to say.

"Let's just take a couple. They were nice enough to trust people," I said.

But that *Twilight Zone* episode where the Devil got loose seemed especially sinister to me because I could see without a doubt that there was evil in the world. Watching the news alone was evidence of that, and there were plenty of things I noticed around me that seemed evil as well. Maybe the Devil really was out there, causing horrible things to happen, like hurting and killing people.

Grandma was looking at me and must have noticed that I was a bit scared, "That makes for an interesting tale, but the truth is there's no such thing as the Devil. People believe in the Devil because they see evil things happening to people and animals, but it's not the Devil who is causing the evil. Ignorant or selfish people are what causes evil. Just be careful of those kinds of people, stay away from them if you can, and don't you worry, there's no Devil out to get you."

What Grandma said reminds me of one of my favorite books, *Black Beauty*. It's a story told by a horse about his life and how people treated him. There is one part where Black Beauty was all overheated from a lot of running, and the young man taking care of him made a mistake and gave Black Beauty too much cold water too quickly. Black Beauty almost died.

Some character commented that it was only ignorance on the boy's part. The gentle coachman, John, erupted into a long speech about how ignorance caused so much misery and tragedy in the world and that ignorance was next to wickedness. His point was that we shouldn't excuse ignorance so easily and that people have to be accountable for the things that they cause through their ignorance. We have to overcome our ignorance and do better.

When I first read the book, his speech made good sense. Now though, I'm thinking that sounds easy to say, but how do you overcome your ignorance if you don't know that you're ignorant? Often I don't know I was ignorant about something until something happens to show me what a fool I was, then it's too late. No wonder ignorance causes so much grief; we don't know what harm we might cause, and we blunder on ahead anyway.

Grandma said that ignorant and selfish people are the real causes of evil, yet somehow that scares me almost as much as the Devil. How do you know if someone is ignorant or selfish before they do something to hurt you? They might seem okay before they cause you grief. Not only that, though, what if I am ignorant or selfish about something myself; evil might happen because of me without me realizing it. Maybe that's why praying to God is so important; otherwise, we are sure to mess things up.

One day Dad dropped Danny and me off with Grandma Babe and took Pap-Pap to a junkyard to pick up a part for Pap-Pap's Dodge van, the green van that said *Gamble Bros.* on the sides in yellow letters, and which they use to pick up furniture.

Over the phone, Pap-Pap found a junkyard in Pittsburgh that had the part, so Pap-Pap and Dad would be gone for a good bit.

While we visited, Grandma decided to tell us a little about her younger days as she called them. Grandma smoked once in a while even though she had emphysema, which is some kind of breathing disease she told us. I asked her why she keeps smoking.

"These days, I just have five a day; one in the morning, one in the afternoon, one in the evening, and two for when I just want to. I cut down quite a bit, but that's the best I can do for now. I know smoking is harmful to you, but I started smoking corn silk when I was about your age, and I've been smoking for over fifty years, so quitting is not so easy.

"So where was I? Oh, I was going to tell you more about my younger days. My mama, that's her picture by the clock, was thirteen when she had me. She was just a baby herself, so my grandma raised my mom and me at the same time. Grandma was a little strict, but she was loving all the same. I was raised in Kansas as a Mormon, so there is not a jealous bone in my body.

"It took me five tries to find the right husband; I guess I was just looking for Harvey, and I couldn't find him for the longest time.

"My fourth husband, Ruben, was a nice man, but he came home one day and saw me wrestling with Bruno Sammartino. That's right," she said, as our eyes must have gotten wider, "Bruno Sammartino, The World's Heavyweight Wrestling Champion. He wasn't actually the champ yet, just a young friend of mine in Kansas, and he was showing me a wrestling move or two when Ruben came home. Wrestling has always been one of my interests, but Ruben didn't care for wrestling, and he wasn't a Mormon.

"That opened the door, and Harvey came into my life. The first day we met was at a family picnic—Harvey and I are second cousins, and he started singing me a song in the middle of a walk we were taking together. There was a small creek nearby shaded by willows; we stopped for a time on the grassy bank under low hanging branches as Harvey sang to me. That was over twenty years ago, but that day always feels close to me.

"Later, we moved here, and it is okay in Pennsylvania, but I get lonesome for Kansas sometimes. The hills here are so confining you can hardly see the sky; they make the world smaller somehow. In Kansas, you can see the sky forever, and the land is nice and flat, perfect for riding a bike or walking, not like here where it's so hard just to get across the block because of all the hills."

When Grandma Babe finished talking, we watched the afternoon movie about a giant tarantula terrorizing a town in the desert. It was called *Tarantula,* of course. We drank cans of root beer with a straw and ate deviled ham sandwiches with sandwich spread on them. A little red devil with a forked tail was on the white wrapper covering the small cans she always bought. I asked Grandma one day why they always put straws in our cans of pop because Mom never did.

"Who knows what kind of dirt or germs get on top of the cans while they are transporting or storing them, and then people put their lips on them," Grandma said. After that, I tried to get Mom to give us straws at home, too; she did for a little while, then quit buying them. Luckily Mom usually buys bottles of pop, not cans. When she does buy cans, I wash mine off in the sink before I drink out of it.

Grandma Babe was just as interested as me and Danny in the movie. She was disturbed by seeing all the animals in cages that the scientist used for his growing experiments. A wolf-sized rabbit was in one cage, and a tarantula the size of a dog in another.

Later, the scientist's partner, who had turned into a monster, attacked the scientist and injected him with the same serum that had turned him into a monster. Then he threw a chair against the glass cage containing the tarantula, and the tarantula escaped. Both scientists died later with horrible-looking monster faces.

The tarantula kept on growing in the desert; eventually, it was bigger than a building. We shuddered together when the tarantula moved all eight legs at once to climb over a mountain smashing cars and knocking down telephone poles.

It's creepy how tarantulas walk. When we lived in Leesville in our duplex, we were all out in the front yard one day. Dad was barbecuing some hamburgers and hot dogs, and he was frowning because one of the hot dogs just rolled off into the coals. "God Damn it!" Dad said. Me and Danny were standing next to the grill with our buns ready, trying not to laugh when Mom screamed out from the small front porch.

"Hon! Look! Watch out!"

We turned, and Mom was backed up against the screen door with her face all red, pointing near the porch steps. A

giant hairy tarantula came out from under the porch, right next to Mom's ice tea, and was crawling right up the sidewalk. He was as big as my hand. The tarantula's legs moved all at once, but slow, like he was the King of the Spiders out for a stroll.

Danny leaned next to me and whispered, "Watch out, I read that tarantulas can jump ten feet in the air."

"No way!"

"Don't believe me," Danny said as he backed away from the sidewalk about ten feet.

Dad put his hand on my shoulder. "Robert, move back with your brother and stay away from it. I'll be right back."

Dad went into the house as we watched the tarantula walk down the middle of our sidewalk like he owned it. Dad came out with a broom and a fresh cigarette a minute or two later. By the time he caught up with the tarantula, it was in the street.

Dad squinted through the cigarette smoke as he took a giant whack with the broom. Then Dad swept the curled-up pieces across the street and flicked the mess into some bushes. I didn't really see the point in smashing the tarantula after he left our yard, but I could tell Dad had his mind made up to kill it, so I wasn't going to stick my nose in.

It would take one heck of a giant broom to smash the tarantula we watched in the movie—I think they finally killed it by jets burning it with napalm, the same stuff they use in Vietnam all the time now. The tarantula curled up as they sprayed liquid fire all over it, and a giant black cloud of smoke filled the sky. That must be a horrible way to die. How can they use something like that on other human beings, just spraying it from planes or helicopters? I've heard that napalm sticks to skin like glue and that even rolling in the grass can't get it off—once it's on somebody that's it—it's not coming off; they just keep burning. No one can tell me that's not evil.

Grandma felt sorry for the tarantula as we watched it collapse bit by bit in flames. She said it wasn't the spider's fault that some crazy scientist made it grow so big. I don't think there is any kind of animal that Grandma doesn't care about. She even had a pet snake when she lived in Kansas. I can't remember what kind of snake she said it was, but she used to let it crawl on her arms and shoulders, which made one of her ex-husbands get so flustered he begged her to get rid of it. Grandma gave it away to a friend of hers to make her husband happy.

She gave me a big hug when Dad got back with Pap-Pap, and we left that day. In all the times we've ever visited, I've never seen Grandma Babe sad or feeling sorry for herself, even when she was obviously in pain from her legs. Sometimes, like that day before I left, Grandma tells me she's always had a special place in her heart for me. I am always happy when she says that—I just wish she wouldn't say it in front of Danny.

It's too bad that Grandma Babe couldn't come to the funeral; her smile would have made things better around here. She would've come if she could because she loves Kansas, all her relatives live here somewhere, and I'm sure Grandma loved Uncle Billy. I've seen pictures of Uncle Billy in front of the giant gold pocket watch, smiling and standing in his dress greens with his arm around Grandma Babe. Grandma Babe's Buddha smile lights up the picture as her head leans against Uncle Billy's shoulder.

Dad said earlier that she didn't come because she cares more about her pets than people, but I know better than that. Dad says, "Your Grandma makes Pap-Pap spend all their money on pets, and that's one of the reasons why Uncle Clarence has a nicer house." I figure that it's their money to spend, and it makes them happy to have so many pets; I don't know why it bothers Dad so much.

Dad just doesn't like her, and that's too bad because Grandma gives Dad advice sometimes that he'd be better off if he took—like about taking things as they come and not letting things get to you. Dad does get upset pretty easily sometimes; he just can't help it. Grandma Babe is not afraid of Dad or speaking her mind, which is probably some of what Dad doesn't like about her. Grandma is a strong person who happens to be a woman, and I get the feeling that rubs him the wrong way somehow.

Me, I like that she is strong because I can count on her if I get in trouble. She would never let me down on purpose. Grandma Babe is deep in my heart, and so is Pap-Pap.

I'm glad Pap-Pap is sitting right in front of me; I can see the black arm of his glasses alongside his temple, the curved part tucked behind his left ear. He seems real interested in what the preacher is talking about. Somehow him being here makes things less scary. I'm sure he's not afraid; he's probably been to plenty of funerals since he is so old. He has his right arm around Grandma's shoulders now because she is crying so much. Funerals are hard things to be a part of, especially seeing other people's grief. I'll be glad when it's over.

Chapter XIII

Moon Puddles

Danny is sitting to my left, looking a bit drippy from his hay fever—must be because of all the flowers. Lucky for him, he always carries tissues in his pocket. Danny sticks his tongue in his cheek when he's worrying about something, and I can see him poking his tongue in there now. He probably remembers Uncle Billy better than me because he is two years older. Maybe he's in the middle of a memory about Uncle Billy.

Danny's brown hair is a little lighter than Dad's, and he has blue eyes like we all do, except Mom, who has green eyes. When we lived in Bad Kissingen, Dad teased us about the green-eyed monster that hid in our closet. He raised his eyebrows real high like he always does when he is trying to be scary, "Green Eyes is hiding. I think I heard it in the closet. Did you hear that?" He'd cup his ear with his hand and lean towards the closet door. "Listen real close, quiet now, shhh . . . BOO," he'd shout out and grab me and Danny, tickling us till we laughed. I knew he was joking, but I couldn't help but picture a monster in my head and feeling a bit scared. We finally figured out he was talking about Mom with her pale green eyes.

Mom's next to Dad. Her eyes are red and wet looking, but she isn't crying. Neither is Dad, of course, but he's looked scary ever since we stood in front of Uncle Billy's coffin, like any minute he could either start cursing or crying.

There are big bunches of flowers on either side of the dark wooden coffin. The bunch Mom and Dad bought is shaped like a heart; a yellow ribbon draped diagonally across the middle says, *Beloved Brother.* Half the coffin lid is open. Uncle Billy is in dress greens with a few medals on his chest. Dad says one is a Purple Heart; there's also a rifle set in a blue rectangle, which shows that he served in Vietnam. Uncle Billy has three yellow stripes on each sleeve; he's what's called a Buck Sergeant. All the brass on his collar is shined up bright— Dad has to shine his with Brasso every so often to keep the tarnish off. God, that stuff stinks. After he shines up his collar brass, Dad always spits-shines his black boots till you can see your shadowy reflection on the toes.

Uncle Billy has a lean triangular face; his light red hair combed straight back like he wore it, and the freckles on his nose (he has the same handsome nose as Pap-Pap) look the same as when we ate the french fries. But I can tell he is dead.

It's different from sleep somehow. When I see someone sleeping, I expect their eyes to open anytime and catch me looking, but there's nothing inside to open Uncle Billy's eyes anymore. Somehow I can see that, and I don't like how it feels. I can see that Dad doesn't like it either as his face gets flat and still. His hand is gripping the coffin edge hard, and for a second, I think I see his eyes look lost and wet, but then we are sitting down. I try not to look at Dad now.

241

This is my first funeral, but it's not the first time I experienced one of our close relatives dying. We lost somebody just last year while we were in Louisiana. Dad couldn't get leave to go back to PA for the funeral because the Army said the person wasn't in our immediate family. Family is family; what does the Army know about families anyway? The way they move people around all the time, they don't seem to care about families.

Take us, for instance; Dad got orders to go to Hawaii when we lived in Virginia. We moved back to PA to visit our relatives while the Army began arranging things for Dad to get shipped ahead of us to Hawaii. For some reason, the Army wanted Dad to go there first, and then we were to follow a couple months later. I started first grade while we waited and lived at 404 15th street in Arnold. I don't think they had kindergarten back then because I went right to first grade, and I know that Danny didn't go to kindergarten either. We were only supposed to go to school there until we got the green light from the Army to board the ship to Hawaii.

Me and Danny would eat breakfast and watch *Deputy Dawg* before we walked to school about three blocks away. Deputy Dawg is a not-so-bright dog who's the deputy of a human sheriff with a big white mustache. A muskrat and a weasel wearing a beret always tried to trick Deputy Dawg—they usually did, and then he'd have to explain to the sheriff what went wrong this time. It gave us a good laugh before we had to go to school.

We got to walk home for lunch every day, but that was about the only nice thing about that school. They had a playground behind a high green fence we would play on before the bell rang. It wasn't so great because the ground was hard cement; I fell off the seesaw once because some kid jumped off unexpectedly, and I scraped my knee on the pebbly concrete.

In class, we worked in workbooks with pictures to choose from because we couldn't read yet; it was kind of frustrating sometimes. We would take breaks from time to time and play London Bridge. I didn't like that game. We would all be rushing under the bridge getting pushed, and sometimes the other kid's arms would bump me in the head when they sang, ". . . all fall down." I didn't enjoy going to school there, so every day, I kept hoping we'd be moving to Hawaii soon. Dad was supposed to get shipped to Hawaii in a week or so, then we'd follow later.

God, we were all so excited about going. Hula dancers with flowers in their hair and grass skirts, palm trees, coconuts, pineapples, beaches, volcanoes, beautiful weather; Dad was especially excited about no more stinking cold Pennsylvania winters. I couldn't wait to go, to have flowers put around my neck by a beautiful native girl welcoming us to their island paradise.

One afternoon after school, we were watching *Beany and Cecil*. Dishonest John, who has the best evil laugh ever— "Nyuh, ah ah," was about to throw a round black bomb onto the Minnow—Beany and Cecil's ship (It was really the Captain's ship, but he always hid in his cabin when trouble came) when Dad came home. He didn't usually come home that early. His face had the same tired look as when our Studebaker's engine died for good.

Mom could tell right away that something wasn't right, "What's wrong, Hon?" She asked.

Dad plopped down on the couch, "I'm sorry, everybody, but my orders got changed. We aren't going to Hawaii anymore. This missile crisis going on in Cuba is shaking things up. My orders got changed; now we have to go to Germany. It's because of that crazy shoe banging Khrushchev getting chummy with Castro and ticking off President Kennedy.

"I guess they want more troops in Germany in case Russia does something stupid. President Kennedy isn't going to take any crap from Khrushchev; it's the Russians' fault; we'll just have to get used to the idea of going to butt-freezing Germany."

It took us a while to get over losing Hawaii and becoming excited about going to Germany—Dad never got excited about Germany, too cold. (He always wears socks in the house to keep his feet warm, even in the summer.) Now I'm glad we went to Germany, but it seemed awful when we first got the news.

That's the Army for you. They aren't out to make families happy, country first, families down the list a bit. Maybe that's the way it should be if I calm down and think about it, but it's not easy to take sometimes.

When we came back from Germany and visited our relatives in PA before going to Louisiana, we stayed at Uncle Bill and Aunt Shirley's house for a while. They have a three-story house on Kenneth Avenue in Arnold. The kind with three or four feet between the neighbors on either side, enough for a sidewalk and a small strip of grass, maybe. They had a cozy front porch with a green metal glider on it and a small fenced-in backyard.

Their garage was right next to the alley, but Uncle Bill always parked his big Chevy Impala out on the street. His garage was full of tools and machines. He cut his lawn with a push mower where the curved blades spin around like an open barrel. His yard was small, so he didn't sweat much, and he had an unlit cigarette in his mouth the whole time. When he finished mowing, he lit up his cigarette. I was watching him from the back porch to see if he would ever smoke it.

Aunt Shirley was pretty with long black hair, and she liked me; I could tell because she tried to get me to talk with her, and she smiled at me a lot. She looked similar to a picture I saw of Grandma Babe when she was younger, same long black hairstyle, similar legs in shorts. There was another picture of Grandma Babe sitting at a table smoking, and for years I thought it was Aunt Shirley until Mom told me it was Grandma. I was surprised. Aunt Shirley is a little prettier than Grandma used to be, but Grandma has rounder eyes and a more beautiful smile.

Aunt Shirley showed me how to cut a pineapple one day in her kitchen. Mom never bought one for us before, so I was interested in how she cut it up. Aunt Shirley gave me some right away, but it didn't taste much like the pineapple in fruit cocktail that I was used to. Aunt Shirley seemed surprised that I wasn't as crazy about fresh pineapple as she was.

Uncle Bill had hair like Elvis Presley, he even had a lock of hair that usually hung down on his forehead like Elvis, but he was more handsome than Elvis was; his face was narrower, and he had sharp eyes like he didn't miss much. Dad said he was the smartest person in our family, a mechanical genius who might have been a great engineer if he could have gone to college.

He smoked as much as Dad did, but he smoked Benson & Hedges 100's. Uncle Bill said he smoked them because they were the longest cigarettes he could find, and that way, he didn't have to relight a new one so often. Uncle Bill had a habit of saying dear and sugar instead of swearing with the d and the s words. I noticed that he used dear and sugar quite a bit when he talked.

Dad really liked Uncle Bill, but there was one obstacle to their friendship. Uncle Bill liked to drink, and Dad was a teetotaler. When they got married, Dad promised Mom he would never drink because of what drinking did to Mom's dad. Mom never asked him to; Dad just did it because he knew what a rough time her dad gave Mom and her family all those years. Besides that, "Beer tastes like warm piss," he says. (I wonder if he really knows what pee tastes like?)

So when everybody started drinking beer at a family picnic or a party, Dad drank his Pepsi. He couldn't really be drinking buddies with Uncle Bill, Uncle Friday (Uncle Friday got the name Friday because every Friday when he was younger, he was out all night at the bars partying, so his friends started calling him Friday, and it stuck), or even Uncle Al, who wasn't that big of a drinker at all. Uncle Al is Aunt Doreen's husband. He has dark brown hair with a slight reddish cast to it and a real friendly manner; he smiles a lot and gets along well with everybody.

Aunt Doreen has glasses, reddish-blonde hair, and freckles, and she is the best baker in our family—though Aunt

Joyce makes the best nut rolls. Aunt Doreen makes berry pies and cheesecakes that are like pies from heaven. I call her my Betty Crocker aunt in my mind because she can bake everything so great. She's always considerate of other people's feelings if they are comfortable or need refreshments when visiting her house. Aunt Doreen sells Avon on the side, and Uncle Al works in an auto body shop fixing dents in cars. All three of their kids, Louie, Patti, and Donna, have red hair and tons of freckles.

Most of our family on Mom's side--the Tinnemeyers, went to Crooked Creek once to have a big picnic. We all traveled in a car caravan of about four or five cars. The Army Engineers had built a dam there, which created a lake that people used for boating, a beach for swimming, and plenty of picnic grounds scattered everywhere. It was a great place for a picnic, so everyone pulled their cars onto a good spot near some shade trees, a big field, and a small creek.

Before we all ate, Ricky, Danny, and me went exploring up the creek. I was looking for salamanders, the shiny black ones with yellow spots; they feel clammy when you touch them, but they are awful slow, no challenge to catch, just a matter of finding one. Danny and Ricky were just walking and talking up ahead when all of a sudden, they both jumped out of the creek and started running. Danny looked my way and shouted, "Wasps!" I hopped out of the creek and followed them at a safe distance until they stopped.

Ricky had stepped on a wasp nest in the muddy bank, and they attacked his leg. Ricky wasn't crying, but I could tell he was hurting from how he winced and the scared look on his face. The pain wiped away his usual wise guy look. He was wearing shorts, so it was easy to see the three stings on his calf. They were swollen already and an angry red color. Danny had escaped without a sting, just mud all over his shoes.

We helped Ricky hop back to the picnic tables, where Aunt Joyce wrapped up ice in a red and white checkered tea towel and had Ricky hold it on his leg. Ricky sat under a tree and rested. I went to play badminton with Louie for a while.

Uncle Bill, Uncle Friday, Uncle Al, even Aunt Shirley were all sitting at a picnic table drinking bottles of beer; Dad was sitting there, too. Mom, Aunt Joyce, Aunt Doreen, and Grandma T were at another table drinking cans of pop. I came by after playing badminton with Louie. He's a couple years younger than me, so I beat him easily, too easy, I guess because Louie's big ears were all red, and I could tell he wasn't happy about losing.

I was thirsty, so I grabbed a can of cream soda out of our ice chest. I glanced over and saw Dad sitting at the end of the table with all the beer drinkers. Dad was sipping a Dr. Pepper. Everybody else seemed to be relaxed and having a good time, but Dad looked so unhappy I felt sorry for him. Dad felt like the odd man out at times like that, and he would get lonely and angry. Later on, he would complain to us about not having any friends, that other guys didn't like him because he didn't drink like they did.

While we stayed at Uncle Bill's, he and Dad got along okay, but I could see that Dad was just trying a bit too hard to be friendly. When a person tries too hard, it kind of makes other people draw back, and then the person tries even harder and feels more frustrated—it can get embarrassing.

We left Uncle Bill's a lot of the time and visited other relatives, like Grandma Babe and Pap-Pap, Grandma T, Aunt Joyce, Aunt Doreen, everybody we could before we had to drive to Louisiana. Dad had bought a Dodge at a used car lot when we first got to PA. Uncle Bill drove Dad there and helped him check out the car to make sure it wasn't a clunker.

One afternoon we left Uncle Bill's and went to visit Grandpap Tinnemeyer. Grandma T had kicked him out years ago, but he still lived in Arnold on the corner of 3rd Avenue and 17th Street, right across the street from where the Alcoa plant finally ended behind a big fence. He had an apartment at the top of a long flight of outside steps that ended up on his porch. Grandpap lived alone, except that Uncle Johnny was starting to spend the weekends with him. The rest of the week, Uncle Johnny lived with Grandma.

Uncle Johnny was there on the Saturday when we visited. He had his own bedroom with a bunch of comics and detective magazines under his bed. Uncle Johnny didn't let us look at the magazines, but we got to read some of his comics. In the living room on a bookcase, he had a super cool model of Godzilla. It was purplish, about 10 inches high with Godzilla's jagged branchy stegosaurus-type spikes down his back and his thick, scaly legs; his sharp-toothed mouth was open as if he was shooting out a blast of electric fire. Uncle Johnny let us play with Godzilla while Mom and Dad chatted at the kitchen table with Grandpap.

Grandpap had a dark brown cane that was always close to him. He needed it for help when he walked. Sometimes he would smack the cane against the table if he wanted Uncle

Johnny to come into the kitchen to get something for him. Grandpap had an A&P shopping cart in his small scruffy back yard that Uncle Johnny used for shopping on the weekend. Grandpap must have gone out sometimes, at least to buy his wine, but most of the time, he stayed in his apartment.

Grandpap Tinnemeyer has short gray hair; he's going bald in the middle, but he still has a little hair in front. He is skinny, and his shoulders are a bit bent like he can't sit up straight. He reminds me mostly of Uncle Bill, with his lean face, and he has the same sharp blue eyes that show he is smart.

Mom said Grandpap had a twin brother somewhere in Cleveland, where Mom was born. His brother was supposed to be nice. I guess Grandma picked the wrong brother. Grandpap could be nice too, but there was often an edge to his voice, and he said things in a way like he expected people to let him down and do something stupid.

We all hugged him when we met; his chin was scratchy with gray stubble, and he smelled a little like wine. There was a half-empty bottle on the kitchen counter. The green bottle had red-looking wine inside, and I could see an empty glass next to it that had red dribbles at the bottom.

"So can you tell me something in German?" he asked me.

"Ah, not too much," I said.

"That's too bad; what did you do with yourself over there then?"

"The usual stuff, school, movies, I read a lot and played baseball."

"Another baseball player, are you any good?"

"I'm OK, not great, but I love to play it."

"Well, at least you are honest. Hold onto that; honesty is a good thing to have, and rare, so don't lose it."

After I went into the living room, I could relax again. I liked Grandpap, but he made me feel like I was a suspect and he was the detective. I felt sorry for him, though; he pretty much lost his family because he couldn't stop drinking. I can tell that Mom and Dad don't feel very comfortable around him. No wonder Dad never started drinking.

"Do you guys know how to play pool?" Uncle Johnny asked.

"We have a small pool table that goes on top of the kitchen table," said Danny.

"C'mon upstairs; I'll teach you guys how to play on a real one."

Uncle Johnny took us up another flight of steps. He was taller than Grandpap already. Uncle Johnny was always ready to smile, and because of his high cheekbones and blondish hair, I was reminded of Lucas McCain from the *Rifleman* every time I met him. Lucas shot with a short rifle instead of a six-shooter, and he was faster than anybody. He had a son, Mark, who was probably thirteen or so. Lucas's wife had died years before. Poor Mark, not having a mom, but Lucas did the best he could raising him.

The best episode was when they camped out one night on a trip somewhere. Before they bedded down, they met Micah, the old-looking sheriff, with a prisoner who had murdered someone. Everyone woke up the next morning except Lucas, who slept in with his hat over his head. After calling his pa's name for a while to wake him up, Mark lifted

Lucas's hat and froze when he saw Lucas's wide-eyed face covered with beads of sweat. Mark didn't understand why his pa looked so petrified until he heard a rattle under Lucas's bedroll—it was a rattlesnake that had crawled inside overnight.

Lucas couldn't move or talk from fear that the snake would bite him. Sweat was dripping off his face as he laid there still as a statue; he didn't even seem to blink. I don't know how he could stand laying there with a snake crawling around in there with him. I'm sure most people would have screamed or moved—I know I wouldn't have been able to stop from shivering or flinching with a snake touching my foot or winding up my leg. Just thinking about it gives me the creeps.

Micah, who was a smart sheriff, came up with an idea. He burned a hole carefully into the bottom of the blanket with a cigar. Then he stuck a bamboo pole that Mark had cut down for him into the hole. Micah blew big puffs of cigar smoke into the hollow bamboo. Hopefully, the smoke would drive out the rattler. When smoke started coming out of the top of the blanket by Lucas's face, though, Lucas started to cough, and the snake started rattling again, so Micah had to stop blowing the smoke.

The prisoner, who claimed he had experience handling snakes, offered to grab the blanket with the snake inside and throw it into the bushes. In return, all he wanted was for Micah to put in a good word for him to the judge so he wouldn't get hung. Micah couldn't try it himself because the prisoner had sprained one of Micah's hands earlier, trying to escape. Micah didn't trust the crook, of course, but in desperation, Micah agreed, and Mark trained his rifle on the prisoner in case he tried something tricky once his hands and feet were free of the chains.

After he was free, the prisoner squatted down next to Lucas and quickly threw the blanket and the rattler away like he said he would, but right at Micah's face, and then he pounced and grabbed the rifle out of Mark's hands. Micah was ready, though, as he sidestepped the flying blanket, shot the prisoner in the heart, and then fired five bullets into the rattler.

Mark ran over to his pa, who sat up drenched in sweat but was too drained to speak. Lucas had plenty of courage to be able to lay still for so long with a rattlesnake cuddling next to him.

Most people don't have snakes to worry about disturbing, but uncomfortable or frightening situations come to most everybody once in a while. Sometimes the only thing we can do is just sit still and bear what life brings, maybe cry for a bit, but it's sure not easy when something awful happens.

Well, Uncle Johnny's long legs took the steps two at a time, his squeaky sneakers echoing in the stairwell. The banister, stairs, and stair poles were dark wood with a strong woody smell I enjoyed taking deep breaths of. It was like the wood smell had been building up inside the air of the stairwell for decades. Everything still seemed solid and sturdy, even though the floors were creaky.

I loved the smell; it reminded me of another old house that some kids lived in on 4th avenue. Me and Danny used to play with them every once in a while. Their house was around the corner from our row-house apartment where I had crashed my tricycle in the alley. They had the same kind of banister going upstairs to the attic we played in, the same old dark woody smell. Dad told us once that when Alcoa first opened and started hiring people, many of the houses in Arnold and New Ken were built around the same time.

A trunk full of toys was next to the window, and we scattered toys everywhere as we looked for fun stuff. There was a Bozo the Clown jack-in-the-box I liked playing with the most. I loved watching Bozo the Clown on TV with his super wide hair and his giant shoes. That day, as I cranked the box over and over, watching Bozo pop out smiling, a parade with a marching band started to pass by outside. We ran down the steps just as the mayor drove by in a convertible; he threw out pieces of bubble gum to all the kids on the street. I managed to get two pieces out of the gutter. They were kind of hard and dry—he wouldn't get my vote.

Anyway, when we got to the top floor with Uncle Johnny, there was a giant space in the attic with a pool table in the middle. It looked old, but the green felt was in fair shape, the bumpers still had some bounce, and we chalked up our sticks with cubes of blue chalk. Uncle Johnny taught us how to play eight ball. Man, was he good! He could crack those balls apart like Minnesota Fats.

I wasn't too bad, at least I could hit the balls, even if they didn't go in like I wanted, but Danny didn't have the knack for it. I always felt bad for Danny when he couldn't do sports stuff very well; he just wasn't coordinated enough or something. After about a half-hour, Dad hollered up for us to come so we could go home to Uncle Bill's. Grandpap leaned on his cane and waved goodbye to us from his porch as we walked down the steps and got into our car. We didn't visit him anymore before we left for Louisiana.

Uncle Bill had two daughters, Debbie and Dottie, and a little boy, Davey. Debbie was the oldest; she was five. She had dark hair cut like Prince Valiant, bangs in front, but longer in the back, a pretty smile with two big dimples, sweet brown eyes, and she liked to run like boys do. Debbie also had cancer in her left knee. The good news was she had been getting better before we arrived. Uncle Bill and Aunt Shirley were happy that her condition was improving and Debbie had lots of energy.

One night both our families drove over to Aunt Shirley's mother's place, which was out in the country a little. They had a big field for their front yard that Debbie, Danny, and me played in as it got dark. All the adults were inside the house playing cards, so they left us alone for a while.

Dozens of lightning bugs scattered throughout the field were flashing on and off. We caught some and watched them light up glowing yellow in our hands; then we'd open our hands and let them fly free in the night air; their wings beat fast, and the lights in their butts hung down a little as they flew away. Debbie had a hard time catching them, so I grabbed a couple for her. She looked at the lightning bugs with an amazed smile like they were little fairies or something.

After that, we found a tree that had dropped buckeyes everywhere, so we collected as many as we could before our parents made us come inside. It was the first time I had seen them, and I didn't know buckeyes was their name; I thought maybe they were chestnuts or something, but not knowing made them even more mysterious and interesting. Dad told me they were buckeyes later when I pulled some out of my pocket to show him.

Buckeyes feel nice and smooth in your hand, even better than a good stone does, and they fit perfect in your palm, great for rubbing or squeezing gently. They are a beautiful shiny brown with cream-colored thumbprints in the middle—I guess they are supposed to look like a buck's eye, but I never saw a deer with eyes like that. Debbie was running all over, excited about all the buckeyes she was finding. Danny had a more slow and meandering way of looking for them, but his pockets were full, too.

"Hey, Bobby!" Danny called out; when I turned to look at him, Danny had two buckeyes stuck somehow in his eye sockets with a goofy grin on his face. He looked like a nut all right.

Debbie pointed at him, "He must be a zombie! Let's get away quick!" she shouted as she pulled me by my arm. We ran for a bit, pretending we were scared as Danny walked after us like Frankenstein till his eyeballs popped out and bounced on the grass.

There was a big pile of wood burning in the next yard, and a lot of smoke started drifting our way, probably because the wood was still a little wet. I could see Debbie watching the fire, sniffing the pleasant smoke smell like I was; Danny was pulling out a tissue from the smoke making his nose run a little.

It had rained earlier in the day, so there were plenty of puddles about, especially in the dirt driveway. I noticed the full moon reflected in a puddle by my feet and another moon reflected in the puddle next to it. I started checking out all the puddles I could find, and sure enough, the same bright white moon was in each puddle. Debbie followed me around.

"What are you looking for in the water?" Debbie asked me.

"What do you see in every puddle here besides water?" I asked her.

She went from puddle to puddle, bending down with her head tilted at different angles, and then she turned to me and smiled her biggest dimpled smile yet.

"Oh, they're all moon puddles, how beautiful!" Debbie said.

I could feel the Mystery coming into the night like it was trying to make me understand something important about the moon being everywhere. The Mystery was rubbing gently inside my head; my temples were pulsing pleasantly as Debbie smiled in delight at the moon in a puddle.

Then it hit me, and I almost lost my balance as a feeling of wonder sunk in. God is like the moon. There is only one moon, but its reflection is everywhere like God is somehow everywhere, but there is only one God. Jesus said the kingdom of heaven is within us. Are we reflections of God, like the moons in the puddles? I was close to understanding more, but Uncle Bill was calling Debbie, so we went inside with our pockets bulging with buckeyes, and the feeling and my train of thought slipped away from me.

But now I remember a couple days ago when we were driving up to Kansas. I was thinking about Tom Terrific; how I thought about God being able to turn into everything; how

I thought God was playing Hide and Seek with us; how I promised I'd grab hold of his sleeve someday and not ever let go. Like the moon in the puddles, God is in all of us, but we can't see him; the puddles can't look inside themselves, and neither can we.

But maybe there is a way to find him hiding inside ourselves somehow; there must be—it's God's game. He wouldn't make a game we had no chance of winning, would he? That wouldn't be fair. I want to see God or feel him, but I don't want to wait until I die. Can't it happen now while I'm alive? Please, God, let me see you and be with you someday.

A couple days after seeing the moon puddles, we were all playing a running game on the side of Uncle Bill's house during twilight. I was chasing Debbie and Dottie, trying to tag one of them. Dottie has light brown hair like me, and she was four at the time. They have a side door and steps that Debbie was running to when she slipped and hit her knee on the concrete stair. Her knee was bleeding, and Debbie started to cry. I could see she looked white-faced scared because it was her bad knee.

Aunt Shirley came out and took her inside to bandage it. I was feeling sick inside because it was my fault that she fell and hurt her knee. I started to worry that falling on it might make the cancer come back again. After ten minutes, some cookies, and some Kool-Aid, Debbie was happy again, but I never forgot how scared she looked; she knew that leg was bad news. That was the last time we played any running games.

It wasn't long after that—we were settling in at our new place in Leesville—when Mom got a letter from Aunt Shirley saying that Debbie was back in the hospital—her cancer was getting worse. Six months later, Aunt Shirley called to tell us that Debbie had died. Mom started crying over the phone. We were all shocked. I snuck away after a while and found a nice quiet place in the pine woods where I could cry by myself. I wondered if it was partly my fault because I made her fall that day by chasing her so hard. I still do.

Now, whenever I think of Debbie, I remember how she smiled at her moon puddles. She was just as beautiful as the moon that night. I'm sure she's in heaven now. Maybe she flies to the moon from time to time with her little angel wings.

Uncle Bill took Debbie's death awful hard. Aunt Shirley wrote to Mom later that she was worried about Uncle Bill drinking so much since the funeral. I guess he had a hard time sitting still and bearing what life brought him; it must have been too awful for him, even worse than a rattler in his blankets.

I wasn't supposed to hear about his drinking, but Mom was telling Dad in the living room, and I had snuck down to the kitchen for a glass of milk. As I laid in bed, I wondered what it must be like for a parent to lose a child. It must be one of the worst things that can happen to a person. No wonder Uncle Bill was so depressed; who could blame him?

No wonder Grandma keeps crying so much now. Uncle Billy is all grown up, but he's still her child. She probably remembers all the times when Uncle Billy was a little boy. I'm glad we didn't go to Debbie's funeral though, seeing Debbie in a little coffin for kids would have been terrible, even worse than seeing Uncle Billy in his.

Chapter XIV

Ben-Hur

The preacher talking is an older man who reminds me of a skinny Art Linkletter wearing glasses. He's holding onto the podium, crooked blue veins in his hands, glancing down at his papers or the open Bible on top. Everyone is looking at him, except Grandma; she's still looking at Uncle Billy. Pap-Pap nods his head from time to time like he agrees with what he hears.

"My friends, seeing a loved one's death reminds us that we must come to terms with our own life, with what is most important. We are all on a journey of unknown duration. Time is relentless, and we have to be careful that we don't waste the gift of life that God has given us. If we want salvation, we have to be like a child and trust in Jesus to show us the way to God and his heavenly kingdom."

The preacher talking about Jesus reminds me of when I first saw Jesus in the movies. I knew who Jesus was, of course, before we saw the movie, even though we never went to church, but watching a movie was the first time I felt moved by Jesus in my heart. That was when we went to see *Ben-Hur* in Schweinfurt.

We went to Schweinfurt every so often to buy groceries, as they had a much bigger commissary than the one at our base. They even had a nursery room for little kids—we never went in, of course, but we would pass by on the way to the shopping carts and see little boys and girls through the giant glass window playing with blocks, dolls, or cars.

Across the giant parking lot from the commissary was a massive square-looking building with the spread wings of a mighty eagle thirty feet across carved in the middle of the granite entrance. Dad said it was the federal building. It was impressive looking. Mrs. Martinez told us in class last year that countries and empires like the United States, Germany, and Rome pick eagles as a symbol to show how powerful they are. She added that the eagle also stands for freedom in the United States, for people's right to fly free.

I believe she's right; somehow, the USA is a special country for freedom, different from other countries. Look at the Statue of Liberty or the Bill of Rights. People from all over the world move to the US so they can live like they dream—a place of hope. Sometimes I feel proud to be born in America. But when I think about Leesville and colored people forced to sit in the balcony, pollution poured into our rivers, or what's happening in Vietnam; I'm not quite so proud.

Back then, though, when I saw that stone eagle across from the commissary, I just felt impressed, and kind of glad that Dad was in the Army, that he was part of something grand somehow, and because we were his family, so were we.

I remember walking into that commissary one day, and we got little toy mail trucks with eagles on them; the back door opened up, and we could put secret stuff in there. I put a tiny green rubber frog in mine that I got in a Cracker Jack box. I'd take the frog out, play with it and sniff it from time to time because of the nice rubbery smell, almost like plastigoop.

Last Christmas, me and Danny got Creepy Crawlers—sometimes we get Christmas gifts for both of us to share. That usually works out OK. We don't usually fight over having to share stuff—we're used to it. The kit has molds for different kinds of insects, spiders and scorpions, even a bat and little snakes. We pour the plastigoop into molds, and then heat it in the metal cooking pan it comes with. When the baking's finished, the insects get solid but rubbery.

They look cool; I've scared a few people because they seem pretty real. The best thing is the plastigoop smell they always have even when they come out of the pan and cool down. My green rubber frog had that smell, not the kind of smell that makes you want to eat something, but the kind that makes you glad you can smell things like Play-Doh does.

We always got comics at the commissary, too. My favorite at that time was *The Legion of Superheroes* with Cosmic Boy, Lightning Lad, Lightning Lass, Sun Boy, Chameleon Boy, and Saturn Girl, who was so smart and pretty with blonde hair in her red and white uniform—Saturn and its ring was between her breasts. She had the coolest power with her telepathy; she could read other people's thoughts and communicate without talking. Those are the kind of powers God must have. I'd love to be able to do that.

The ride to Schweinfurt took us about a half-hour through German countryside—Dad drove a small gray Opal back then. After we left Bad Kissingen, we'd take a winding road over the giant hill where our hiking castle was. We could see the tower poking out above the trees. Beyond the hill, there was a flat plain. We'd look at open fields of green and gold crops and great hills off to the left. About halfway there, we always started watching for our special house. It was at the top of one high hill.

The blue and white house looked like a face with a hat—like the Tin Man in *The Wizard of Oz* with a long chimney poking up in the middle and windows spaced just right. It was sort of a contest every time to see who could spot it first and holler out, "There's our house!" Danny usually won. The trip wouldn't have been complete without seeing that house, and it always made us all smile.

Tractors pulling manure wagons gave the air an "oh-my-goodness-smell," Mom called it, that made us roll up the windows, especially when we got stuck behind a wagon for a while—which seemed to happen every trip. Dad called them honey wagons. Secretly though, I liked the smell as it seemed so earthy and German somehow, and I snuck deep breaths of it.

We always passed through one small cobble-stoned village with a white mermaid fountain that had water tumbling and splashing wet across her beautiful body. She was holding up a small fish on the palm of her hand that was squirting out a thin stream of water. The mermaid was smiling like an angel with long curled locks like waves as she reclined on a dark gray boulder. Water gushed like a waterfall over her and the rock; her tail flipper was spread flat on the wet stone.

There was a bakery past the fountain that always seemed to have its front door open. I always stuck my head out the window a bit to catch a whiff of fresh-baked bread—nothing smells as good as hot German bread. The bread smell even overpowered the smell of the pastries, cookies, and cakes inside. At the end of the village, turnips piled up against one house like coal.

When we got close to Schweinfurt, we passed a few American monuments from the war. They had a giant green cannon with two huge rubber wheels, a small fighter plane with shark teeth painted on the nose cone, and a massive green tank; they were all placed in a big grass circle that traffic went around.

Those weapons were such giant pieces of hard lethal-looking metal. Sometimes I stared at them and tried to imagine what it must have been like to be a kid living there when the Americans invaded Germany, to see and listen to a tank or a plane coming after you, or hear cannon fire and wonder if the shell would land close by. It must have been terrifying.

This drive to Schweinfurt was different than usual, though, as it was turning dark, we couldn't see everything as well, and because we were going to the movie theater, not the commissary. Army bases get movies that have been around for a while—I guess to save money, but the movies were always new to us, so we didn't care. *Ben-Hur* was playing, and Mom said it had won the most Oscars ever; it even had an intermission because it was so long. That was good news for Dad as that meant he would be able to smoke a cigarette or two halfway through.

Mom knows everything about movies. Ask her about any movie star, and she can tell their life story, what movies they were in, who they starred with. Especially old black and white movies with people like Clark Gable and Ingrid Bergmen—God, she was beautiful; talk about looking like an angel. She was Dad's favorite actress until she did or said something he didn't like—about communism, I think. Now he can't stand her. I say (in my head, of course, not to Dad) who cares about that, it's a movie, look at her and enjoy her beauty.

Sometimes when I come out of a movie theater, I have a strange feeling for a few minutes. It's a sensation like I'm still in the movie somehow, that my life is a movie and I'm watching myself. It's weird, and the feeling fades away quickly, but it has happened plenty of times. Hey, maybe God makes a movie of everybody's life, and after you go to heaven, you get to watch your whole life over. Some of it might be kind of embarrassing or painful to watch. I hope none of the other angels get to see it, too.

Mom can usually figure out what will happen next in a movie because she has seen so many; she says you get a feel for things after a while. When she was a kid, they didn't have a TV at all. It was either the radio, with great-sounding shows like *The Shadow,* or the movies. Mom said back then movies were super cheap, ten cents for two movies, cartoons, shorts—some of which were about what was happening with the war—the whole matinee lasted most of the day on Saturdays. Popcorn was five cents a box. That must have been great.

Candy and gum were cheap back then, too—and I guess she ate a lot of it because Mom lost all her top teeth as a teenager and had to get dentures. I don't know if she got her dentures before or after she met Dad, probably before, I guess, or he might not have wanted to kiss her. No one can tell they're not her real teeth. She never lets us see her without her dentures, but I saw them in a glass of water one night while she was sound asleep, creepy looking.

So Mom went to the movies whenever she could, partly to get away from her dad, I bet. That makes me wonder, she says she lost her teeth because she ate too many sweets, maybe so, but her dad was pretty mean when he was drunk. Maybe he had something to do with her losing teeth somehow, and she just doesn't want to tell us that because he's our grandpap?

No, it probably was the candy; she has quite the sweet tooth. When we get hungry before supper, and it's going to be a while before the meal is ready, sometimes she gets tired of us moaning about how badly we are starving, and she makes us a sugar bread snack. Mom puts margarine on a piece of white bread and then spoons sugar on top. It cuts the edge off our hunger and quits our complaining, but it's not exactly tooth-friendly food.

Mom pointed over to the right, "There it is, Hon." Mom is always Dad's co-pilot when we go somewhere new; she is good with maps and gives Dad directions, so he doesn't get us lost. When we pulled into the parking lot me and Danny were super excited; we had heard about the chariot race from Terry Macintosh, who lived across the hall from us. He had seen the movie a couple weeks before at another Army base.

Terry had a crew-cut of light blonde hair and the biggest head I've ever seen on a kid, but he was lots of fun. He had the games Mouse Trap and Operation, which we played in his room, and he was the third member of a comic book club that Danny started. Danny was the president, me and Terry took turns being the vice-president or the treasurer—since we didn't have any club money, no one wanted to be the treasurer.

We would bring some of our comics to our clubhouse, which was in a corner under the basement stairwell of our apartment building, near the cages with everyone's storage stuff and the laundry machines. We would share comics and talk about how great they were. Sometimes we would pretend we were our favorite superheroes fighting some villain—we took turns being the villain.

A year or two later, we actually found Terry living in Leesville as his dad got stationed at Ft. Polk, too. All of us went to visit his family one day in a trailer court. I couldn't believe how small the rooms were; when he showed us some of his toys, he could hardly open the built-in dresser drawer without hitting the bed. He seemed to like the trailer, and there was something cool about having wheels on your house, but it was too cramped for me. I don't know how Grandma Ludwiczak can stand her tiny one.

We played outside mostly by a small pond in the middle of the trailer court. Tall scruffy-looking pine trees surrounded half of the pond, and a muddy dirt road circled the green water. We found jellied strings of tadpole eggs and cute baby frogs. There were at least a dozen or two. They were the color and size of chocolate Necco wafers, hopping in the wet mud by the shore.

I sat in the car on the way home thinking about how different things were in Louisiana than when we played together with Terry in Germany, how time changes things, how life never stops moving—until your life ends, I guess. We never saw Terry again after that day.

It was a mild evening, but Mom made us take jackets out of the car for later since it was such a long movie. Dad was smoking one last cigarette as we walked across the parking lot. The theater was much newer and bigger than the one at our base. There was a long line of people outside; they all seemed excited too, as they talked and smoked on the sidewalk. The whole front of the theater was glass, and inside the carpet was deep red, like blood.

Once the movie started, I fell in love with Charleton Heston. It was the first time I had seen him, and he was so handsome and strong-looking, so sure and confidant about everything he did. I'd love to look something like him when I'm grown-up. Our hair is about the same color, though mine is lighter, similar cheekbones as well.

There was a girl in Copperas Cove with long brown hair who reminded me of Charleton Heston, the way her cheekbones were, her nose, her wide smile, and how her hair swept back from her forehead. I only saw her a couple of times, but I was smitten. I called her Charlotte Heston in my mind.

The first time I saw her, Charlotte was shopping with her mom in Piggly Wiggly wearing a blue cowboy shirt with white strips hanging from the pocket flaps and jeans. Piggly Wiggly is a big grocery store with a giant picture of a funny-looking pig over the entrance. It was mine and Danny's favorite store, mostly because we liked the name and the pig picture, but also because it was full of good food, snacks, and candy.

I was cashing in empty pop bottles at the check-out counter. We got two cents a bottle, so we would go around Copperas Cove collecting bottles all over, wipe any dirt or gunk off, and turn them in for candy money—sometimes they would refuse a bottle or two because they didn't sell that kind at their store.

Charlotte didn't even see me, but she was taking my breath away. I was trying to convince the mean-looking clerk that we bought all the bottles there, and Charlotte was looking at a girl's magazine in the next check-out line. When she turned sideways, the resemblance to Charleton Heston was especially striking—she could have passed for his daughter.

The other time Charlotte was just walking across a field by the library. She was wearing white shorts and a green shirt, with her Charleton Heston face making my heart flip—almost as much as it does when I watch Haley Mills and listen to her sweet British accent. I followed her for a little bit trying to get up the courage to talk to her. She had slender strong-looking legs like she was used to running. When she turned her head in my direction, my courage faded, and I ducked into the library. That was the last time I saw Charlotte, but I'm hopeful I might see her again after our trip. If I do, I'll say something nice to her—I hope I can anyway.

Ben-Hur was powerful, no doubt the best movie I ever saw, and full of the Mystery. I never forgot one sentence from the beginning of the movie. One Roman soldier told another about this son of a carpenter going about teaching people that "God is near, in every man." After the movie, I thought about how God could be inside everybody—talk about a Mystery.

The most amazing scene was when Ben-Hur was in a chain gang walking through a desert. They were all stumbling from thirst. The guard let everyone have a gourd full of water except Ben-Hur. He collapsed and laid on the ground gasping, about to give up, it seemed, as they showed Jesus' back with his long brown hair coming out of an open-air carpenter's shop. Jesus walked across the sand, knelt, and then cradled Ben-Hur's head, pouring water over it and smoothing his hair. Jesus helped Ben-Hur take a long drink from the gourd.

We never got to see Jesus' face in the movie, but when Ben-Hur looked into it, something moved him to reach out and stroke Jesus' hand gently, the same way Jesus had touched him. Then the mean guard came swaggering back with a whip threatening Jesus for giving Ben-Hur a cool drink. The expression on the guard's face as he looked at Jesus was remarkable like he couldn't understand what he was seeing, but he was awed, shamed, and powerless against it. The guard turned away from Jesus and cracked his whip for the prisoners to get moving again.

There was also a scene showing Jesus surrounded by hundreds of people drawn to come and see him. They were scattered around a hill just sitting on the grass or big rocks, all their eyes eagerly looking at Jesus, waiting quietly for him to speak to them about God.

They must have wanted to hear the truth from Jesus about how to live, love God and get to heaven. I wonder what that would've been like in real life. I wish I could have been there. I would have gotten up as close as I could to Jesus so I could look into his face and see what Ben-Hur and the guard saw.

Later, Ben Hur found his mother and sister in a giant cave for lepers with his girlfriend's help. They had become lepers by being imprisoned unjustly years before. Ben-Hur took them out of the cave, and then his girlfriend urged the two women to seek Jesus to find the peace she felt when she saw Jesus and heard him speak. When they got to the city, they heard that the Romans had arrested Jesus. They rushed to find him and managed to see Jesus carrying his cross up steep stone steps, but then he stumbled and fell.

Ben-Hur rushed up to help Jesus but was pushed away by a guard into a small stone water basin. Ben-Hur grabbed a gourd out of the basin and stumbled over to Jesus, offering a drink. Once again, he looked into Jesus's face, and their hands touched before Ben-Hur got shoved to the side. What did Ben-Hur see in Jesus's face that moved him so? What mystery did Jesus have, or was it that Jesus was the Mystery?

When Jesus made it to the top of a hill, they nailed him to a cross; the sky was dark and purplish behind him, yet glowing with a strange light. People stood around weeping and wringing their hands. Ben-Hur had followed and watched as Jesus hung there dying. How could people be so cruel to do that to him, someone so full of the Mystery, someone so holy? I felt wounded somehow, too.

Then Ben-Hur's mother, sister, and girlfriend, who were waiting below in the shelter of a stone arch, saw the sky light up before a dark storm came. The storm struck after Jesus' death; when it died down, they saw that they were miraculously cured of their leprosy by Jesus or God and made beautiful again. The mother and daughter looked and touched each other's faces in joy. Later, Ben-Hur found them transformed after he made his way home and was reunited with them. Ben-Hur had been seeking revenge against the Romans all through the movie for what they did to him and his family, but Ben-

Hur told his girlfriend that right before he died, Jesus had said, "Forgive them, Father, for they know not what they do."

Ben-Hur added, "And I felt his voice take the sword out of my hand." How could Ben-Hur ever be the same again after seeing the miracle of his loved ones made whole again and after being with Jesus? He had to believe in God with all his heart; he had to change.

I came out of the movie theater stunned by what I had seen. The cool dark air seemed so clear, fresh, and sparkling somehow. I couldn't talk. I just breathed in the night and felt something precious inside of me, like I was different somehow, too. I curled up in the dark of the back seat, looking at stars, letting scenes from the movie sink into me, feeling a sense of wonder and a quiet comfort.

No one is talking. I glance up to see the preacher close his Bible and walk to his seat. People are starting to stand up in the back and walk up the aisle towards Uncle Billy. A line forms as men and women begin to pay their last respects to him. We are in the second row, so we won't have to go for a bit yet.

I look across the aisle, and I see Aunt Cora and Uncle Chick, and in front of them, Aunt Elaine, Leonard, and their four kids; the baby seems to be sleeping. Darla has a dark blue dress on with tiny white polka dots. I wish I could be sitting next to her, my shoulder against hers, holding her hand. Maybe things wouldn't seem so sad then.

After *Ben-Hur,* things changed for us. We never did go to church, but Danny and me decided we wanted to go to Bible School for a few days during summer vacation. They had us color pictures and make folded stand up displays after the teacher read us stories, mostly from The Old Testament, like David and Goliath, Samson and Delilah, and Lot and his wife—not so much about Jesus, who I was really interested in, but it was OK.

After Bible School one afternoon, we saw the German peddler pushing his big cart stacked full of all kinds of toys, gadgets, and utensils—he came on Post from time to time, just like the German chimney sweeps did, all dressed in black with their top hats and stiff wire-bristle brushes. It was good luck to touch their soot smeared clothes, which they usually let kids do. They smelled like coal dust and sharp musty leather. We ran over to see what the peddler had and discovered gray plastic swords and small shields; the swords even had scabbards that you could loop through your belt.

Me and Danny ran home after asking the price and begged Mom to give us the money to buy them. She finally gave in when we got on our knees and promised to do extra chores around our apartment. We caught the peddler near the edge of Post and had a swordfight right away. I always imagined myself to be Sir Lancelot or Ben-Hur, the Ben-Hur who fought before changing at the end of the movie. After Jesus, Ben-Hur must've given up sword fighting and become a man of peace.

Mom and Dad bought us each Bibles for Christmas; they had a color picture of Jesus on the cover surrounded by children and color pictures scattered inside. I kept the Bible near my bed and tried to read it from time to time, but mostly I just liked looking at Jesus' picture on the cover and the colored pages of Jesus in The New Testament.

Jesus' pictures didn't really match the face I figured he must have in *Ben-Hur*; in my imagination, his face is full of some holy light, the Mystery pouring out of his eyes is making people kneel in love just from looking at him. The Bible pictures helped me remember Jesus, though, and a little of what I had felt watching *Ben-Hur*.

Later on, I got a small black pocket version of the New Testament. It didn't have any pictures, but because it was small, it was more inviting to read somehow, and I could carry it around in my pocket. Plus, it was all about Jesus, his life, what he said and did; no other Bible stories got in the way.

Mom and Dad also bought both of us an angel picture. Mine was prettier, with her golden hair and lovely wings watching over a boy, and a girl in a red, black, and white dress, walk across a rickety bridge above rushing water. I wonder if I had an angel watching me sometimes in my life. I must have when I fell out of my bunk bed or almost got run over by that tractor-trailer truck in the alley.

Not long after *Ben-Hur*, I also found a cross with Jesus on it, a silver figure nailed to dark wood in the middle. I imagined that the wood was a small piece from Jesus' cross. It was lying in the big field next to the helicopter pad and a large puddle that always covered over with ice in the winter. I was caving the ice in with big rocks and my black rubber boots when I saw the cross stuck in some mud; I couldn't believe my luck.

Or maybe it wasn't luck. It's strange sometimes how things I think about seem to bring stuff to me at the right time that's somehow connected to what I was thinking about. I wonder if that happens to other people, too.

Mom gave me one of the chains in her seashell-covered jewelry box to put the cross on; I loved wearing it. One day though, months later, I came in hot and tired from playing outside all day, and at bedtime, I noticed the cross was missing. I cried quietly till I slept. I never found it again. Maybe someone someday will be lucky enough to find it like I did, or maybe someone's heel smushed it deep into some mud where it will stay hidden forever.

Losing my cross was almost as bad as when I had to give back my holy medal. I was playing marbles with Walter, who I liked, and Perry, who was a bit of a bully. He was from Puerto Rico, with light brown skin and curly hair. His brother, Hector, was a bully, too. Hector was in the same class as Danny and sat behind him. Danny said Hector was always picking at him, tapping his ears with a pencil or something. One day Danny got so mad he just had it, and he turned around and smacked Hector right on his nose and bloodied it.

Danny said Hector never bothered him after that. I was surprised that Danny did that as he's not the fighting kind; he must have really been holding it in for a while. It's also a wonder he didn't get in trouble for smacking Hector, usually, the good kids get caught when they defend themselves against bullies; they aren't as good at being sneaky.

Well, Perry made a deal with me. He had this really cool holy medal that I just had to have. It was almost the same size as a Ben Franklin half-dollar, and it showed some saint walking across water, with a halo around his head (I think it was Peter). I managed to get it in a trade with Perry for eight of my best marbles, including my favorite spaghetti marbles.

I was thrilled, and I carried that medal in my pocket for a few weeks, rubbing it and taking it out every so often to admire it or just to make sure that I still had it in my pocket. There was just something about that medal that felt holy and made me feel closer to God somehow.

Then I made a dumb mistake. I was at school bragging about the trade I had made with Perry, gloating like a fool. Perry overheard me, and I guess he realized I had gotten the better deal, so he wanted the medal back. I said no way; we made a deal. I headed for home, afraid he might try to beat me up and take it.

Perry actually followed me home and knocked on our door after I closed it in front of his face. I asked Mom not to open the door; it was just some creepy kid, but after he knocked again, she opened it. He told Mom that I had his medal and he wanted it back. I explained to Mom what the deal was, and I expected her to back me up, but she didn't. She told me to give the medal back. Perry handed me some marbles I didn't even look at, and I had to place my medal in his cruel hand. I was crushed.

When Mom's birthday came that March, I was looking through the PX with what little money I had, trying to find a special gift. I wanted to get her something other than the usual bath crystals or Turtle chocolates she liked. To tell the truth, I especially enjoy giving gifts that I like myself; it makes the present feel more special. Then I saw what I wanted, a painting of Jesus sitting at a table with his disciples. Jesus sat in the middle, and they were about to eat a meal on the long table before them. The picture cost two dollars and eleven cents, four cents more than what I had on me.

A lady clerk with tall, teased yellow hair told me it was called *The Last Supper*, painted by Leonardo da Vinci. It was beautiful; the colors were striking, and Jesus looked magnificent. The painting was attached to a thick 3" x 8" shiny piece of dark wood. A thin sheet of glass covered the front of it, so it was easy to clean. When I counted out my money and told her it was for my mom, I must have had a pitiful look on my face. She said, "That's close enough; Merry Christmas. I'm sure your Mom will like it."

Mom loved it. She still hangs it up in every place we live. She also has a white hanging plate with a picture of Jesus' head and shoulders in the middle. The edge of the plate is gold, and Jesus' robe is red and white. She's always had it hanging near her bed over the years. I don't know where she got it, but it must be special to her to have kept it for this long.

Mom and Dad both believe in God, but for some reason, they don't talk about God, and they never go to church. They just take it for granted that we all believe in God, and God will take care of us. I think it's because Dad works so hard, and when he gets a chance to sleep in on Sunday mornings, he takes it. He likes lazing about, sipping coffee, eating a leisurely breakfast, and reading the Sunday paper. So does Mom.

It's funny how one experience can change a person's life, and after it happens, somehow, things move forward in a different way than before. Going to see *Ben-Hur* was like that for me. I've always had the Mystery with me; it's part of who I am, of how I experience the world. But after *Ben-Hur*, Jesus somehow became a piece of the Mystery, too. I didn't feel like singing hymns or praying all the time, but the wonder of Jesus' life sank into my heart and merged into the beauty of the Mystery around me.

Chapter XV

Soldiers

Dad's getting up. Our turn to look at Uncle Billy for the last time is coming. Across the aisle, Aunt Cora is peeking over the pew at Aunt Elaine's baby, who must have woke up. Aunt Cora is making silly faces and sticking her finger out, which the baby has grabbed onto. His little hand is so tiny; I can still see half of Aunt Cora's finger poking out of his hand. I'm surprised he hasn't cried much; he's so helpless, so new. One life ends, and another one is just beginning; I hope it turns out better for him than it did for Uncle Billy.

I shuffle behind Dad, glancing over at Pap-Pap. He is holding onto Grandma's hand as they stand in the front row. How can he be so caring about Grandma, like he was still married to her? He must have tender feelings for her even though they are divorced, or maybe it's just because Pap-Pap is always kind to everybody.

I only saw him get mad once in my whole life. He had made me and Danny these cool hot-dog pillows out in his shop. It was when we came back from Germany, a few days after we gave him and Grandma Babe the cuckoo clock we brought for them. They put it up almost near the living room ceiling, on the wall across from the couch; being so high up and away from any furniture, the clock would be safe from cats trying to get the cuckoo or mess with the pine cones on the chains.

I guess the pillows were a welcome home present. They were awful fine presents, especially since Pap-Pap made them himself. Our pillows were waterproof because when I spilled something on mine, the water rolled off. Danny's was blue, and mine was red, our favorite colors at the time; they even had buttons sunken into them. (Nowadays, I'm leaning more towards green than red.)

The pillows are about as long as our arms and as wide as our hands. After our visit, we took them home—I still have my pillow, of course. I keep it in my room and use it as a bed pillow when I'm reading or a floor pillow when I play games. Sometimes I stand it up and pretend the pillow is a tall building or a tower, and then Garloo topples it over, crushing a green and brown village made out of Lincoln logs or some green army men.

When we first got our pillows, we were on Pap-Pap's flowered claw-footed couch watching *Bonanza*. Hoss was my favorite because he was so big and strong, yet gentle at the same time. He had a sweet smile (made special by him missing some front teeth) and a soft heart, but he could be fierce if he had to be, scowling and wearing his tall white ten-gallon hat as they rode after outlaws. Grandma Babe liked Little Joe the most; she said he was prettier than most girls. I couldn't agree with Grandma; I could see he was handsome all right, but not prettier than girls. Danny liked Adam the best, who dressed in black all the time, and was Pa Cartwright's oldest son. They were all lightning-fast drawing their six guns, protecting their giant ranch, the Ponderosa, from the bad guys who wanted some of what they had.

During a commercial, one of us whacked the other with his pillow; I'm not sure who, and soon we were going at it, bonking each other with our new pillows. Dad was in the kitchen getting a drink, and Mom was talking to Grandma. Pap-Pap hopped out of his easy chair and snatched the pillows out of our hands.

"I'm disappointed in you, boys. You don't deserve these right now," he said.

He didn't even raise his voice, but him saying that hurt my heart even more than Dad's belt hurt my butt. I could tell he was mad because his usual relaxed and friendly expression was gone, replaced by piercing eyes and a slight frown. Then he put the pillows in the other room out of our reach. My face felt as red as a beet, and my ears were hot from shame.

A while later, after he saw the looks on our faces, I guess, he gave us back the pillows, and we shared some of his oatmeal cookies that he always keeps in a tin by his chair. He also gave us cans of root beer with straws. Pap-Pap couldn't stay mad long; he's just naturally happy inside. His face soon became relaxed and eager about watching his western again. He even started singing a song later when the Cartwrights galloped across the Ponderosa after the bad guys.

Besides always having oatmeal cookies handy, Pap-Pap is predictable in other ways, too. Pap-Pap always wears blue jeans, a big buckled belt, and a white T-shirt. Except in the winter when he always wears a long-sleeved flannel shirt. If Pap-Pa is working, though, he takes off the flannel and shows his white T-shirt—sort of like Superman revealing his ever-present costume when he goes into action.

If Pap-Pap is watching TV or a movie, chances are it's a western. He never gets tired of them; Grandma Babe seems to like them, too. Hopalong Cassidy and Randolf Scott are his favorite cowboys. In pictures that I've seen of Pap-Pap when he was younger, with darker hair and more of it, he kind of looks a little like a very short Randolf Scott. Pap-Pap also likes the old singing cowboys, Gene Autry, Tex Ritter, and a lot more from all those old B westerns. He sometimes sings along with them, loud and clear; he seems to know all the words to their corny songs.

Of course, he thinks John Wayne is great, too, especially when John Wayne was younger in movies like *Stagecoach*. He likes *Gunsmoke* even more than *Bonanza* because he thinks Matt Dillon is the best sheriff ever and that his deputy, Festus, is a real authentic-looking cowboy who makes Pap-Pap laugh with his talk and how he makes such funny expressions on his face. Pap-Pap says Festus is even better than Chester, whose place Festus took after a few years.

I must say *Gunsmoke* does have some really gripping episodes; it's a well-done show all right, and one thing you can always count on with each show is that Marshall Dillon will do what is decent and right every time. He's a lot like Pap-Pap that way.

One day Pap-Pap was driving down the hill into downtown New Ken to buy some electrical parts for one of his machines. Danny and me tagged along. After he bought the parts at a hardware store, where the guy behind the counter talked with Pap-Pap about how he and Uncle Clarence were doing, Pap-Pap stopped at White Tower to buy a bag of burgers.

They were fifteen cents apiece. Pap-Pap thinks White Tower makes the best burgers because they always grill the buns for him without having to ask. I guess they know him pretty well there. Grilled buns do make burgers more delicious.

After they stuffed all the burgers into a white bag, we walked outside, turned the corner, and saw an old man sitting against the side of the white bricks. He had the skinny wasted look of an alcoholic. He was wearing old smelly worn clothes, had dirty greasy looking hair, and wrinkled tan skin from being outside so much, I guess. He glanced our way as Pap-Pap walked over and squatted next to him.

Pap-Pap took two burgers out of the bag and offered them. "Tommy, I need a little help here. I bought too many burgers, and I don't want them going to waste. Now, how about eating these for me, c'mon now, here you go," Pap-Pap placed the burgers in Tommy's gnarled hands and stood up.

The man stared vacantly for a moment, and then he smiled, showing ugly yellow and brown teeth, "Ok, Harvey, if you say so."

"I do, by crackey. You take care now." Pap-Pap patted him on the shoulder and slipped a dollar bill into Tommy's shirt pocket.

When we got in the car, Danny asked, "Do you know that man Pap-Pap?"

"Yes, I do, kind of, you see, Tommy used to be a soldier during the war, but a shell got a little too close and rattled his brains, and then he went downhill. He spends most of his time by the Tower, so I try to buy some extra burgers for him when I go there. It pains my heart to see a good man end up like that."

On the way back to Pap-Pap's, I kept thinking about that man being so lost. He fought for our country like he was supposed to, yet look what happened to him. Who knows what kind of life he could have had without that shell messing him up.

I also thought about other people I'd seen in my life living on street corners, mostly driving through Pittsburgh, New York, or other big cities. I always keep away from them when we get out of the car, but I must admit I've felt disgusted, disturbed, and a little scared by how they live. I'm sure they didn't plan on ending up on a street corner or in an alley when they were kids like me, but there they are. I don't want that happening to me or anybody I know. Maybe if I knew their stories, how they got the way they are like I do Tommy, they wouldn't give me the creeps, and I'd just feel sorry for them, too. I'm sure Jesus would.

Another thing Pap-Pap loves is antique cars. We've often bought him models of antique cars for Christmas or birthdays—the kind that are already put together and painted nice, and he puts them out on bookshelves or desktops. I wouldn't be surprised if he plays with them when nobody is around.

Dad, Danny, and me took Pap-Pap to an antique car show once for his birthday. He was as excited as a little kid, climbing inside cars when he was allowed to, making comments about how fine different things were and how he used to drive a car like this one or that one.

He sat in the plush leather driver's seat of a green Packard for the longest time of any of the cars. He was rubbing the steering wheel and looking off in the distance—to some other time, I imagined, as I sat in the back seat. The car had a good smell from the leather; it reminded me of my baseball glove. Dad and Danny had gone on ahead to look at a banana and white-colored Mercury next to the Packard.

"Did you have a car like this one too, Pap-Pap?" I asked.

"Oh . . . yes, it was a dandy all right, a dream to drive; it feels good just to hold the steering wheel, and touch the seat, ain't that the most comfortable seat you ever sat on? Baby and I drove around in one like this when I was courting her in Kansas. Then we drove it back to Pennsylvania when we moved."

"What happened to the car? I asked.

"We kept it for some time, but eventually it got wore out like most things do, broke down, and that was it."

Dad stuck his head in the window. "Hey, you guys up for a hot dog?"

"You betcha, by crackey!" Pap-Pap said.

They had all the cars parked in big grass fields close to the Allegheny River in Oakmont. Every once in a while, we could hear the horn of a barge going under the Oakmont Bridge. Sometimes the whining whirr of speedboat engines and the smacking sound of their boat bellies slapping the water would reach us as we walked from one car to another. We stayed there for a long time, eating hot dogs with mustard and onions that they sold at the show and drinking pink lemonade, while Pap-Pap gave each car his careful appraisal.

Dad nudges me, and I see that it's our turn to say goodbye to Uncle Billy. Dad is holding Mom's arm; Danny looks sad too, like everybody. The bottom half of the casket is closed. Is that normal, or did something happen to Uncle Billy's legs that they don't want us to see?

Mom has a few tears dripping down from the corner of her eye as she and Dad pause in front of Uncle Billy. Mom doesn't have a black dress, so she is wearing a dark blue one and carrying a black purse. She snaps the silver snap open and pulls out a tissue; I can see it has some red lipstick on it, but she uses a clean corner to wipe her eyes. Dad rests his hand on Uncle Billy's chest for a moment, rubbing it gently. His eyes are shiny with tears, but nothing comes out; he looks like he is thinking about something, probably some special memory of his brother.

Danny's face is a bit pale, but that's normal for him. He gives Uncle Billy a small wave like he is saying goodbye. While I take my last look next to Danny, I wonder if they have french fries and ketchup up in heaven. Maybe Uncle Billy is looking down at us right now, sharing a big bowl with Tequila and Jesus.

When we turn around to start leaving the church, I see some soldiers standing in the back, near where people sign the guest book. They have on dress blues. Each of them has a blue hat with a black bill in one hand and a pair of white gloves in the other. All of them are very tall, with shaved heads and grim-looking faces.

I wonder if they are army buddies of Uncle Billy. Did any of them see him die in Vietnam? Maybe one of them carried Uncle Billy out of the jungle and tried to get him to a hospital. Probably not though, they might have to do this at other soldier funerals, too. That wouldn't be a pleasant job to have, going to funerals all the time, but soldiers don't have much say in what they have to do.

Dad took me and Danny to Tigerland once. It was Dad's day off, but he had to pick something up from headquarters, and since we were going fishing for the first time afterward, he took us along.

Our fishing adventure was a disaster, though. Dad bought us black and white Zebco fishing rods and reels for something we could all do together, but me and Danny found out we didn't really care for fish fishing; (crawdad fishing was totally different and great for me) we couldn't get over the hooks going into the poor fishes' mouths. Once a hook went into a fishes' eye—horrible, and it turns out Dad didn't like fishing either because the fish smell was too much for him.

It was a giant lake, so we walked around it, trying to find good spots to fish. There were a few dead fish washed up on the shore of the lake, bloated and white like they'd been lying there for days. Dad walked past them as quick as he could. Dad can't even stand the smell of an orange being peeled in the same room when we watch TV. The hot sun reflecting off the water made the fish smell even stronger.

Danny got his finger pricked by a hook when he was trying to put corn on it. He had to wrap a Kleenex around his fingertip to stop the bleeding. After I cast my line once, I got snagged on a tree branch under the water. Dad yanked my pole so hard to free it that the branch popped up, the line snapped, and his loafer slipped on the slimy mud shore right into the lake. "God damn it to hell," Dad said. Finally, we all had enough of fishing and went home.

So the rods stayed in the garage after that, and we just never got around to going again. On the way home from the lake, though, we were thrilled when we saw a roadrunner for the first time. It was running alongside the road over the rocky sand. God, it was breathtaking how fast he zipped down the road—no wonder the coyote in the cartoons could never catch the Roadrunner—"beep, beep." A real roadrunner isn't that big, though; they are more like the size of a falcon than a turkey.

A few miles down the road, there was an apple cider stand under a big tree with four or five cars parked in front; it must have been good cider that people were eager to buy. Dad pulled over, and we all walked into the shade. A man with a big tan cowboy hat offered Dad a jug of cider to look at.

"This is the best cider in the county, Mister. Drink it slow, though, so you can savor the taste, and let it chill first before you open it." The cider was brown-looking and cloudy; it seemed like bits of apple were floating inside. When we got home, Dad did chill it till after dinner. The cider was as smooth and quenching as could be, and the apple smell and taste was like heaven. Dad, Danny and me must have drunk a little too much, though, because the next day, we all spent a lot of time in the bathroom.

Well, before we went to the lake and found out that fishing wasn't for us, we entered Post and drove past row after row of green and white buildings until we came to another gate by a large PX. This giant word TIGERLAND was on top of the gate; a snarling painted tiger was crouching on the word. As we drove under the tiger, Danny asked, "What's Tigerland, Dad?"

Dad pulled his cigarette out of his mouth and pointed it out the window at the gate, "Once a soldier passes through this gate, it means he has orders to go to Vietnam where your Uncle Billy is. Tigerland is their last home in the States. They won't go out of this gate until their training is over. Then they'll be bussed straight to the airfield where they'll board a plane and fly to Vietnam or the coast so they can take a troopship over. By the way, I heard they are using the Darby now—the ship you went to Germany on—to transport troops to Vietnam."

At the top of a hill, Dad turned off the road into a small parking lot. Down the other side were hundreds of soldiers doing jumping jacks. Some were short, some tall, some wore glasses, some had different skin colors, but all of them had shaved heads, white T-shirts, green fatigue pants, and black army boots that made them all look pretty much the same.

We walked down the hill around them towards a green brick building with a rounded metal roof. Dad nodded or smiled at some of the soldiers we walked by. A drill sergeant was on a raised platform in front with his hands on his hips. He dressed like everyone else except for his Smokey the Bear hat like Dad has.

When we got closer to the front, he yelled, "Well, well, lookee what we got here, men! Sergeant Gamble brought his boys over to see what kind of soldiers you are! I think we ought to give them a little demonstration, to show them what you're made of. Don't you?"

"YES, DRILL SERGEANT!"

"What was that, ladies?"

"YES, DRILL SERGEANT!!"

"On your backs and assume the dying cockroach position!"

The soldiers flopped onto their backs and stuck their legs and arms about six inches in the air, wiggling and waving them about as if they were dying cockroaches.

They were all kind of half-laughing about it then, but by now, all those soldiers are in Vietnam, sweating and fighting in that jungle. Who knows what they are going through, what they might have to do. I wonder how many of them will end up like Uncle Billy.

Dad has a platoon he's in charge of training, about fifty soldiers, but he works with other drill sergeants and trainers, too. One day, not long after visiting Tigerland, while we drove to Ft. Polk, I asked Dad what he does with his soldiers to get them ready.

"No one's ever really ready for war, but here are some of the things we do: we march them to the firing range where they learn to shoot; run them through the obstacle course; take them to different classes about weapons, like grenade throwing, shooting M-60's (machine guns) and bazookas, setting explosives, wearing gas masks, how to take their weapons apart, clean them and put them back together quickly, classes on first aid. We show them how to dig a foxhole, crawl on their bellies with their weapon, and camouflage themselves. They learn to bivouac outside for days at a time; we teach them hand-to-hand combat and to march as a unit.

"We also wake them up in the morning, march them to the mess hall, inspect their lockers, their equipment, and many other things besides. In short, we try to teach them what it means to be a soldier and be part of a unit that depends on each other.

"You know what, I sure do enjoy teaching them, especially in a classroom situation; sometimes when I'm teaching, I think maybe I should have been a teacher instead of a soldier—too late for that now though, but I do enjoy seeing them get what I'm trying to teach. Altogether their training lasts a couple of months, but it's not really long enough to prepare them for what's ahead."

I think about what Dad told me then as I stare at the soldiers in blue. They are trying not to look at everyone in the funeral; they probably don't want to intrude on us paying our respects. A few of them have their heads bowed; some look sad, some bored; some seem to be thoughtful.

Everything Dad does with his soldiers adds up to a lot of time that Dad spends with them. In all that time, he must get to know what they're like, how they're different from each other. Dad probably jokes around some with them, too, I imagine; Dad likes people to like him. So he must start to care about them. How could he not? After their training is over, they all get sent to Vietnam, and he gets a new platoon.

That's probably part of what Dad was talking to Mom about the other day in the kitchen, why he is thinking about getting out of the Army; it's not only because of Uncle Billy getting killed. It must be hard on Dad to keep sending kids— as he calls them, over there, knowing that some of them will not be coming back. Dad pretends he's tough, but he has a soft heart inside. I wonder if Dad ever finds out which kids from his platoons get killed in that jungle. It might be better not to know.

We walk past the soldiers and go outside into the bright sun. I hear a bird singing from somewhere; cars are whooshing by on the street. Everyone is getting into their cars. Darla is ahead of us, climbing into the back of a green station wagon with wooden panels on the doors; I hear Grandma sobbing behind us.

Me and Danny climb into the back seat. Dad has both his hands tight on the blue steering wheel, staring at the entrance to the funeral parlor. Mom looks like she expects something to happen. Pap-Pap and Grandpap Steve walk past, helping Grandma to the expensive funeral parlor car behind the big black hearse. Grandma slowly gets in first as we wait. Everything is real quiet.

In a few minutes, the soldiers come out of the building carrying Uncle Billy's coffin, three of them on each side, with their white-gloved hands. An American flag covers the coffin. I can hear the soldier's shiny black shoes clicking on the sidewalk. Two more soldiers are in front, opening the black doors of the hearse.

As they start loading the coffin into the hearse, Dad lets out a moan and smashes the dashboard with his fist. His shoulders start shaking, and for the second time ever, I hear Dad crying, sobbing like Grandma.

Mom puts her arm around him gently. Me and Danny are frozen. Danny peeks at me with his worried look, afraid to look at Dad. The dashboard is caved in, and as Dad's sobs ease up, he says, "He was my baby brother, Joan." I look away after Dad raises his head. He has tears on his cheeks, and I don't want him to think I'm staring.

The first time I saw Dad cry was at the movie theater on base in Bad Kissingen. We'd all gone to see a movie called *The Black Zoo*. The preview looked good a few days before, but they must have crammed all the movie's action into the preview to make it seem exciting; it was the only minute of the whole movie worth watching. Mom said it was a melodrama. I'd say it was one of the worst movies I ever saw. Some crazy doctor (The same actor had played a mad scientist in *Konga*, who injected a chimp with something that turned it into a giant gorilla.) had these lions, tigers, leopards, and a regular gorilla murdering people at night in this gloomy zoo.

The movie plodded along in dark night scenes. We could hardly make out what was happening because of all the black shadows at night, and the movie was so boring it was making me half-asleep and depressed. Danny kept rolling his eyeballs at me like he couldn't believe how bad it was. Finally, we could escape into the lobby, but it turned out to be much worse in the lobby than watching the movie.

The short movie theater guy with the crew cut started talking to people in the lobby as they came blinking out of the theater. When they heard what he said, people looked shocked, some of them burst into tears. A few of them shouted in surprise or disbelief. Someone had shot President Kennedy—in the head. People started talking, asking questions in hushed voices.

Dad looked devastated; tears trickled down his face; a soft low moan was coming out of his mouth. He thought President Kennedy was the best president ever. Mom's face was all red and crumpled, with her lips quivering. Danny was looking at me like he couldn't believe what was happening. Dad grabbed Mom and hugged her tight. It felt like the world was ending.

No one says anything during the short drive to the cemetery or walking between the gravestones to the giant hole someone has dug up. Grandma, Pap-Pap, and Grandpap Steve are right next to the coffin. Grandma's short gray curls are poking out from under her black pill hat. Pap-Pap's wispy white hair is blowing from the breeze. The preacher is talking again as we all stand around the casket in a horseshoe shape. It's closed now, no more wind on Uncle Billy's face, ever.

Everyone's heads are bowed down, except mine—and Darla's. She is across from me, sharing her shy, sweet smile, not caring who sees. It's the first time we've looked into each other's eyes since that day last year at the creek. I must be smiling back because she smiles even sweeter. She looks so pretty in her blue polka dot dress; the wind is playing with her long hair. I never saw her in a dress before. She's holding a small white purse. We're just standing here enjoying each other's company; nobody even notices us, of course. I don't feel guilty for smiling; I need her smile right now. Maybe she needs mine, too.

After a while, the preacher stops talking, and the soldiers march over, lining up off to the side, near a big old oak tree. There are seven of them looking so sharp in their blue uniforms and white gloves. They all have a few colored ribbons on their chests. Each of them has a rifle in their hands. A colored sergeant, standing apart from the seven, with a rocker under his stripes, like Dad has, barks an order.

The soldiers raise the rifles to their shoulders, pointing them high to the sky. The sergeant grunts something else that I can't make out, and the soldiers draw back the bolts on their brown guns and then snap the bolts shut.

"FIRE! . . ."

"FIRE! . . ."

"FIRE!"

Twenty-one shots fire in honor of Uncle Billy—one shot for every year of his life. My ears are ringing; there's a smell in the air—like when we smash rolls of caps with a big rock, and I feel a tear sliding past my nose. Bluish smoke floats above the soldier's heads.

The sergeant and one other soldier approach the coffin. They take the flag off gently. Then they carefully and slowly fold it tight, working it back and forth into a triangle. After he inspects it, the sergeant puts the flag into a plastic case and snaps it shut. He walks over and bows down in front of Grandma, holding out the flag to her. Grandma hugs the flag to her breast as Pap-Pap holds onto her elbow. Grandma isn't the only one crying now.

Chapter XVI

Mother

Dad is quiet as we drive away from the cemetery. Other cars are following us; Uncle Chick's green Buick is in front. I can see Aunt Cora looking behind to see if we're keeping up. She gives us a slight wave; I wave back, and so does Mom. I hear Dad's Zippo click. He shoots a double-barreled blast of smoke out of his nostrils and catches me looking at him from the rear-view mirror. He tries to smile and gives me his wink like everything is okay. I smile and lean my head back against the seat, letting my body relax as the car rolls along.

Danny is looking out his window, and so is Mom. We pass a pond off to the right with plenty of shade trees around it. I see a few kids along the shore with fishing poles propped up by sticks. Two of them have gloves on and are tossing a baseball back and forth as they wait for their rods to bounce from a fish. An older man is walking with his Irish Setter snuffling along the shore. The dog must have been splashing in the pond because the bottom of its coat is all wet looking. It's just a lazy summer's day for everybody else. Life is going on just as it always does; one person's death doesn't slow anything down.

A teenager and his blonde-haired girlfriend, sitting on the trunk of their car at a gas station, turn from their Coke bottles to look at us and the other funeral cars passing by. Everyone knows what those purple flags on car antennas mean.

Mom turns around, "We're going to a church now to eat, so if you're hungry, there will be plenty of food. Do either of you want something to drink before we get there?"

"I'm okay, Mom, thanks anyway," says Danny.

I just shake my head as I don't feel much like talking right now.

"How about you, Hon, care for a Pepsi or anything?"

"Thanks, dear, but I'll just wait till we get there."

Mom goes back to looking out the window like me and Danny. The sound of rubber rolling along the concrete and the soft whooshing of air outside the windows fills the silence. Everyone seems content to be quiet.

Cornfields take over, high and green on both sides of the road. Tucked away under floppy green leaves, I can see corn silk spilling out the tops of sturdy ears. How could Grandma Babe smoke stuff like that? There's no way it could taste good. I wish she was here; I sure could use one of her smiles. She would know what to say to make me feel better about the funeral. She believes in heaven, and she doesn't believe in the Devil, so she must not be afraid of dying so much. There's no Devil to get her, and she knows she will be with God in heaven because she's been good and kind to people and animals all her life. For her, what's to be afraid of?

I'm afraid, though; I don't want the Charcoal Man sneaking up and touching me with his cracked black hand of death. I love being alive, and I've got lots of things to see and do. I haven't even kissed a girl yet. The world is such a wonderful place to explore and experience, with the Mystery peeking out in beauty now and then, thrilling yet oozing peace. I'm not ready to go like Debbie and Uncle Billy, no way, but Debbie's death shows that being young is no protection from the Charcoal Man. There's nothing that says we have to be alive tomorrow. Death can happen to anybody, anywhere, anytime.

We pass by a fruit stand selling watermelons near the edge of the cornfields. There must be a hundred watermelons piled up under a tan canvas tarp shading them from the sun. A station wagon and a Chevy pick-up truck have pulled over. A family with a few kids and an elderly couple stop knocking melons to watch our convoy go by. The old man has a frown on his face as he looks up at us. Maybe he feels his time growing shorter now that he is older—who likes to see death rolling by. A little girl about Debbie's age points at us; she must wonder why so many cars in a row are driving past.

The corn and the watermelons fall behind as buildings pop up ahead. About a dozen people turn to look as we go through the main road of a small dusty town. There's a Murphy's Department Store with a hot dog stand outside. A few people have paper cups and hot dogs in their hands as we pass them. Flags from the Fourth of July are still hanging from the streetlights even though that was three weeks ago. Most people look, but no one is smiling or waving at us as we pass by.

We're a grim reminder of what's happened to some of their loved ones, what will happen to their children someday, what will happen to them. That preacher was right, "We are all on a journey of unknown duration. Time is relentless. . .," sooner or later, one way or the other, we are all going to end up like Uncle Billy, and there's not a thing we can do about it—except turn to God.

My head is resting sideways against the cushioned back seat. The blue and white checkered vinyl is nice and warm against my cheek; bright sun closes my eyes; soft bouncing of the car makes me drowsy. As we roll along, the jiggling of my body loosens me up and seems to be coaxing me to let go, to surrender, to become empty.

Bright whiteness floods out everything for a few moments; then, it focuses into pure white snow. The snow is covering the ground by some woods, pine trees mostly. Skinny dark trees scatter before the thick woods ahead. In front of some holly bushes, up a small rising slope, there's a figure sitting cross-legged on a blanket of snow—a white shaft of sunlight centers on the person. The snow is sparkling so much I have to squint a bit.

As I move closer, I can make out that it's a woman who seems to be gently waving at me to come to her. Something about her looks familiar. She's dressed all in white down to her ankles and has long black hair and dark brown skin, like a colored woman. An eagerness begins to well up in me as her features become clearer. I remember now. I have seen her before; I dreamt about her rocking me back when I was four or so. I couldn't see her face clearly then, but I can never forget how she made me feel; my leaping heart can't be wrong—it's her.

This doesn't seem like a dream, though; this feels real somehow, real as the wet snow trickling into the top of my sneaker. She has no shoes; her bare feet poke out of her white dress, resting on the snow as if the cold doesn't touch her at all. Her hair is parted in the middle, covering her ears, brushing against her cheeks, flowing behind her back.

God, she has the most beautiful face I've ever seen, her closed lips showing what a smile should look like, but it's her eyes that I can't look away from. They are brown with dark circles underneath and have a look of love and understanding I've never seen in anybody's eyes before.

As I stop in front of her, I realize that no one has ever looked at me so thoroughly and completely, as if she knows everything about me, even things I don't know about myself. Her eyes make me feel vulnerable yet cherished like I belong to her somehow. Love, soft, like light, pours out of her eyes at me, pulling my eyes irresistibly to hers; I could look into them forever.

Now I understand what the guard with the whip saw in Jesus' face; how could he do anything against such a look? This is the Mystery in full bloom, beauty from somewhere beyond the world we usually see, not peeking out in glimpses that we catch from time to time, but beauty pouring out in constant gentle love.

She pats her hand in the white snow inviting me to sit next to her. When I do, she puts her arm around my shoulders; her touch is light, calming, and she smells like a room full of roses. I snuggle up against her, and I feel complete like this is where I belong, what love is supposed to feel like.

I look up into her eyes. I want to ask her who she is, but I forget how to talk. I wrap my arms around her waist and rest my head on her soft breast. Peace seems to soak into every pore of my body. Time fades away as I hold onto her beauty, as I feel her love engulfing me, making me hers. She is my whole world; every breath is only to breathe in the smell of her; every touch is only to feel her against me; every sound is the slow, steady beat of her heart under my ear or the soft rustle of her clothes as she caresses me; whoever I am doesn't matter. I want nothing but to be with her always.

Slowly time creeps back, nibbling at me, and I start to worry that she will leave me. She must know what I am thinking because she whispers into my ear, "I am your mother, and I am always with you, my darling; do not worry."

Suddenly, she's no longer next to me, and I'm in the car again. Danny is across from me, staring out the window at the bright blue sky and the trees flashing by. Gone. Dad is still smoking and driving the car. Mom is chewing gum and looking ahead. Gone. The car is rolling along the concrete; a mile marker flicks past. Gone. She's gone. Why am I here without her? Why did she go? Why didn't she take me with her?

Grief overwhelms me, and I burst out crying; the loss of her is too much; I don't even try to stop the hot tears from streaming down my face. Mom reaches back and puts her hand on my leg, "It's okay, Bobby, it's okay." She must think I'm crying about Uncle Billy; she has no idea who I was with, who I lost. I feel lost as the tears keep pouring out. My sobs are the only sounds to be heard now as Mom rubs me gently on the back.

It's a while before I can stop, but finally, I run out of tears, and everyone is quiet while I start to recover. I can see the startled surprise on Danny's face. Dad keeps glancing at me in the mirror to see if I'm OK now, and Mom hands me some Kleenex to wipe my face.

There's no way I can tell them why I was crying; how can I explain what I experienced with—with Mother, without them seeing her themselves? They would just think it was some dream and pooh-pooh it. I don't want anybody to say anything against what happened between me and Mother. It feels holy, sacred. It's better just to let them think my crying was from Uncle Billy's funeral.

There's no question in my mind about Mother being real; I know she is; it wasn't a dream. My brain couldn't make up anyone so beautiful, so full of the Mystery, so full of love. The memory is clear, whole, alive. I can still smell her scent of roses, feel her touch, her soft body under my arms and my head, see her eyes loving me. She is more real than anyone I've ever known, solid like the earth somehow, yet softer than a pillow. I wonder where she is now; is she in heaven or on Earth somewhere? Maybe she's waiting for me to find her one day.

Mother said she was always with me. What does that mean? How can that comfort me when she is not next to me anymore? Part of me knows that I've just received a great gift, but most of me just wants her back—right now. I felt so happy and complete feeling her against me; now I've never felt so alone.

It's not long before the car slows, and Dad turns off the road and bumps to a stop under a shady tree. We're in a parking lot next to a white church with a tall pointed steeple and a brass bell at the top. I see other cars with little purple flags on their antennas rolling in, kicking up great puffs of sandy dust.

I get out of the car, feeling a little unsteady. I look in Mom's side mirror to see if people will be able to tell I was crying so much. Tear streaks are all down my face. I point to my face and look at Mom. Mom goes back in the car, wets a cloth with melted ice water in the cooler, and hands it to me. I wipe my face and the back of my neck. The cold water helps me focus on the moment, on moving somewhere, and the streaks are mostly gone. "Thanks, Mom."

We start walking towards a building off to the side of the church. Danny comes beside me in his white shirt—we left our suit jackets in the car, and whispers, "Hey, what happened, are you okay?"

He must suspect something. Danny knows me better than anybody, and it would be strange for me to cry that much about Uncle Billy. I shrug my shoulders like I don't know, "I'm okay." I hope he lets it go because I don't want to talk about it to anyone right now, or I might start crying again.

Dad comes up on my other side and puts his arm around my shoulders. Mom must be behind us, slowed down by her high heels. We walk under a wooden roof with thick beams showing, and before long, we are seated in a long pavilion with a cement floor full of picnic tables. Someone has spread out fresh white tablecloths on all the tables. They probably belong to the church. In the center of each table is a small vase full of daisies.

Aunt Cora comes in with Uncle Chick, who is carrying a big blue cooler. Uncle Chick has his suit jacket off, too. Looking so dignified and calm in her black dress, Aunt Cora starts pulling out bowls full of fried chicken and potato salad. Aunt Elaine seems to be setting down a big pot of macaroni and cheese and a heaping plate of sugar cookies. Other people are dropping dishes off, too.

Soon, we are filling up our plates. People are talking softly to each other as they wait in line. The different smells of all the food starts my stomach gurgling. I realize that I'm awful hungry; crying always seems to make me hungry once I calm down, but how can we eat like this after the funeral? We just seem to be leaving Uncle Billy behind. Yet, what else can we do? We have to eat. Our bodies make us keep going, even if our minds just want to curl up somewhere and be alone.

Mine sure does; in my mind, I keep seeing Mother's eyes looking at me, her smile thrilling my heart. I keep remembering the feeling of surrendering to her touch, to her love. I need some private time to think about her, remember everything I can about her, try to understand, to hold onto her somehow even though she is gone. Maybe on the drive to Aunt Cora's later, or when I'm in bed tonight laying alone quietly in the dark.

While I'm chewing on a chicken leg dipped in baked beans, I wonder how many of these I'll have to go to. I wish my first funeral was my last one, but I know that's not possible. For the rest of my life, funerals will pop up from time to time, probably without much warning, I'm guessing; there's no getting away from it. The Charcoal Man gets around to everybody eventually. Who might be next? I don't want to know. I just hope it's a very long time from now.

Suddenly, Pap-Pap is patting my shoulder, "My, aren't you two the most handsome boys I've ever seen. It tickles my heart to see you here. Now you eat up all this good food. Don't be shy and don't forget dessert. How are you, Joanie?" Pap-Pap adds, giving Mom a hug and a peck on the cheek. He pats Dad on the shoulder, "I'm so glad you could make it here, Bobby." Dad squeezes his hand as Pap-Pap moves on to the next table to chat with Uncle Chick and Aunt Cora.

I watch Pap-Pap as he works his way around the tables, stopping to say a few words to almost everybody. His suit jacket is a little oversized, and that makes him look younger somehow, like a kid wearing his brother's hand-me-downs. His black tie has a big knot that shows he's not too good at tying. The breeze keeps his thin white hair busy. He is smiling for the most part. People seem to lighten up and start talking more after he moves on to the next table, towards Grandma.

Grandma is sitting with Aunt Elaine, who brought a plate over for her, encouraging Grandma to eat, but Grandma doesn't seem interested. Pap-Pap comes by and kisses and hugs Aunt Elaine, who lights up with a pretty smile. Then Pap-Pap says something in Grandma's ear and kisses the top of Grandma's head before he moves on. Grandma stares after him for a moment, then she picks up her fork and starts eating. I wonder what Pap-Pap said to her.

I realize that going around the tables talking and touching people is Pap-Pap's way to comfort everyone. Uncle Billy was his son; he'd have the right just to sit quiet and poke at his food feeling sad, but not Pap-Pap. Pap-Pap has some kind of cheerfulness in his heart that he has to let out and share. Dr. Blake cures people, Pap-Pap cheers them up; they are both worthy of that hammer. I'm sure Jesus and Mother are saving a spot for Pap-Pap, but someday far, far away, I hope.

After I finish my third sugar cookie, I slip outside with Danny, who is halfway through a chocolate brownie. Darla and

Lenny are already out in the playground by the church. It has a slide, swings, a seesaw, and a giant sandbox. Darla is swinging, and Lenny is playing in the sandbox. Danny plops down on the edge of the sandbox and starts talking to Lenny about building a castle together—they better be careful not to get their good clothes too dirty.

I hop on the swing next to Darla and try to catch up to her. She's already way up there. The chains feel good and strong, twisting slightly in my hands. After pumping my legs hard for a couple of minutes, I'm almost at Darla's height; it feels like I have hair made out of wind; my toes are pointing at clouds lit up from the sun behind me. When I rush backwards, my stomach flips a little from how high and fast I'm going.

Darla is right across from me now; we are matching each other as we pump to get even higher, abandoning ourselves to the thrill of flying together. Her hair is streaming straight back, and then it falls to her shoulders when she goes backwards. Her eyes close from time to time; now and then, she glances at me and smiles. The sky, the wind, the swings, and each other, that's our world right now—it's enough.

After a few minutes, Darla flashes me her smile and then signals by pointing at the church and to me and her. She starts slowing down, and so do I, then Darla scoots off the swing. It's tempting to jump off the swing as she is ahead of me, but I don't want to mess up my pants. Darla runs fast, even with blue dress shoes on, then her polka dot dress disappears behind the white wooden church.

When I catch up to her, she is waiting in a courtyard in front of a white statue. An arch of red roses wrapping a green lattice surrounds the statue. It's Mary, Jesus' mother, about

four feet high, standing on a stone pedestal. She is looking down a little, and her arms are pointing downwards, too. Mary has a soft and gentle smile on her face that makes me feel peaceful right away. Her robes have folds that look like the wind could blow them.

Darla and I sit on a marble bench with no back that's in front of Mary. A handful of bees are buzzing around the roses, whose sweet smell makes me breathe in deeply. The scent reminds me of Mother; is the rose smell just a coincidence, or does it mean something? Is Mary connected to Mother somehow? Maybe roses are the flowers that Queens of Heaven love the most or that have enough beauty to be near them.

I feel Darla's hip next to mine, and before I know it, we are holding hands again; hers is so soft, yet strong, warm. I can feel her heartbeat in her hand, or is it mine? Mary is looking down on me, pulling at my heart as well; I catch a glimpse of Mother in her face, the Mystery somehow caught in Mary's loving expression. Darla must feel it, too, the way she is gazing at Mary's face with a soft smile and adoring eyes. Maybe that's why she brought me here, to share Mary with me.

Long sweet minutes pass. Darla rests her head on my shoulder. I consider telling Darla about Mother, but it feels right not to. We don't really need to talk, but I do anyway. "We're heading on back to Texas tomorrow morning."

She squeezes my hand, "I know. It's been so nice to be with you again. Don't you forget, you hear."

"I could never do that, I promise."

"Bobby!" Danny's voice is calling me.

Before I get up, I lean over and kiss Darla on her lips, my heart is flipping and twisting from how soft and good her lips feel against mine. I can't believe I'm kissing her, that she's letting me. She pats my cheek and rubs her nose softly against my nose, and then I jump up and run towards the playground before Danny sees us and teases me forever.

Danny's goofy face suddenly pokes out from the corner of the church.

"Time to go," Danny says.

It's a quiet ride back to Aunt Cora's. We must all be a little worn out from this day. I understand now what Grandma Babe means about the sky in Kansas. I can see hundreds of puffy white clouds stretching for miles and miles in every direction. The ones close by are enormous, like floating mountains or islands; the ones far away by the horizon are puppy-sized, glowing orange and red on their bellies from the sinking sun.

I keep going over Mother's words. She said she was my mother, and I believe her, but Mom is the mother of my body, so Mother must be the mother of my what? Of my soul? Yes, that feels right, but if she is the mother of my soul, then she must be like God or Jesus, or maybe she's an angel sent by God? No, an angel wouldn't say she was my mother; she's bigger than an angel.

The sun is barely peeking above the horizon now; violet light swallows up the clouds and the red sky. The dark violet shadows of the puffy clouds keep swelling till only a short, thin red line holds onto the edge of the world, like a pair of red hands about to slip off out of sight. I bet angels are flying up there now. If I was an angel, I'd fly in that sky, amongst those clouds, in all that beauty. God can make a living masterpiece like that sky without even trying. God can do anything.

It's all too big for me to get, but if God can be a father, why not a mother, too? I prayed to God to let me see him and be with him someday; maybe that just happened with Mother. Isn't Mary called the Mother of God? God came to people as Jesus; why couldn't God come as Mother? Mother is so overflowing with love and the Mystery that they must come from God.

There is no question or doubt about one thing, which is clearer than anything else: I love her, desperately. She said she was with me always and not to worry; that means I am never really alone, even if I feel that way sometimes. So I'll try to believe her and not worry. I'll just love Mother and hold onto her in my heart, remembering and feeling her presence as much as I can until she comes back. Maybe that's all I'm supposed to do anyway.

The headlights lead the way through the growing dark; trees by the side of the road start to become dark shadows bunched together. I see small frogs hopping across the lighted road once in a while; a moth splatters against our windshield—light pulls all creatures towards it. Dad lights a cigarette, and his face glows yellow in the dark for a moment. Dad, Mom, Danny, me, all four of us are separate in the dark, yet bouncing along together, connected by birth, blood, and all our years of being with each other.

Who knows where we will end up as time keeps pushing us forward into one experience after another. One thing I'm sure of is that just as we keep leaving beauty behind, the days ahead will be full of beauty as well; we just have to pay attention and soak in the Mystery when we can.